Stephen Blanchard

THE PARAFFIN CHILD

VINTAGE

Published by Vintage 2000

2 4 6 8 10 9 7 5 3 1

Copyright © Stephen Blanchard 1999

First published in Great Britain in 1999 by
Chatto & Windus

Vintage
Random House, 20 Vauxhall Bridge Road,
London SW1V 2SA

Random House Australia (Pty) Limited
20 Alfred Street, Milsons Point, Sydney
New South Wales 2061, Australia

Random House New Zealand Limited
18 Poland Road, Glenfield,
Auckland 10, New Zealand

Random House (Pty) Limited
Endulini, 5A Jubilee Road, Parktown 2193,
South Africa

The Random House Group Limited Reg. No. 954009
www.randomhouse.co.uk

A CIP catalogue record for this book
is available from the British Library

ISBN 0 09 928925 3

Papers used by Random House are natural, recyclable
products made from wood grown in sustainable forests.
The manufacturing processes conform to the environ-
mental regulations of the country of origin

Printed and bound in Great Britain by
Cox & Wyman Limited, Reading, Berkshire

To my daughter Lili

THE PARAFFIN CHILD

Stephen Blanchard is the author of, *Gagarin and I*, which won the *Yorkshire Post* Best First Book Award and was shortlisted for the Whitbread First Novel Award and *Wilson's Island*. He lives in South London with his partner and three children.

ALSO BY STEPHEN BLANCHARD

Gagarin and I
Wilson's Island

1

I burned little Pearl's photos very soon after my mother died. While Rosemary Shand was in town and my father took his nap I went through every room and released her pictures from their frames. I took the bound albums from their shelf above the trophy-cabinet and opened them on Dad's snooker table. Panting like a dog I tore the prints from their mounts.

Then I climbed the stairs to his room – the double bedroom at the front of the house. Dad was sleeping in one side of the bed with his head dead-centre on the pillow, nose pointing – what he called his afternoon recovery. In an hour or so he'd wake and call himself revived but now when I bent down I could see the tremble of an eyelid and, inside, a line of pinkish white like shell.

I took the wooden picture frame from the bedside table, teasing the corner from a fold of the curtain. A flash of daylight. The photo was of Pearl and my sister Marion in the garden, that summer I had brought her home. She would have been two then, two and a half. She sat easily in the crook of my sister's arm, looking up at her, and Marion was smiling towards the lens of Dad's elderly Pentax. Dad made a noise, a sigh like he was deeply satisfied by something in his sleep, while I was busy at the back of the frame with my thumbs, turning down the little brass catches. The photo slipped out, given a curve by the salt damp in the air. Dad didn't stir.

I put it with the rest in a Circle Mart carrier-bag. *For Every Day and that Special Occasion.* That was the last one I knew about. Marion had a couple in her flat in town but she would keep them to herself after this – out of harm's way. I picked up the metal wastebin from the kitchen as I went by and I'd already stood half a gallon of paraffin by the back door to the garden – the blue stuff, not the pink.

Outside, I tipped the photos into the bin and splashed on some of the paraffin. The fumes took my breath for a second. I'd chosen the paved yard in the shelter of the house, where the drain breathed a smell of sudsy water. Marion's window was open above because Rosemary had been cleaning her room for a visit – dusting and hoovering. I struck a match. The sun was shining but then a cloud went over and I could see the little blue bead of the match-flame with a paler blue inside. Then the bin was full of flames and when the sun came out again they were invisible and I could only feel their heat – different from the sun's because it wasn't gentle. It gave no warmth but only pain. The photos were curling and turning a black so matt that it looked like nothing – black scraps of nothing twisting in the bottom of the bin.

2

Oh John, are you surprised at this letter? Maybe you won't even read it. Or I won't send it. I don't know. Sometimes I don't think of you for quite a while. Hours. Days. Then when I do it becomes very strong, like I've swallowed the wrong medicine and it's too late now. Too late.

I have to tell you this, inform you, because we're still together to an extent. In memory? In spirit? Together, anyway. I know of course that it (he/she) will not be Pearl. Sometimes I hope there will be no resemblance and at others I'd like more than anything to see that – just a look of her, nothing more. The eyes or the mouth, you know. I'm already three months and everything is okay. If you're wondering about the father his name is Gerald. While we're still alive we go on doing living things (loving things?).

So I hope you're well and happy, as I am sometimes – we need to keep a little of that in store, I've learned. Like keeping a fire burning. I've moved three or four times since it happened – this thing that I'm mentioning only as a point in time. I live in a nice house in a nice town and soon I'll have a nice baby, so isn't life like magic sometimes, like a fairy-story! Gerald is a manager for a firm which makes and installs the boilers for central-heating. He's divorced and nearly fifty but in a few years I'll be forty myself. Ha.

When the child is here I could send you a photograph, if you can face that. Until then I want

3

you to know that it's inside me, making itself by whatever means they use.

Be happy as I am sometimes. Be as well as you can.
Love,
Anna

The speaking clock talks. Papa Gosse's voice announces eight o'clock, twelve, three in the morning. The mechanism lurches, uneasy on its mountings. Salt-eaten recording wire winds from spool to spool, across the magnetic heads. Square horns at the corners of the clocktower broadcast the croak across the estuary towards Four-mile Town, along the front towards the OKO plant and Maurice's Beachcomber Bar. With a carrying wind you can hear it at Whiteheads. The last echoes die towards the chain-bridge.

Papa Gosse the father, Baby Gosse the son. Teddy Sandringham as holy ghost.

Dad and I sat on the bench above the sands, watching the rows of little waves on the estuary – silver or bruise-blue according to how the light struck. Behind us were fields with nothing growing but caravans.

IN DELECTABLE MEMORY OF
LILIAN ROSE DREAN

The inscription was incised in square letters along the back of the bench. Other words had been added later, in a freer style – *Rene Sucks. Terry and Linda 4 years and years* – scratched by knife and pen-point. Dad wiped a drip from his nose. April, and the wind was in our faces.

'Did you remember the milk, John?'

I opened the sports bag I'd packed the flask in. The zip stuck halfway and I had to tug at it. My hands felt numb and clumsy. The flask had two mugs which I set between us on the bench. The milk was in a screw-topped jar. I poured the sweet coffee laced with rum.

4

'Cheers, Dad.'

I'd used the wrong word exactly. Dad lifted his plastic mug. 'To your mother then. To Lilian.'

'That's right, Dad. To Mam!'

Dad sipped and smacked his lips. He had the collar of his coat turned up but he was still shivering, starting circles on the top of his coffee. He sat leaning forwards – big-shouldered and big-handed, the weight in his arms and upper body. He'd be seventy on his next birthday but he still had the stocky, stable build of a man in his fifties. Only the ash-grey tufts above his ears gave it away. Something about his manner also, the way he faced stiffly forwards, lifting his chin towards the wind.

'Two years and it doesn't seem like five minutes! There's still days when I expect her to walk through the door.'

'I know, Dad.'

'She'd be carrying something – like she always was. Her hands would never be empty.'

'That's right, Dad.'

He was looking across the river towards Four-mile Town and the ferry terminal. The water would be dull and then show a web of light like a net floating a fraction above the waves. 'There's someone else I expect, as well . . .' He looked sly then, as if he was withholding it. 'Do you know who that is, John?'

I shook my head, then swallowed some of the coffee, glad of the rum in it.

'I keep her in mind, though. I'd like you to know that,' Dad said.

I drank the rest, knocked it back even if it scalded my throat. I put down the mug and stood up. Dad looked away and then back at me, as if he were daring me to say something, start some performance.

'You can leave me to it, if you like . . .'

I was already walking back to the car, letting myself down the slope of the dyke. Fucking caravans for miles –

the only sign of life! The ground was slipping, loose with blown sand, so that I had to dig in the heels of my shoes.

We'd come in the old Rover, the car we'd used years ago for family outings. Dad had had a couple of cars since and for ten years it had stood on blocks in the garage with a pool of black oil below the sump. Then when Mam fell ill and Rosemary Shand came to the house he'd had it serviced so that she could use it for trips into town. He didn't go there much himself nowadays – for a haircut, a visit to Dr Spelling – and even then Rosemary would usually drive. I got back inside and the interior smelt of old leather and groceries. The wind was blowing across the top of the dyke and rain or spray specked the windscreen. I knew Dad wouldn't sit there for long in weather like that – no more than five minutes. Two.

I went back after ten. One mug stood where I'd left it on the seat but the other had fallen into the grass near the buffed toes of Dad's shoes. I picked it up and the last cold drop of coffee ran along my wrist.

'Let's go now, Dad – it's starting to rain!'

He wouldn't look at me. I didn't know where he was looking. Not at the smooth patches of water above the sandbanks. His hands were open on his thighs – blue and white below the dark cuffs of his coat.

'Dad?'

He didn't answer for a second. I had to bend down and peer into his face. His eyes had a lost look and then they focused.

'I'm all right.'

'Are you sure, Dad . . . ? I'm not sure that you are.'

He made a noise then, a gravelly clearing of the throat. He looked at me spitefully, hatefully. I thought it was better to spit than to send a look like that.

I put my hand on his shoulder. 'C'mon now, Dad. You'll catch a chill . . .'

He was better later. He was usually better after his nap so

maybe it was tiredness that brought it on. The post had brought letters from the Labour Party and the Snooker Association and he read them under the lamp, sighing to himself.

'Another do that I'm invited to – a dinner and dance!'

'Will you be going, Dad?'

He looked impatient. 'Who would I take with me nowadays? D'you think I want to go on my own?'

He put me in a joking mood. 'You could ask Rosemary!' I said, knowing it was her day off.

'To keep an eye on me, you mean?'

'She might enjoy it, Dad.'

He folded the letter and slipped it back into its envelope. 'Oh, I don't think so! She must think she sees enough of me as it is – more than enough . . .'

We played snooker on the half-sized table in the front room, under the long lamp with its fringed shade. I could play to a certain level but never above that. My positional play let me down, my fundamental grasp of the game. I could never think more than a shot ahead and Dad would beat me with ease.

'You never address the ball properly!' Dad complained.

'How should I address it?'

He shook his head that I should ask. 'With respect but as if you meant it – as if you meant to take charge of the game!' He held up a finger. 'You never act as if you're master of the situation.'

He bent over the table with an air of demonstration. He pocketed a stray red and sent the white spinning off the cushion. It stopped on the spot like someone had put a meaty thumb on it.

'Rosemary's a better player than you,' he said. 'Not now, I mean, but she has it in her. A bit more practice and she'll leave you behind.'

'Don't say that, Dad.'

He decided on the green and sent it to the pocket, brought the cue-ball back towards the pack. 'The real difference is that Rosemary has humility enough to take advice.'

He moved about the table, rolling his shoulders. I could see the way each shot he played gave him delight, surprised him even if the ball did exactly what he intended. He laughed and sent the pink into the middle pocket. I heard a car on the gravel road through the caravan-site.

'That might be her and Marion, Dad!'

'Oh?' As if he had no interest suddenly.

'There was a party at Maurice's and Marion invited her.'

He glanced up. 'What sort of party?'

I was sure Marion would have told him. 'Something Maurice had arranged. He has trouble keeping that place full out of season.'

'Then you should have gone yourself. There was no need to keep me company.'

'I thought her and Rosemary might enjoy a chat together.'

'About the pair of us, no doubt,' Dad said. 'Or do you think that's claiming too much?'

'I can't see Rosemary gossiping.'

'Can't you? She'd find it a relief, I should think. These close-lipped types usually do.'

'I wouldn't call her that, Dad.'

He shook his head, looking about the table. 'Your mother and Alice Sandringham were the same. They'd draw to one side to have their little exchanges. And maybe they weren't so little. Maybe they were the important things and me and Teddy were wasting our breath . . .'

I wanted to tease him then, knowing it was dangerous. 'They had their secrets then, Dad?'

'Oh, that's what marriage is all about – bloody little secrets!'

He split the pack, impatient with the poor standard of play. The balls cannoned noisily. I could hear Marion parking her car in front of the house. She was singing as she opened the door and after a second Rosemary joined in – her high amateur pitch and Marion's throaty, confident voice.

'Sounds like they've had a skinful!'

'Why not?' Dad asked. 'And a skinful is no way to describe it.'

Marion was still humming to herself when they came into the hall, carrying on where maybe she'd forgotten the words. Dad put down his cue and started to fidget with his hands like a child waiting for a treat. Sometimes she had that effect on him. Then she breezed into the room and kissed him on the side of the mouth. She smiled across the table at me. Her big, slightly uneven teeth looked brave.

'You should have come with us, John!'

'So Dad was saying, but I wasn't in the mood.'

She clicked her tongue. 'That's the thing about a drink, isn't it – to put you in the mood?'

She took off her leather coat and her bare arms were freckled as far as the elbow and then smooth, shining in the guarded light from the table. Dad was smiling at her, bashful as if he were paying court. Rosemary stood in the doorway, watching them. She had taken off her coat in the hall and wore a simple print dress and cream, low-heeled shoes. She might have been dressing down as policy.

Dad beckoned her into the room. 'So did you have a nice evening, Rosemary?'

'Oh, it was a night out, George.'

'No more than that? You didn't enjoy yourself?'

She smiled and didn't speak. I supposed she must have had at least a few drinks but she had the look of the housekeeper on her suddenly, as if she'd been keeping it under her coat.

'I think the answer is yes,' Marion said with a touch of impatience. She went to the radio and turned it on, trying to find some music she liked.

'You can rely on Marion to enjoy herself,' Dad said. 'That's one thing she has the knack of.'

'One of many, I'm certain,' Rosemary said.

Marion took hold of my hand now, squeezing it. I felt a twinge in the flesh where it was not properly healed. She might have seen my flinch because she hooked my arm around her waist and put her cheek to mine. The music was playing fast and low – Latin hour from the local station. Her dark hair had the pub smell, like candy-floss and smoke.

'A dance!' Dad called, taking hold of Mrs Shand. 'Would you dance with me, Rosemary?'

'Give her a chance,' Marion told him. 'Let her get her breath first!'

Dad grinned at his partner. 'Why? Why should she have a chance? I never gave your mother one.'

'Shut up, Dad!' Marion said, dragging at my arm.

Dad was holding Rosemary's hand high now, nearly against his lips. She stood stiffly before him, smiling. 'Let me make us all some coffee, George! That's a better idea . . .'

'Oh, let the old fool dance if he wants to!' Marion told her. She bumped me with her hip, sweeping us into the space in front of the snooker-table.

Dad and Rosemary started to turn. Their steps made the cups and figurines shiver on the glass shelves of the trophy-cabinet and I noticed how his hand was spread at the formal centre of her back. Rosemary was smiling but with little patches of heat on her cheeks.

'So how was the pub?' I asked Marion.

'Oh, the pub was fine but Maurice wasn't. I think this is a hard time for him because of the dog.'

'Dog?' I was still enjoying the smoky smell of her hair.

'Oh, he's still upset because of his dog being run over.'

'He shouldn't care so much about a dog. It could have been him that stepped out.'

'He might have preferred that,' Marion said.

I watched Dad and Rosemary at the other end of the

room. Dad was holding her at arm's-length now, leaning backwards. She smiled when he spoke to her quietly.

'He's been more upset about the dog than when his wife walked out,' I said.

'I never really liked his wife,' Marion said. 'I thought he was better out of that, anyway.'

'I don't think Maurice saw it like that. When she left I think he fell back on the dog – for affection, I mean.'

Marion laughed. 'Poor Maurice . . .'

I held my sister by her full, sliding waist. She was lost in the dance for a minute, humming to herself. I could feel the vibration of her throat. She'd reach a drunkenness of mind and body and then she'd suddenly sleep and I was jealous of this power of sleep. I glanced across at Dad, then spoke quietly into her ear. 'So was lover-boy there?'

She stopped and then turned again, taking me with her. 'Who is that?'

'Baby Gosse, I mean.'

'Will you give him his proper name, please?'

'Okay. Was Tony there?'

'Why would he bother himself with that place?'

'You mean he wouldn't like to be seen in a dive like Maurice's?'

'Whether he would or wouldn't doesn't concern me,' Marion said. 'He's other commitments as you know.'

The music was slowing, stopping. Dad laughed and bent to kiss Mrs Shand on the forehead. She stiffened but he still smiled at her, tilting his long head. 'So, Rosemary, did you dance with anyone else tonight?'

She shook her head. 'Oh, it was enough to see Marion enjoying herself, George.'

Marion looked irritated, as if her good humour had ended with that particular tune. 'It wasn't that no one asked her,' she said over her shoulder. 'She'd decided to take no offers, that's all.'

'Then she's only being wise with that crew,' Dad said.

11

'Half the scum around here use that place. You've only to drive past and watch them fall out of it!'

Marion sighed, teasing the dial of the radio again. 'You can spend your life being wise, Dad. And then it's over.'

3

I'd feel myself falling, but then I'd wake. Dr Spelling's little pills would start to send me off but I'd fight. I didn't like the whisper in my ear – the dopey little tune they started in my head – so I'd check myself. It was an instinct with me – to try and not go down that particular road.

I'd deny myself.

A heavy step and then a light down the rocky road of sleep.

No.

'Here,' Rosemary said.

'What's this?'

'What do you think it is?'

She dropped it into my palm – a capsule half black and half grey. I was judging only by touch.

'It'll help you get off,' she said.

'I'm not sure if I want to, Rosemary.'

'That's your problem, you see – lack of conviction.'

'And I've tried something already.'

'Oh, this is better altogether – I'd recommend it to you!'

She was leaning over me, dark-faced and dark-haired. 'How did you know I was awake?' I asked.

She smiled in the dark. Her cigarette smile. 'Aren't you usually at this hour? What were you thinking about?'

'I wasn't thinking.'

'You wouldn't tell me if you were.'

Dark Rosemary, Mrs Shand. I swallowed the bitter tasting pill. It had no taste so it must have been my throat that was bitter. 'Where did you get these?'

'From a woman at the hairdresser's. She has the same problem herself – it's a bloody epidemic in this town . . .' I put my hand up to her cheek and she leaned back a fraction. 'You're getting as bad as your father.'

'No, I'm not as bad as him.'

'I've a son nearly your age,' she said.

'That can't be true.'

'Actually, I think of you as being related. As if you were his unlucky elder brother.'

'Why am I unlucky, Rosemary?'

'Because you won't allow what luck you've left to flourish . . . Drink something now.' She held out half a glass of water.

'You're mad, Mrs Shand. You're mad and bad but not sad.'

'Marion makes me feel as if I'm sad.'

'She does that to people – she can't help it.' I sat up and spilled water on the quilt.

'Careful!'

'Could you stay for a minute, Rosemary? Just for a minute?' There was enough light to see the outline of her face but not the expression. I'd settle for the outline.

'Okay. Did you think I was about to leave?'

'You've a history of it, haven't you? Because you must have left somewhere else to get here.'

She laughed. 'You're being too clever for me now!'

'Sorry . . . So was Dad giving you a hard time tonight?'

'That's just his way!'

'He should mend his ways then.'

'That's not for me to say.' She cleared her throat and looked about the room.

'What's the matter?' I asked, teasing. 'Is there something that you've lost?'

'John, have you one for me?'

I reached into the drawer of the bedside cabinet and took out a pack of cigarettes. There were a couple left – one she'd smoke and one I'd save for the morning. I passed her my lighter and heard her light up. The burning paper made a silvery tinkle.

'So tell me a story then, Rosemary . . .'

'Is that the price you charge – a bedtime story?'

'No – I'm begging really.'

She drew on the cigarette again. I inhaled some of the smoke which started my own cravings but I resisted.

'The three of us were changing trains. I wanted a cigarette.'

'Where?'

'Where doesn't matter. Call it the Midlands. Call it Crewe.'

'Crewe then.'

'There for the sake of argument. Our connection had been announced but I knew I couldn't wait. I left them and ran into the buffet. Barry shouted after me – he was always so nervous about missing trains while I was exactly the opposite.'

'Barry?'

'You think that's a funny name, don't you?'

'There's something about it that makes me smile.'

'Then you're soon amused . . . I was at the counter and a train was stopping at the other side – a commuter train, not an express. I could see it through the glass doors. The people rushed on and the guard was already slamming the doors of the carriages.'

'But it wasn't your train, yours and Barry's?'

'It was the one I got into. I knew that if they saw me I could say that I'd been confused, mistaken the platform. I had the pack of cigarettes in my hand and I was stripping off the plastic wrapping. All of a sudden I was ravenous for one. It felt like the start of an addiction. I hadn't realised until that second that I'd wanted to do it – leave Barry and my little boy, I mean.'

She sniffed and then breathed out smoke.

'How old was the boy?' I asked.

15

'Nearly four. He had his father's chestnut hair and my dead mother's eyes. It broke my heart to leave him.'

'I believe you . . . But where are they now, Rosemary?'

'I have this idea that they're still there on the platform, still waiting for me. I've tried but I can't think of them as being anywhere else.'

'And this place you got off at?'

'I'd changed a couple of times before then. It was a bank holiday and the trains were short of staff . . . Finally though, the man was coming to collect the tickets and he was a carriage away when the train started to slow down. I waited near the door. No one else seemed to be getting off there and I didn't know the place from hell. A place called Opley. Ever heard of it?'

'No.'

'A few houses and not even a pub. I crossed by the bridge and walked down a lane. There was an alley-way alongside the wall of a garage and a man was doing some welding inside the doors. I stopped to watch and the flame left a yellow mark in front of my eyes.'

'You shouldn't have looked . . . So you stayed there a while?'

'The only shop was half a post-office and half a grocer's. I bought another packet of cigarettes and I had about twenty-five quid left in my purse. The post-office part had a board with notices and a respectable old gentleman was asking for a housekeeper . . . At least that's how he'd described himself. I pretended that was the thing I'd got off the train for and the woman behind the counter stepped out of the door with me and pointed the way. The start of my new career . . .'

'And you found your way here eventually? To Dad.'

'To this present post. Marion was doing the inter-views . . .'

'It was her that talked Dad into it. He was looking after Mam himself and she insisted that he needed a woman around the house. I suppose she didn't want to be that herself.'

She flicked ash into the brass bowl I kept beside the lamp. 'And you were still on your travels, John.'

'That's right. I was incommunicado.'

She let that go, never pushed me on that. She would let me decide to talk about it and sometimes I didn't. 'I don't think Marion liked me much at first but then she sat up when I told her I enjoyed a game of snooker. Barry would take me to the hall on Saturday mornings, you see, at least until I was good enough to beat him. And if it hadn't been for that I don't think I'd be here . . . Do you believe in fate, John? Something that acts to draw people together?'

'No, I don't.'

'Good.'

A first cig in the kitchen with the fridge's hum for company. Before even Rosemary stirred. Then the gravel road through the big field, the sun just above the dyke and the caravans locked against the chill, windows misted. Tony Gosse bought the big field and small fields as overspill for Sunnylands, where the visitors came. The people at Whiteheads were mostly long-stay tenants with the odd weekender. The caravans were old now and small, patched with canvas and bitumen and parked where the scrubby ground allowed. There were sandy holes and licks where the water leached below the dyke's foundations – muddy patches that would dry in summer with a glaze of salt. All the house had left were its garden and a right of access to the coast road.

I drove a couple of miles towards town, then turned at the entrance to Sunnylands towards Teddy Sandringham's cafe and arcade, nursing the car over speed-bumps. A tractor was towing a mower between the rows of 'vans, the driver hunched down in the open cab. A couple of cars and a white van were parked outside Teddy's. I went through into the cafe and Bilko was playing one of the machines. I said hello and he lifted his hand to me without taking his eyes from the display. His wife Fiona was talking to a woman I didn't know behind the counter and a couple of drivers were eating breakfast near the long window. It wasn't eight and the chairs were still stacked on top of the tables at the other side.

'Alex Vosper wants a word with you,' Bilko said.

I stood behind him and watched the lights. 'What about?'

'He said he had a couple of fares yesterday and he couldn't get you on the radio. He wondered if you were feeling ill or something.'

'I'd turned the thing off, that's all.'

Bilko nodded as if it didn't concern him. He had piles of silver lined up on top of the machine and he kept reaching for a coin and feeding it in, pushing the buttons with the heel of his hand, feeling for another before the tumblers settled.

'Had breakfast yet?' I asked.

He slapped his belly. 'I was waiting for you.'

Fiona served us, setting the plates down with a bang. Bilko was smiling to himself and I wondered what had been going on between them. Then instead of joining us she went behind the counter again to whisper to the other woman who looked slight and pale beside her. She had her back turned and I noticed only a head of shortish dyed-blond hair that was nearly white above the blue coat. Fiona noticed me looking their way and smiled, keeping it separate from her man. Bilko started talking about work and Alex Vosper again but I interrupted him.

'Is Teddy in?' I asked.

Bilko shrugged and I looked towards Fiona. She pulled a face. Her make-up was bright for the morning – set for the day ahead, the battle. 'Oh, he'll be in his office, I suppose. He hardly ever leaves the place nowadays. I'll swear he sleeps there sometimes.'

'It's anywhere but home for some people,' Bilko put in.

Fiona still wouldn't look at him. 'He's worried and that makes him hide himself away.'

'Why's he worried?' I asked.

The younger woman had been listening but she turned away now, as if this didn't concern her. Her shoulders looked fragile under the thin blue coat.

'Take a look at this place,' Fiona said. 'Wouldn't you be?'

'What about you, Fiona? What do you think?'

'Oh, the way I see it I can always get another job like this. There's always opportunities in catering.'

'Opportunities for slavery,' Bilko said.

Fiona ignored him again, as if her eyes wouldn't turn that way. The other woman was cooking something on the range that might have been her own breakfast.

I thought of calling on Teddy but decided not to. He had his funny, reclusive moods. I walked outside with Bilko. After a full breakfast and two cups of coffee I felt half-crazed and half-torpid – no condition in which to start the day. Bilko opened the door of his bronze Orion and a plastic cup rolled out. He kicked at it and sent it rattling across the concrete.

I asked, 'Could you do me a favour, Bilko?'

He looked irritated for a second and I hoped it still might be the thing with Fiona. 'What's that, John?'

'A dozen would do. Just to carry me over.'

I must have looked desperate enough because he closed his lip and slipped his hand into an inside pocket. He brought out a little bag of cloudy plastic, folded at the top.

'These aren't the usual but they're okay.'

'As long as they'll do the business.'

Bilko laughed. 'Oh, I think I can promise you that.'

He counted out twelve and I pushed a couple between my lips for starters – eating out of his hand nearly.

'Like feeding the five thousand,' Bilko said.

I was still struggling to swallow. 'What?'

'Never mind . . . You ought to go to see Vic, you know.

I can't be bothered with this, really . . . I'm a bag of nerves as it is.'

Victor owned the car-breaker's beyond Whiteheads and ran a pharmacy as a sideline. 'I don't think he likes me, Bilko. That dog of his doesn't anyway.'

'That's the first sign of madness,' Bilko said. 'Thinking no one likes you.'

'First sign of sanity as well.'

The pills made a little teasing burn as they went down and just the feel of it put me in a better frame of reference. Bilko was watching my throat.

'Don't tell your big sis about this, will you? She'd break both my legs,' he said.

'Are you scared of her, Bilko?'

'Everyone is around here – everyone loves her, that's why. And there's a little bit of fear in every love.'

'You're a philosopher, Bilko . . . But what's between you and Fi this morning?'

He looked displeased that I'd asked, uncomfortable. 'Oh, the usual shite . . .'

'Is it?'

'No . . . It's worse than that really. What happened is she told me that I disgusted her.'

'When?'

'A couple of days ago. Nights. I put my arm around her and she told me that.'

'Had you been arguing about something?'

He shook his head. Through the open door of his car I could see a rubbish of plastic cups and tin-foil trays, old receipts and newspapers. 'She said it right out of the blue. She said she'd been feeling like that for a long time and she'd just decided to tell me.'

'Buy her some flowers, Bilko.'

'I've tried that. And underwear.'

'Tell her you love her then.'

He shook his head, laughing, turning back to his car. 'You've just no idea about this, have you, John?'

I could feel the cosy heat of the pills in my belly. 'Sorry, Bilko.'

'You're not a well man, are you, John?' Alex Vosper said.

'It comes and goes . . . I'm just learning to live with it.'

I looked through the hatch in the wall into the waiting room. A couple of drivers were sitting on the bench, breakfasting on dispenser coffee and bacon rolls from greasy paper bags, watching the TV in the corner which was never switched off. One of them saw me looking and winked. I smiled back.

'You seem to find amusement in this,' Alex said. 'We can't afford to lose customers, that's all. People have to be satisfied so they come back. That's the basis of any business that wants to stay afloat.'

I didn't answer, just looked at the timesheets on his desk and the little figures he'd pencilled in so that he could change them later. A few minutes here, a quarter-hour there.

'I think you're your own worst enemy, John,' Alex said.

'I'm not sure about that.'

He put his fingers together. 'You seem happier when there's a strain between us. But I don't like that, John – I don't care for it at all because I want things to be smooth . . .'

'I'll try, Alex. I'll try to do better in future.'

'I've got plenty of respect for your family, John. For your father in particular,' Alex said.

'Not for me, though?'

He sighed, fiddling with a pen, tapping it against the desk's scabby veneer. There were crumbs of biscuit down his shirt-front. Jaffa Cakes. He got through half a dozen packets a day to stop himself smoking. 'I didn't say that, did I?'

'You implied it.'

'Look, you seem to want an argument, John! All I really had in mind was to give you some advice . . .' A message

21

from one of the drivers was coming over the speakers but he ignored it. 'I want you to do yourself a favour and take this work more seriously. We can all have a few laughs and still do the job, can't we? I'd like you to try and develop that attitude.'

'Okay, Al . . . Anything for me at the moment?'

He half closed his eyes. The phone started to ring and he put it to his ear. He wrote down the address and called through for one of the other drivers. I took the hint and started towards the door.

'Hey, where are you going?'

'For a coffee. If you've nothing for me then I'll sit out in front.'

He shook his head. The phone had left a white mark on his fat cheek. 'Do you know who I was talking to the other day?' he asked, and I knew he'd been saving that up.

'Don't know, Alex . . . No idea.'

'I was talking to your sister. Marion. I saw her in town and we had a bit of a chat about things.'

'What things?'

He flexed his fingers. I could see he was dying to start on another packet of biscuits. 'Look, John, I can understand it if you're still finding life a bit difficult. A lot of people do for different reasons. Especially the men in this office, it looks like . . .' The other driver was waiting at the hatch and he handed the slip to him. 'I want you to know that I'll always understand that.'

'Did Marion tell you?' I asked. 'Did she tell you I was finding life difficult?'

Alex looked hurt and soft-mouthed. 'It's what I've noticed for myself, John. Give me some credit, at least.'

I had a couple of fares from the station and then one out to Hooperstown, over the toll. Then a long run to the hamlets near the ferry terminal. My appetite was still dead but I had a coffee and a bun in the cafeteria, just to keep up my sugar level. From a seat near the window I could look out over the water and see where the sections of the chain-bridge end in mid-stream and never meet. The light was fading by then and the superstructure was very dark against the sky. Red and green warning lights flashed at the broken ends.

I drove back into town to fix another shift and deliver my timesheets. Then out again, towards Whiteheads. My concentration was starting to go and I swallowed another couple of Bilko's little helpers. They were more sudden and savage than the ones I was used to; you'd have a couple of hours of feeling nearly immortal and then it would drain away and leave you stranded. You could swallow another or have a few drinks to smooth out the fall.

I stopped at Maurice's. One corner of the car park was flooded like it did after rain, Maurice was always talking about putting in a new drain. The lounge bar had its feel of off-season slackness. You'd get to like it that way and then the visitors would start and fill the place up. The big screen in the corner showed the racing from Caister with the sound turned down, so that the commentary was only a murmur under the soft belt of music. The part-timer was on duty and Maurice stood in his spot below the portrait of the slaughtered Dobermann. The bottom of the frame was decorated with a wreath of mixed blooms.

'You look pale,' he told me. 'Has somebody been upsetting you?'

'I think it's just lack of sunlight.'

Half a dozen men from the OKO plant were playing sudden death on the pool-table – jeering at each other's shots, most of them still wearing their red overalls with the blue company logo on the back. Maurice wandered across to say something to the part-timer and then came back again. I looked up at the dead dog. The flowers must have been there for a couple of days because some of them were already limp.

'A nice job you made of that, Maurice.'

He looked over his shoulder at it. 'Fiona gave me some

advice about it. I'd have been lost otherwise – it's so easy to go wrong with flowers. Go over the top, I mean.'

'Well, you've avoided that, Maurice. I think you've managed to catch a balance.'

He looked pleased, then as if his eyes were pricking. He had a doggish look himself for a second – like a fat and sentimental hound. 'A few people have sent me cards, you know. Condolences. She didn't deserve that, you see – not a hit and fucking run ... I know that breed has a certain reputation but she was as mild as a lamb herself.'

'Give a dog a name,' I said.

The portrait was misty and air-brushed, enlarged a stage too far. Maurice had probably paid a packet for it at some studio in town. Even the shine added to its eyes wasn't enough to give the dog a look of alertness. One of them even seemed to be misshapen ... As I watched a bulge to one side separated and floated slowly across the neutral background, as if part of the emulsion had come loose.

'Headache?' Maurice asked sympathetically.

'A bit of one coming, that's right.'

'You driver-boys work too hard ... Shall I get you something?'

'I'll be fine. I'll take some air instead.'

'Sensible man,' Maurice said, disappointed. Then he smiled again. 'Marion was in here the other night.'

'So I heard.'

'And the other lady ... What's her name?'

'Rosemary.'

'That's right ... *Rosemary*.' As if he was in love with her and he wanted to repeat it. 'She's a fine-looking woman as well – for her age, I mean. Your dad's lucky to have someone like her looking after him.'

'She looks after the house, Maurice. My dad looks after himself more or less.'

Maurice nodded. 'He must be getting on now, though. How old is he now?'

'He'll be seventy next birthday.'

'Well, we'll make an event of that. Even if he never sets foot in here.'

'You know what he's like, Maurice. Set in his ways.'

'Oh yeah . . . Your dad was the best council leader we ever had, you know. Everything ran like clockwork while he was in charge. Never any trouble about renewing licences . . .'

Which was funny because I knew there had been.

'I'll tell him you said that.'

'Oh, he doesn't need to hear it from me. I mentioned as much to Marion, anyway . . . She was sweet as well,' Maurice said. 'She was very sorry about the dog, I could tell.'

'You've still got hopes in that direction, haven't you, Maurice?' I said to tease him. I knew I was on stronger ground there.

I saw him blush and he looked down the bar at the OKO men still laughing and arguing. 'Oh, years ago I might have had – back in the Stone Age . . . I've had enough of that now, you see. It's too much of a shock to your system, John.'

'There's only one man for her anyway,' I said.

'Is that right?' As if he didn't know.

'You ought to book her for a night, Maurice. She'd still fill this place, I reckon.'

Maurice looked sorrowful. 'She reckons she's concentrating more on the agency side nowadays – more money in it, she said.'

'She does a night now and again – just to keep her voice in.'

'Oh, she'd a lovely voice back then!' Maurice said. 'She had a voice like an angel . . .'

'I know, Maurice. I know.'

'She'd a voice like fucking Joni Mitchell.'

4

In a cottage. In a wood. Lived the woodsman and his wife. Their daughter Pearl. In a little house in the heart of the wildwood lived the woodsman and his love Anna. Their little girl Pearl. In a house called Redwood in the Christmas-tree forest.

The woodsman left early for work, while it was still dark – before even the shy creatures of the forest stirred from their nests. Only his headlights on the narrow road through the dwarf-firs, the trail of shining cat's-eyes. He'd enter the deepest part of the wood and cross the small bridge the commission had made. The noise of his engine would come up sharp from the black water. By first light he would be taking his equipment from the lock-up – his saws, his safety-helmet, his harnesses.

And then Anna had her job. She went every day to the city in her small car, a Fiat, while the woodsman had his bigger car, a green short wheelbase Land Rover. Anna would clip little Pearl dozing into her car-seat to drop her first at the nursery before she went to the office a short drive away. Anna's job was in data management.

Night-time, and the day was done. A flower of passion in the wildwood, its blooms fleshy and strong. In a cottage in a wood, they kissed like they were drinking beer, champagne, spring-water. Taking big greedy draughts of one another, bite-sized portions. In the early hours, in the chill before they lit the woodstove and nothing yet on the road. In the cold and silence they were hot and alive, noisy. Ah! cried the woodman's wife. Ah! he echoed. John Drean and his Anna. The numerals shone on the radio-alarm. In the chill before the stove was lit she cried for happiness, the hour changing. A car on the road with its headlights sweeping, through the room and across her belly. A rackety VW engine – a campervan or similar. The noise woke the child. She called to them from the other room, across the empty landing.

Dad sat in the kitchen in an odour of bath-oil. The collar of his striped robe had slipped and I could see the grey hairs below his throat. Rosemary had put the gas jets on to warm the high stone-floored room. She sat on the other side of the big table, filling in the columns of her book of accounts.

'You're too studious, Rosemary!' Dad said, teasing her. 'You could speak to us instead of that.'

Rosemary sniffed. 'You and John might like to talk.'

Dad pulled a face. 'Oh, we never say much of importance!' He closed his eyes, leaning back in the chair like a sun-bather. 'You say Teddy wasn't there, John?'

'Fiona reckoned he'd be in his office but I thought I'd respect his privacy.'

Dad looked pleased with himself. 'I'll need to pay a call on him myself soon, anyway. Before we both get too old and soft . . .' Rosemary tutted and he smiled across at her. 'Oh, you've a right to be soft when you're old, Rosemary. Soft or hard, as you might choose.'

'Like an egg,' I said. 'Whichever you prefer.'

'You shouldn't neglect your friends,' Rosemary said. 'You've no excuse for that, have you?'

'Oh, what would we talk about, Rosemary? Old times? I've my own view of those and so has he. We won't be converted now.'

'You'll be getting your hair cut today,' I said. 'You could look in on Teddy on the way.'

'No . . . I don't think so.'

'You told me he was your oldest friend!' Rosemary said.

'Well, that's a good reason to avoid him . . .' He winked at her, flirtatious now. He still had the rosy shine of heat on his face. 'What Teddy should do is retire or else die!'

'You could spare us that kind of talk!' Rosemary said after a little laugh.

'A thing's either true or it isn't, Rosemary. That's all we should need to consider.'

'But you might have something good to say, George.' She looked round at at me for help.

'Don't involve me, Rosemary!'

Dad laughed and looked satisfied with her, that she'd shown fight. He drew the robe around his throat and settled himself. 'Oh, things would happen when Teddy and I were together and you couldn't always choose the direction of it! We finished our national service like a pair of tomcats let out of a bag – that's what I remember best.'

Rosemary let her lids droop. 'You were young, George. You had an excuse.'

'Oh, we didn't need one – Teddy especially. John Gosse and I had joined together and we had our release on the same day. Teddy was a week later but we were still drunk when he tracked us down. We stayed drunk for most of a month.'

'Is that all you could do with your time?' Rosemary asked.

'Oh, that wasn't all. I couldn't tell you the whole of it! Things would happen when we were together. You couldn't always choose the direction of it . . . In the camp they called us the Three Zouaves.'

'So what is a Zouave?' Rosemary asked, charmed by the word.

I got up from the table to pour myself coffee from the jug on the side. I was on a late shift and I'd heard the story before.

'The Zouaves were Algerians recruited by the French,'

Dad said. 'They were known for their bravery and their waxed moustaches. I suppose it started as a joke between us – a bit of competition between lads to see who could grow the finest moustache. Johnny Gosse and me shaved ours off as soon as we were demobbed but Teddy could never bear to get rid of his. He was already courting Alice when he came up from the Black Country and I suppose she must have told him that she liked it . . .'

'Some women do like a moustache,' Rosemary said. 'But then what, George? After a month of drink, what did you do?'

Dad's eyes were shining now and I could see that he was pleased by her prompting. 'Oh, we went out to make our way then, Rosemary. To make a future for ourselves . . . And Johnny Gosse and I had to find wives.'

'Well, you made your ways all right,' Rosemary said.

'Except for Teddy,' I put in. 'Teddy didn't end up with much.'

Dad sighed at the interruption. 'Well, Teddy was always one of life's passengers. He was a good laugh but I could see there was nothing to him, even back then. Johnny Gosse and I kept him for his company, I suppose – he'd find a funny slant to most things and you could rely on him to liven up a dull day. But then if there was serious business his chat would turn wearing . . .'

'He made a good husband, I heard,' Rosemary put in, and I knew that she and Marion must have discussed Teddy.

'Oh, I'm not saying that he didn't have a clever side to him,' Dad said, 'but it came out more in talk than thought – like his tongue did the thinking. He'd say whatever came into his mind and wouldn't leave it there to gather a head of steam . . .' He turned to me suddenly, squeaking the feet of his chair across the red tiles. 'You say he's got another woman working there now?'

'That's right.'

Dad laughed, enjoying himself now. 'Some waif or stray

30

he's taken on, I suppose. He could never resist them – human or otherwise. Alice was always complaining about the types he invited back home – he liked to feel he was important to someone, I suppose! Them having no children might have been the cause of that.'

'Some people choose it that way,' Rosemary said.

Dad glanced at me, then shook his head. A clever glance from his reddened eyes. 'Not Teddy and her. It was always a sorrow to them.'

I drove Dad into town and parked near the front. The tide was low and a yellow digger was working on the sands, bringing up ballast and blocks of concrete to extend the sea-wall. Dad eased himself out of the door in his dark overcoat, then drew back his sleeve to compare his watch to the talking clock, angling his head because only two of its four faces were ever reliable. He took a breath and I could see the folds of dissatisfaction around his lips.

'The air isn't so salt now! It used to take the paint off a door in six months.'

'You tell me things I'd never want to know, Dad.'

He pointed a finger at my chest. 'Marion is a good girl to me, that's all I can say!'

The clock started to call the hour as we walked up from the car park – a distorted quacking from the matched horns at its corners. Eleven o'clock. You had to know how to interpret the different sounds.

Dad put his hand to his ear, smiling. 'I'll bet Johnny Gosse is spinning in his grave!'

'Why would he care?'

'Oh, he took pride in himself as a public speaker, you see. I thought that he sounded only pompous but that was one of the few faults in him and we're allowed a few, aren't we?'

'A few each, Dad. Yeah.'

'He'd put in these little jokes he mostly stole from me or Teddy and tried to adapt to the occasion.' He laughed.

31

'Teddy would slide about in his seat at the way they were being slaughtered . . .'

'Like father like son,' I said.

'What do you mean?'

'I mean if you get a joke out of Tony Gosse it usually makes you cringe.'

'But you're in no position to criticise,' Dad said softly. He stopped to talk to a woman of his own age walking a Jack Russell. 'My boy's brought me here for a haircut, Mary.'

Mary smiled and blushed at Dad passing the time of day with her. The terrier nosed about their ankles. 'Well, he could do with one himself, George . . .'

'Leave me!' Dad said while he was waiting his turn. 'Go have a drink or do a bit of shopping!'

'No, I'll wait.'

We sat on the padded bench with our backs to the window. The room was heated by a paraffin-fire and the glowing ring of the element kept drawing my eyes. The warm air smelt of oil and lotion. Just one of the two chairs was in use and the hairdresser was leaning over a customer, questioning him quietly with a look of concern. The sideburns to mid-ear or shorter? That okay? He stepped back and started work again. His hands looked fluttery and unsteady, moving the comb and shining scissors over the man's head.

'He's getting too old for that game,' I whispered to Dad.

Dad frowned and reached for a magazine. 'The way you're going you'll never reach his age.'

When it was his turn he hung up his coat and let himself down into the chair, settling while the hairdresser fussed. 'Do what you want with it! Whatever takes your fancy!'

Eric tucked the sheet close. Dad's face looked pink and congested above the white linen. 'All I'll do is my best, George!'

'Do your worst if you like – it's all the same to me!'

Eric laughed and turned to smile at me. 'You're next, are you, son?'

'Not today, thanks.'

'He's afraid of cold steel,' Dad said.

I leafed through a magazine, listening to the quick snip of the scissors. Eric asked Dad something and I could hear Dad's grumbling reply. Then the bell above the door rang and another customer walked through – a short old man with a stick. He hung up his coat, then lowered himself on to the bench, sighing. A radio played from the corner of a shelf but so softly that I hadn't noticed it before and Eric was talking close to Dad's ear now, leaning over him. The magazine slipped from my lap and I reached down to pick it from the floor.

There was something wrong. 'Dad?'

Dad's head was forward and Eric was holding a grey paper towel to his ear. I saw the rose-shape of blood on the grey paper. A few red drops had fallen on the white sheet.

'I've just nicked him,' Eric said, matter-of-factly. 'He let his head fall forward.'

Dad sniffed then – a draining, dragging sniff. He sat up and the sheet slipped from his shoulders letting fall hanks of his greying hair. The back of his head had already been trimmed and I could see a wrinkled hollow just below the bone of his skull. Eric was struggling to hold the towel against his ear.

'Leave him now!' I ordered. 'Leave him alone!'

Dad was smiling to himself in the mirror. He put his fingers up to the towel. The old man pushed himself up from the bench for a better view, his mouth open.

'It's only a little cut with the ends of the scissors,' Eric said. 'I just caught the tip of his ear, that's all.'

'You ought to be shut down!'

He clicked his tongue, as if he thought I was making myself ridiculous. Dad still had his smile but his eyes were vague – old man's eyes in a face that had turned pale. He got up from the chair and looked as if he might fall for a

33

second until I stepped forwards and caught him around the shoulders. Eric let the paper towel fall and blood was welling from a crosswise gash at the tip of Dad's ear and collecting in the folds further down, like something filling a maze.

I put out my hand for the towel. 'Give me that!'

'It's okay – it's stopping now,' Eric said.

'Just give it to me!'

Instead he shrugged and crushed the soiled paper into a ball. He flung it backhanded into the wastebin, then tugged a fresh one from the dispenser and passed it to me. His hand was shaking with anger or fear. There was a smear of Dad's blood against the lapel of his white jacket.

I kept the towel against Dad's ear while I helped him on with his coat. He accepted it with a look of offence, rounding his shoulders. Eric was keeping his distance now, as if he thought I might attack him. The old man who had been waiting his turn was already slipping off his jacket for the vacant chair. Then Eric sighed and stepped forward to open the door for us, making the cracked bell chime. He kept his injured expression and averted his eyes as we went out.

There were a few drops of rain in the air, petrol smells. I felt better then, more able to cope. 'Are you okay, Dad?'

He didn't answer. I didn't like the pleasant, musing expression on his face. It was as if he had seen something in the situation he knew I wouldn't be able to appreciate.

'Dad?'

'I'm all right, son.'

A car stopped to let us cross the road. Maybe the driver had seen the blood on Dad's face, because she was staring at us through the windscreen. I still had my arm around his shoulders and I kept the towel against the side of his head. As we reached the opposite kerb I put my foot between his so that he stumbled and I had to hold him against me. His mouth was open and he was looking at me half in fear, as if I were a stranger who had taken hold of him.

'What happened there, Dad? Did you fall asleep?'

He stared and didn't answer. He looked like he couldn't for a second, it was stuck in his throat. His face was still a staring white. 'All right . . . I'm all right,' he managed.

I was still angry with Eric, because it was better than being afraid. 'He'll cut somebody's throat soon! I wouldn't let him trim the lawn!'

Dad shook his head. He put his hand to the towel and flinched.

We walked the hundred yards to the car park and I unlocked the car and helped him inside, leaning over him. It was nearly twelve by the talking clock. 'I'll take you to the hospital, Dad.'

He settled back into his seat, sighing. 'No . . . Take me home.' He took the towel from his ear and frowned at the drying blood. 'It's only a cut.'

I started the car. The radio came up and I turned it off. 'Somebody ought to take a look at it!'

Dad shook his head. He looked better now, as if he'd passed a crisis. His face was still pale but his eyes were alert again, ironical. 'No need – all it wants is a strip of plaster.'

I reversed from the spot and drew away. I had a dread of the talking clock starting again – Papa Gosse's cracked voice booming over my distress. Then we were somewhere in the centre of town but I couldn't for a second tell where. Whenever I turned my head I could see the glow of Dad's blood like a red lamp.

'What was that he said about letting your head drop, Dad? Did you feel faint?'

Dad was leaning back in his seat holding the towel to his face. 'It wasn't that exactly.'

'What was it?'

He shrugged. 'I lost the thread, say. I lost the thread of my own thoughts.'

'You're making no sense to me, Dad!'

35

'Oh, Rosemary will take care of this . . . Just see me home, will you?'

'He's sleeping like a babe now,' Rosemary said.

'How's that, Rosemary, when he's turning seventy?'

She tightened her lips as if she thought I was being unhelpful. 'Whatever happened must have taken it out of him. And he might have been tired to start off with.'

'Didn't he sleep well last night?'

'As far as I know he did . . .' She leaned forwards, anxious herself now or she had been hiding it. 'But what else could it have been, John?'

'Don't know . . .' I picked up an empty cup and my fingers were trembling. I put it down again. 'Maybe I should phone Marion.'

'You should phone Dr Spelling,' Rosemary said. 'You should tell her what's happened at least.'

I shook my head. 'I'd like to talk to Marion first.'

'Okay.' She stared at me for a second then turned away. 'That's right – I'm only interfering! I'll take another look at the patient, shall I?'

She went out into the hall and I heard her start to climb the stairs. I wanted to call her back but I didn't. I felt in a panic then, as if I'd touch something and it would break, keep on breaking . . .

Things would break and the rooms would be empty.

I called Marion from the phone in the hall. She wasn't in her flat and so I left a message then dialled the number of her mobile-phone.

'Why should he do that?' she asked. She must have been in her car, because the signal kept coming and going. 'Why should he faint? He hasn't done that before . . .' She left the trace of a question.

'I'm not sure.'

'John?' She was the elder sister now, despite the failing signal.

'He seemed a bit shaky that day we went to Mam's bench. I thought he was just a bit tired.'

'And was he tired this time?'

'I don't think so . . . He seemed all right on the way there. We even had a bit of an argument so he was his usual self, you could say.' I laughed and then wished that I hadn't.

'What about?'

'Oh, the usual shite – you know Dad . . . I can't even remember now.'

'So he was upset when he went in there.'

'He wasn't upset . . . Are you saying it was my fault now, Marion?'

'I'm just trying to make out what happened.'

'He fainted, fell asleep . . . Look, I don't know what happened to him. He let his head slip, that's all maybe . . .'

'So what did he look like afterwards, after it happened?' Marion asked after a silence.

'Oh, pale and a bit like he'd surprised himself.'

'And he had trouble walking?'

'I think it was just the shock of it – that old butcher nearly slicing off his ear . . .'

'Have you called Dr Spelling yet?'

'Not yet. Dad said he didn't want a doctor.'

Her voice started to rise then. 'Look, you two are as bad as each other! If you don't phone her then I'll do it myself. I've some business out of town but I'll turn back now if you want . . .'

'I'll do it, Marion. We don't need a gathering, do we? We don't want to give him the feeling he's at death's door.'

She was quiet for a second. 'Is that a joke, John? I hope so.'

Dr Spelling called that evening, parking her Audi next to Dad's salt-rusted Volvo. I answered the clatter of the door-chimes and she swept in in her bottle-green suit.

'So, how are you, John?'

'I'm fine, doctor; I'm fine myself.'

She peered at me with her small, sharp eyes. Her forehead was convex and glossy between frosted wings of hair. 'And how have you been sleeping?'

I laughed. 'Okay. Dad's the patient today, doctor!'

She nodded. 'Oh, yes . . . And how is he?'

'Oh, he says there's nothing the matter. Rosemary persuaded him to stay in bed but it was a struggle.'

I let her start up the stairs with her case and then followed. She must have been near retirement but she still had the heavy grace that I remembered from years back. Rosemary was doing some washing and the twin-tub was slushing below in the kitchen.

Dr Spelling stopped on the landing, lowering her voice because we were only a flight from Dad's door. 'Marion told me he had some sort of collapse.'

'Marion phoned?' I supposed she'd been making sure.

'A couple of minutes after you did. She was very worried . . . She was concerned for you both.'

'Why both?'

'Oh, she's concerned for you in general, John. You can understand that, can't you?'

I looked at Dad's door and didn't answer. It was open an inch. 'I didn't tell her he'd collapsed.'

'That might have been the word Marion used. She sounded very upset about what had happened. The more so for not being here . . .'

We went into Dad's room and he was sitting up against his pillows. Rosemary had put a neat plaster across the top of his ear and that and his half-cut hair made him look clownish. He sent Dr Spelling a dismayed look and then sighed, as if he might have expected this. He must have heard us coming up the stairs anyway. Dr Spelling sat carefully on the edge of the bed and lay her flat attaché beside her.

'You seem to think I'm wasting your time, George!'

'Oh, it's more your time I'm thinking of, Margaret. We've less to spare than these youngsters, you see.'

Dr Spelling leaned forwards, blocking my sight of him with her tailored back and shoulders. 'But now I'm here we may as well try to find out what happened to you . . . First of all I'd like to take a look at that ear.'

'Oh, Rosemary's already dealt with that!' Dad said with a touch of pride.

'Then I'll admire her skills.'

I saw Dad flinch once while she removed the dressing and then she was opening her case, snapping back the catches. I thought of his head tipped forward in the barber's chair and the exposed hollow at the base of his skull.

'A clean cut. Very nice. Nothing to worry us there . . .'

I went back downstairs. Rosemary wore one pink rubber glove and held the other in her hand. The washer was rumbling and shaking as the tub spun, rattling against the tiles.

'So is he ill?' she asked, and it seemed a strange word to use of Dad, as though he'd broken the habits of a lifetime.

'You don't think they'd tell me, d'you?' I looked into her face. 'Have you been crying, Rosemary?'

Her chin was set now, a firm pebble. 'It'd be hard, wouldn't it? If he started to be ill now . . . Just when he's getting over your mother, I mean.'

'All this is Marion's little exercise, Rosemary. Because she isn't here herself she wants the rest of us running around in a panic.'

'Well, she's succeeding with me! Oh, she's done that all right!'

I was still surprised by her, that she should cry while she was doing the washing. 'He's probably right about it, Rosemary, and we're making a fuss over nothing.'

'Do you believe that, John? Really?'

'I don't know what I believe.'

39

She laughed. One glove off and one glove on. The machine finished its cycle and she started pulling out the ropes of damp clothes, digging in her thumbs and separating them for the line.

'He'll lead that doctor a dance,' she said. 'He'll make a bloody mystery of it because that's his nature!'

5

I *nibble pills because I have terrible indigestion as
soon as I lie down. That's one of the signs, John. One
of the drawbacks of being pregnant. It keeps me
awake at night so that I'm able to do a lot of thinking.
In fact I'm not able to stop.*

*Gerald sleeps like a dog, with the same sort of
noises. I was going to say log but what does that tell
you? I'm weeping as you might have guessed from my
flippant tone, not yet absolutely but I can feel it
coming on – that sweet-and-sour feeling in the
sinuses. It's not out of sadness but tiredness, I think,
and it's a sort of bliss when I let myself go, like I'm
floating down a river of tears.*

*Does it hurt you, my expecting a baby? In a way I
hope so. Not because I want you to suffer but because
it would be a feeling between us – a wire connecting
us with the current still flowing. It would be impossible anyway not to tell you. If I say anything about
myself then I have to say that.*

*What I really want to tell you is I met one of our
policemen the other day. The younger one. The nicer
one. Do you remember him? I think you must do. I
say our policemen because we were so close for a
while – closer to them than a father or a brother.
Intimates.*

*We were in town, in a cafe near the square with
glass tables and wall-mirrors. Gerald always says it
reminds him of a hairdresser's. I've already reached
the stage where I'm nervous about spilling coffee over*

41

myself – for the shock it might give to the baby, if I can use that word so soon . . . And you know the way I like my coffee – very hot and black, with four sugar-cubes dissolving. I shouldn't take so much caffeine but that I'm useless without and anyway I've given up booze and cigarettes and I think that's enough for the sake of one little person . . .

So the younger copper, the nicer one, was standing beside our table – quietly, as if he wanted me to say the first word. He was smiling and because of that it took me a while to know him. Because he'd always looked so serious before, in those circumstances. And the time of course – years having passed. I mumbled and nodded. How are you? But I still wasn't sure. His face seemed to clarify, become itself, only after Gerald had stood up to let him take a seat. And even then I wouldn't have sworn it on oath.

He'd left the police, he said. Now he has his own firm advising on security, which involves a lot of travelling, which he said he likes. He told us security was now the only safe business and Gerald saw the joke before I did, which is unusual.

The copper's name is David Ordish. You'd think I would have remembered that but I didn't. Ex-copper, I should say, though isn't it a bit like having been a priest? While Gerald went to the counter he told me that he still thought about her a lot. Our little lost Pearl. And a look came over his face – a sort of sweetness I didn't trust but which made me feel sorry for him. This sweet, sorrowing look about his nose and upper lip. He glanced towards Gerald who had his back to us and told me that he thought sometimes he saw her in the street – just thought, you under-stand. Saw her from his car, say, passing by with other children. He saw her not as she was but as the child she would have become. Nearly seven years since – a lot of becoming.

So how was I to take all this, John? How would you? We were still talking when Gerald came back because it was like you couldn't interrupt his flow. And between us we were reckless about it, flaunting the subject. You see whenever it threatens to come up Gerald starts to be quiet and tactful, takes a deep breath before he speaks like he has that policy towards it. You must know the type of thing! He was like that for a few minutes, over his cake and coffee, while we raved on. Then he put his hand on my arm, his gentleman's hand, and asked, Are you sure you're not getting upset, Anna?

It takes Gerald to ask such a question! Which is in no way a criticism because obtuseness like his is something precious.

No, I told him, not in the slightest.

Sunday, Monday. Alex beckoned me over to the hatch. I had to wait until he swallowed a piece of Jaffa Cake. 'There's been a couple of messages for you, John.'

'Oh?'

'Marion wanted to speak to you and then the woman who does for you and your father called.'

'Thanks, Alex.'

He smiled past me at the drivers waiting in the front room. 'I wish I could afford to keep a woman.'

'You should find a better business than this, then.'

I jogged someone's elbow on my way to the phone and he stared after me. He was new that week, a thinnish wall-eyed man called Sylvester. I'd already had an argument with him over a fare.

'Marion just left . . .' Rosemary said. She was out of breath so she must have come downstairs to answer. 'She was trying to reach you earlier.'

'I was out and about.'

'She tried a couple of times. She wanted to speak to you.'

'About Dad?'

'That's right. About your father.'

I leaned into the booth. There were a couple of cards for hand-valeting and one for massage. 'Was she home for long?'

'Oh, a couple of hours. They were talking in the living room and then she came out in tears—'

'Why? Why was she crying?' I leaned further into the booth. I wanted to ask stupid questions to give me time to think.

'She wants you to meet her later, John. She's working somewhere tonight . . . Let me get the name for you.' She left the phone and then came back and told me.

'I know it . . . So how's Dad, Rosemary?'

'Oh, he's in the garden at the moment . . . He's fine himself, John. I think Marion is the one you should be concerned about.'

A pub in the streets away from the front, the type you can't get an idea of until you're through the side-door, and then it's too late and you have a drink anyway. Just one. I must have arrived during the intermission because the crowd was gathered around the bar and not the kidney-shaped stage in one corner. A full-length mirror was angled against the wall and a man in camouflage dungarees was working on one of the tall speaker amps with his tools laid out on the floor beside him – pliers, a small file, a roll of solder. The smell of flux was in the air, sharper than cigarette smoke.

A stocky man with dark, crimped hair made way for me at the bar. He smiled, then nodded towards the stage, swinging the little gold dangle of an earring.

'They've got a stripper on later!'

'I thought there was a singer tonight.'

'That should be now but the sound went. She wasn't much, anyway.'

'I've heard she's okay.'

He worked a pint glass towards his mouth. 'She might have been once. She's still got the looks but the voice is going. That's what places like this do to your throat – she'll sound like a bloody hog in a couple of years.'

I bought myself a drink. There was a shriek from the speakers and then whistles and applause as Marion came back on stage. She looked nervous for a second, barely glancing at the crowd and fiddling with the height of the microphone stand.

'Hello again . . . Hi!'

She put up her hand to shade her eyes but I thought she wouldn't be able to see me among the crowd at the bar. The couple of spotlights made spangles shine from her hair and her lime-green dress. She'd put on weight lately and the dress looked tight around her hips. The stocky citizen was half-turned on his stool now, so that he could look towards her and still keep track of the talk along the bar.

'So what's the stripper like?' I asked.

'Not bad. I've seen her a couple of times – nice little bod but she won't go all the way . . .'

'Oh yeah?'

Marion had started her warm-up routine. The man who'd repaired the amplifier was leaning on top of one of the speakers, watching her with a glass in his hand. One of her tapes was playing as background.

'She leaves her G-string on,' the citizen said. 'I've never seen the point in that myself. I mean why go through with all that if you're going to leave out the last bit? That's the important part for me – what it's all leading up to.'

'Like Hamlet without the ghost,' I said.

He beckoned me closer, nodding towards Marion. 'Do you reckon she's wearing a girdle?'

'Dunno. She could be.'

Marion started the joke about the old girl and the crocodile. Man goes into a pub with a crocodile on a leash.

'I reckon she is,' he said. 'I reckon that's all that's keeping her in place.'

So he pours the drink into the ashtray and the crocodile laps it up. Then he orders six packets of crisps . . . I had nearly a full glass in my hand and while Marion was still halfway through the joke I tilted over the bar. A flat wave spread over the zinc top and made a little rill against the man's fat back propped against its edge. The blue cotton of his shirt started to darken and then he snatched himself away as if the stuff had been scalding instead of chilled.

'Aaaah!'

The stool tipped under him and fell. He looked back at me – my hand still sloping the glass. Marion had stopped because of the disturbance but I'd heard the joke already.

I found her car and waited there. The back seat was a jumble of clothes and blankets, as if someone had been sleeping in it for a week, and I noticed that her tax-disc was out of date. It was drizzling now and I could feel the drops like tiny flakes of ice against my face. After about ten minutes she came along carrying her costume-case. The man in dungarees was following behind wheeling her speaker and amplifier strapped to a folding trolley.

She opened the back and I helped them pack away her equipment. 'Harry,' she said. 'This is my kid brother, John. You'll have to excuse his behaviour earlier.'

Harry shook my hand. 'I didn't notice any behaviour.'

He gave Marion a peck on the cheek and started to walk back to the pub. She shouted out to him when he was a few yards away. 'Hey, thanks for all your help!'

He shook his head and then started running, a skipping run along the wet pavement.

'He does well to run,' I said.

Marion blinked her eyes. 'He does the bookings for there and a few other places. I made him promise that my fool of a brother hadn't buggered my chance of a repeat.'

'You should stop playing these places, Marion. Telling jokes to drunks.'

'They're not all drunks, and I need the jokes now. When

you've been around for a while they won't take you straight any more – they won't pay just to hear you sing.'

'Give it up then! Maurice was saying you were doing well as an agent.'

'I enjoy it, though – that's my problem . . .' She hugged herself. She'd replaced the shiny dress with a dark top and tracksuit trousers.

'Are you finished for tonight?'.

'I've finished work, yeah. I said I might meet Tony later. After that I'll come to stay the night, if I may.' She looked at the little gold watch Tony Gosse had given her.

'Rosemary told me you were there today.'

'That's right . . . she finished off his hair for him and she said she might do yours next. I reckon Rosemary's the best chance he's got, don't you?'

I ignored that because it was too complicated to think about. 'She told me he had you in tears,' I said.

'Oh, I might have shed a few – I wasn't counting . . . Dr Spelling thinks he should take it easy for a while, until we know more about what's going on.'

'You've spoken to her?'

'I phoned her a couple of hours ago. We had quite a long chat . . .'

'I thought you might have. She thinks you're more responsible, for fucksake!'

Marion leaned to kiss me on the cheek. 'She's old-fashioned, you see. She thinks this is woman's stuff.'

'And she's had a little chat with Rosemary. I think I'm the only one being left in ignorance.'

'Rosemary looks after him. That's her job.'

'She's a housekeeper not his nurse. Unless that's going to change.'

'Dr Spelling wants Dad to go to the hospital for tests,' Marion said.

I looked down the wet street and back again. 'What sort of tests?'

'To see what might be wrong. To see if his vagueness

might be caused by something physical . . .' She pursed her lips. 'If it might be a medical problem.'

'Vagueness?'

'That's the word she used . . . Haven't you noticed it lately?'

'He nodded off in a chair, that's all I noticed.'

'You know he's ill, John! We both know.'

She stared at me, wanting me to speak. There was a white edge to her lips.

'So Dr Spelling thinks it's Alzheimer's or something?' I asked.

'She didn't use that word.'

'She wouldn't, no! They say the minimum and leave you to work things out for yourself.'

'She said it could be a number of things.'

'So tell me what else!'

Marion sighed and looked at her watch again. I thought she might have been thinking of Tony Gosse but then I saw that she was doing it only out of numbness and her eyes hadn't registered the time. 'Do you want to know what Dad said to me, John?'

'What?' But I wasn't sure I wanted to know and it was her look that warned me.

'He said that the second before he blacked out he saw little Pearl.'

I did the thing again of looking both ways along the street. For help or something. Distraction. 'Where . . . ? Where did he see her?'

'He said he looked in the mirror and caught sight of her outside – just for a second as she passed by the window.'

Behind me, as I was sitting over *Practical Motoring*. 'What did he say she looked like?'

'Like she does, did. A child.'

'She would be, wouldn't she? She would be a child! How old did he say she was?'

She shook her head. 'He wasn't sure, John . . . He said about four or five, that kind of age.'

'How could it be Pearl then? How could it have been her?' She would have been older than that. She wouldn't have stayed still.

'That's what he said, John. I asked him what happened and he said that.'

'So was she on her own?'

'It was a child walking past the window, John – someone who reminded him of her . . . He might even have fallen asleep like you said and dreamed it.'

'She wouldn't have been on her own, though. Four or five. A child that age wouldn't have been walking on her own.'

Marion put her finger to her cheek and I could see that she wished she hadn't started this, that she and Dr Spelling had kept it between them – my father's private sickness. 'She might have been, I don't know. Maybe she was with someone.'

'Who? Who was she with?'

'I think you're approaching this from the wrong end, John. The real problem is that Dad's ill, not . . .'

'Not that he saw Pearl, right? That isn't a problem.'

'Look, I'm sorry . . . The last thing I wanted was to bring this up. I thought you needed to know, that's all. I thought you'd be able to—'

'Understand. You thought I'd understand . . . So why didn't Dad tell me this?'

'He wouldn't, would he?'

'*Why?*'

She looked exasperated now, anxious to clear up this little problem and be gone. 'Because you're the one he can't mention her to, John! Because he's *frightened* to. Because she can't be between you for a second—'

My hand hit her chest and she covered herself and stared back at me. I think it must have hurt because her mouth was open.

'I'm sorry,' I said. 'Sorry, Marion.'

She was still staring and then she swallowed and nodded, as if she'd learned something. 'Okay, John.'

'Look, I'm sorry . . .'

'I don't want you to be sorry!'

I couldn't look at her now, my beautiful sister.' But you shouldn't, you shouldn't have started on about that . . .'

She put her hand on my arm. I could feel that she was trembling or I was. 'Look, I'm going now, John. I'm going to see Tony, okay?'

I was glad of that because it gave me the chance to be angry. 'Go there, then! Sod off!'

She got into the car and switched on the engine. It didn't catch for a second and I started to hope it wouldn't. Then it roared when she put her foot on the pedal.

I went to Maurice's after that and Bilko's flame-red Orion was parked outside. As soon as I pushed through the revolving door I saw him beckon to Maurice and Maurice snapped a glass for me down from the shelf. Double shot of brandy, which is the cabbie's comfort.

'Here's blood in your eye!' Bilko said, lifting his own.

'Yeah . . . Cheers, Bilko. I'm not surprised if there is.'

He brought his big soft face close to mine, peering, concerned. 'Have you been upsetting people again?'

'I don't know what it is I do, Maurice. That's the truth.'

I had a couple of drinks, another. Went to the gents, came back. I noticed that Maurice had taken the flowers away from the portrait of the dog and that the shift must have changed at the plant because there was a crowd of them at the bar.

I got into an argument about something – continental shoe-sizes, dog-handling, quickest way to Carlisle. Some pushing and shoving along the front of the bar and Bilko and one of the barmen were restraining me with Maurice hanging back as if he wouldn't soil his hands. He never would on occasions like that.

The next thing I was driving alongside the dyke and

couldn't put my finger on where I'd made the transition. I was thinking about a joke of Marion's: Man goes into a pub with a fish in a glass of water. The concrete slabs rocked when I crossed one of the little bridges over the Course and the water was high because of the rain so that I could hear it rush under the belly of the car. I was on the caravan site then and the white sides of caravans threw back the light of the lamps. I wound down the window to let in air and I could feel a sore spot on the tip of my chin where I'd skinned it on something but I couldn't remember the event.

Man goes into a pub with a rabbit on a piece of string . . . I followed the gravel road for a while and then turned off, with this idea of stopping and taking a recuperative walk along the top of the dyke. Lights were on in a few of the 'vans and the clothes on a line looked filled for a second when the lamps touched them. The sea was invisible but the sky was lighter above the line of the dyke, like it had caught a shine from the water. There was something pale to the side of the track, a rag of mist. Then it swung towards me.

I tried to stop dead and the car clenched and jolted another few feet. She was holding the child's head against her throat, tucked for warmth below her chin. Its red knitted bonnet had worked to one side and she put up a hand to set it right. The lamps were trained at the height of her belly so that I couldn't see her face clearly but the cloud of her breath floated back. I wasn't sober but some clarity had slipped over the drink. I switched off the radio and I could hear the child then – a long cry and then a catch, another cry. I pushed open the door and climbed half out, holding on to the edge of the door.

'Are you all right?'

She started and shook her head. The child was still nuzzling at her, kicking its feet in their red woollen bootees – not a baby but more of a toddler, so that it was a weight in her arms. The wails it was sending out were shocking in so much silence and the door of one of the caravans opened and levered out light. Whoever it was stood there for a second and then it closed again.

'You're not hurt, are you?'

She jerked her head so that her hair whipped. I was getting used to the dark now and her face looked dead white, tight as a fist. 'You nearly fucking killed us, you prat!'

'Ah . . . Sorry. All I can say is I'm sorry.'

She wouldn't look at me. She was petting and cuddling the child, rocking it like a quick little machine. For a minute she was giving it her whole attention and I thought I could have got back into the car and driven quietly away.

'Where are you going? I'll give you a lift if you like . . .'

'Do you want another try at killing us?'

The child turned its head then. Its mouth was still open but no sound came, as if it had screamed itself breathless. I could see now that the woman was the one who had quietly cooked her breakfast behind Fiona's counter.

'I know you, don't I?'

She stared at me over the child's woolly cap. 'You don't know me.'

She shut her eyes, blinking me away. The toddler was pressing its face against her throat and making soft little grunts.

'Okay, I don't. I'm sorry anyway.'

'I'll bet you're pissed, aren't you?' She shook her head. 'People like you ought to be banned!'

'Look, you were standing nearly on the road! You must have seen me before I saw you.'

She looked past me to the car and I wondered if she was memorising the number-plate. 'You don't live here anyway, d'you?'

'I've got a right to drive through.'

She turned away then, as if I wasn't there, as if that attitude had removed me. I watched her walking towards the dyke. She had a strong, sudden step. Her dark coat had

52

bands of velvety trim that shone in the lamps. The child's red woollen cap showed over her shoulder.

6

You could think there was nothing wrong at all. If you were careful you could work your way into that frame of mind. It went on like that for days, for a week. Marion stayed for a couple of nights and then had business out of town. I thought that Tony Gosse would have the same, away from his wife Julia and the kid. I did my shifts, then I watched the small TV in the kitchen while Rosemary and my father played snooker in the front room. I would let the room go dark except for the light from the screen and blue flame of the pilot-light in the water-heater. I'd hear Dad calling encouragement when Rosemary made a shot he liked, then he'd slam the butt of his cue on the rug.

'You're giving me a game tonight, Rosemary!'

The trundle of the ball across the bed of the table, the roll and clack as it fell into the net. I looked up from the set and saw Rosemary standing at the door, an off-duty cigarette in her mouth.

'You're in the dark tonight, John!'

I smiled up at her. 'Am I though, Rosemary? Did you win?'

'Oh, if I did you'd see him sulk for a week.'

I laughed at that. I'd had a couple of drinks on the way home, sitting at the bar before Maurice's boss-eyed stare. 'He ought to marry you, Rosemary!'

I swore she blushed in the light from the screen. Then Dad called her and he must have been standing in the hall and peering at the way she had gone. She pulled a face, rolling her shoulder against the door-frame. Then Dad called more quietly, softly as you'd coax a cat.

I took my breakfasts in Fiona's. I noticed that Bilko had his in town now so that things must have been getting worse between them. The cafe would be quiet until the men from the plant came in and then she would be flitting between the grill and the hotplate, the dishwasher, serving and clearing the tables. Cursing below her breath.

'Where's the help today, Fiona?'

She laid a tray of dirty plates on the counter. 'Do I have any help, John? That's news to me.'

'The girl you had here. The quiet one.'

'Oh, her.' She let her lids close, gathering contempt about the lashes. 'She hasn't been in this week, so I don't reckon I'll see that one again.'

'Has she been ill?'

'I wouldn't know if she was or not . . . Teddy's the one who hires and fires, so you can ask him if you're interested.' She gave me the clear look that always unnerved Bilko.

'Is he in?' I asked.

'Oh, that place is his castle nowadays. He hardly shows his nose outside.'

'Why's that, Fi?'

She shook her head. One of the OKO men came to the counter and she gave him a weary look. 'Yes, love?'

I put my change in the box for the lifeboat appeal. 'Okay, bye, Fiona. I hope the kids are being good.'

'Better behaved than this lot,' Fiona said.

I walked through the arcade and out through the automatic glass doors. A couple of children from the site were playing the machines, standing on tiptoes to nudge the bars. Teddy's office had a separate entrance at the side of the building and a man with an attaché case was sitting on the low wall of the car park just around the corner. He gave me the nod as I went by. It might have been time for one of Teddy's naps because he took a while to answer the door. Then I heard his stockinged feet cross the rug and he blinked at me around the edge.

'Is this a bad time, Teddy?'

'You tell me when they're good, son!'

He took a glance past my shoulder and let me inside. The room was dark except for both bars of an electric fire shining in front of the desk. He went to fiddle with the blind and pale light entered. The window had a view across the car park towards the slope of the dyke. There was a sweet smell of drink – sickening at first but then you could get to like it.

'Dad likes the same tipple,' I said.

Teddy brought the fat bottle out from hiding. 'That's right – we developed the taste together. Want some?'

'Just one. I'm working today . . . So who's the character in the tin suit?'

Teddy stood a plastic mug next to a souvenir beaker and poured. 'Still there, is he? I was hoping he'd have gone by now.'

'He's waiting you out, Teddy. I can see that from his face.'

'I haven't got what he wants,' Teddy said. 'I've already told him that.'

'I could tell him again for you.'

'Don't bother, son. Whatever you do don't intervene!' He took another swallow so that his glass was nearly empty. I used to worry about Teddy's drinking but then he was too old and sly to be an alcoholic. He'd slip away from the drink, sidestep it.

'Bad as that, is it?'

'It's fucking worse, John. I used to owe Tony Gosse and that was bearable but now someone's bought out the debt and they're starting to be serious.'

'An agency? And Tony put them on to you?'

He spread his hands. 'Something funny's been going on with him lately. I'm starting to wonder if he isn't clearing out altogether.'

'Why should he do that?'

'Maybe he wants a new start.'

The rum had a soft, heavy feel and little Pearl touched me like she did sometimes. During moments of ease and relaxation. I suppose I'd already been thinking about her and Dad.

'You might be in a trance but I'm not,' Teddy said.

'I was thinking.'

'Start to do that and you're fucked – I'll give you that advice!'

'Thanks.'

'Look, you don't have to thank me for anything – you're my godson.'

'I didn't forget that, Teddy.'

He looked offended. 'Well, make sure you never do!'

There was a knock at the door then – not loud but abrupt. Teddy put out his hand for silence.

'Mr Sandringham!' a voice called through. 'If you're indisposed then I could call on you tomorrow or the day after.'

'I might be indisposed for the rest of the week,' Teddy said. 'You can slip anything you've got for me under the door.'

We heard him fumbling and then a tongue of paper showed at the bottom of the door.

'Thank you,' Teddy called. 'I'll deal with it when I'm feeling better.'

We listened until a car started on the forecourt. 'You've ground him down, Teddy.'

Teddy closed his eyes and leaned back in his swivel-chair. 'I'm too fucking long in the tooth for this hide-and-seek shite. It's undignified as well . . . I suppose Fiona's been giving you an earful about it.'

'She was complaining about the help you found her.'

Teddy shook his head. 'There's another one that's been a disappointment to me! She seemed like she needed the work but then she started playing silly-sods. It kills your faith in human nature.'

He sipped his drink, trembling as he felt the heat of it. His fingers found the tip of his moustache.

'Dad was talking about you,' I said.

'Then I'm privileged.'

'He was saying it was too long since he saw you.'

'Well, he knows where he can find me.'

'He needs an invitation though, Teddy. I think it'll need to come from you first.'

'I could let sleeping dogs lie,' Teddy said. 'Maybe that's the best thing.'

'It'd be good for him, I think. I mean there's no one to check him now. Now that Johnny Gosse's dead.'

'You mean he thinks I'll do now that he's gone.'

'He needs somebody to compare notes with, Teddy. Otherwise he loses track.'

'That's what I've heard,' Teddy said.

'What have you heard?'

He shook his head, then put on a foolish, old man's smile. 'I've heard nothing. D'you think anyone bothers to inform me?'

A coffee, a fare, a cheese-and-ham sandwich, another coffee, another little pill. I watched a bit of telly in the front office. Then a call came in and I was out of the door again.

A reception near Hooperstown, waiting with the engine running while the fare made his goodbyes and swayed down the garden path. The front windows were open to let out the smoke and buzz, empty glasses balanced on the sills.

He swore when he kicked over a potted plant, then nearly fell trying to right it. He brushed spilt earth towards the border with the side of his shoe.

'Where to?' I asked.

'Oh.' Shooting his chin forwards. He named a street about half a mile away and got in the back.

I pulled away. 'Hardly worth your while, was it? Waiting for a cab, I mean?'

'Why walk when you can ride?'

He was about my age – a couple of years older, say. He wore his hair slicked back in oiled wings so that in the mirror it had the look of black mouse ears. I must have been staring.

'Something the matter?' he asked.

'Nothing is . . . Nice party?'

'Oh aye. Very nice.'

'A relative, are you?'

'Not really. Not as such. Not theirs.'

'Someone else's then?'

'What?'

'You must be someone else's relative.'

I couldn't stop myself from glancing through the mirror at him, seeing if I could catch him with the ears again. He must have noticed because he started to look grim and set his face. His wings of hair shone.

'There's something wrong with you,' he said.

'I'm sorry you think that.'

'I'm bloody sure of it!' he said.

'You're the customer.'

He started to look through the windows then, turning this way and that. 'So where the fuck are we?'

I'd taken him him a mile or two out of his way. 'Dunno, friend – I'm as lost as you are.'

'You're a fucking freak, that's why! Call yourself a fucking driver!'

I could feel him staring at the back of my neck. Another second and he started rapping at the windows. A ring was cracking against the glass. I didn't know if he was trying to break his way out or only attract attention. Summon help from passers-by.

'Okay! Stop the car! I'm not being driven about by a fucking nutcase!'

I tucked my head down and speeded up – the response you make to that level of abuse. We were at the outskirts of town now, passing rows of semis behind overgrown hedges, moving into shadow and out of it. Then the fare reached forward and slipped an arm around my throat.

'*HEY!*'

I stamped on the brakes. The car went into a skid and the back slewed round. He was on top of me before we'd stopped moving, pushing at my back and shoulders as if he were trying to force me down on to the mat. His mouth was exploding with fucks and I could feel the spit hitting the side of my face. I covered the back of my neck but the fare was hitting me now with something hard, grunting every time he let loose and still shoving at me with his free hand and elbow. I squeezed myself as tight as I could into the space between the seat and the pedals.

Finally he let up and I heard him open the door. He stepped out and started to walk back along the road, the soles of his dress shoes scraping the gravel. Then he must have changed his mind because he turned and marched back. He was still panting with exertion. I waited for another round of cuffs but instead I was hit by a shower of silver and coppers. They sprayed about me like bullets. Silver bullets for the vampire. With my eyes squeezed shut I felt one cold coin slip down the back of my collar.

7

So do you remember him, John? Was it hard cop/soft cop like you see in the films – and he was the nice one you were supposed to trust? I don't know what they put you through because you wouldn't speak about it. Because it was unspeakable.

I was walking in town when I saw him again. I was in town and walking quickly through the rain. It doesn't matter to where. Or what really happened was that he saw me first and tapped on a window with a coin. I went inside – to the warm room of detergent smells and rumbling machines.

I was scattering drips. The brisk walk had made me daring. I asked if he always did his own laundry.

'Oh aye. I don't have a machine – or a wife.'

There were a few other customers, old and young. David Ordish was sitting on one of the benches in the sort of mismatched clothes you wear when they're the only ones clean. And a funny thing I noticed, John: his trousers were too short and riding up above his socks, as if he'd recently put on a spurt of growth. He moved up a foot on the bench and it seemed a shame not to sit down. Because of that pitiful inch of bare shin.

'Your husband might be doing for himself as well,' he said. 'I mean the first one.'

So I reminded him that we were never married, that we hadn't thought it important at the time.

He nodded his head a few times. 'That's right – I

forgot that little detail. But you do now, I suppose? You believe in the sacrament of marriage?'

A funny way of putting it – to a woman with a bump. It saved a lot of awkwardness, I said.

'Hmm. So are you still in touch with him? The first one?'

How would you have answered? If you had been me, John, what would you have said? Sometimes I write. Sometimes I write and don't send, or only think about writing – about the things I could say should I decide to. Sometimes I feel strong enough to do none of the above.

I said I wrote to you sometimes.

'But he doesn't write back?'

He must have read that from my face. His pale eyes make me think of blindness but also second sight, John – one sense compensating for the lack of the other.

Not so far, no.

'But you live in hope?'

I had to laugh. I said hope wasn't the word.

The wash finished and he took his things out to transfer them to the drier. A few damp handfuls of clothes.

Is that all the clothes you have?

He smiled. 'What am I – a bloody mannequin?'

You could keep yourself covered, I said.

'Don't you think I'm decent then?'

I wasn't sure that I wanted to be playful, start the flirty stuff with him. You never know where that might lead. I watched his few clothes falling past the door of the drier. Some bright, expensive-looking socks seemed to be the only luxury he allowed himself. But then it's like that with men and socks.

He touched my arm and I jumped. 'You're deep in thought.'

I said I ought to get on. I'd been sitting there for ten minutes already.

'More like twenty. You go on your way, then.'

Yes, sergeant. Teasing.

He laughed but I could see he didn't like it.

You can't give it up though, can you?

The drum was slowing and he got up to feed in another coin. 'I can't give your little girl up, if that's what you mean. Or the others.'

Others?

'Oh yeah – it's an expanding field.'

Then I asked if it was mostly kids, because I was starting to be worried by that concentration, wondering what his reasons might be.

'Kids and young women – they're the ones who disappear.'

And never men?

'Oh, they do. But it's usually because they want to.'

I told him I couldn't see the point. Because it wasn't his job any more and they weren't his kids.

He moved closer then, so we were elbow-to-elbow. He was so confidential that I couldn't lean away. 'Oh, because I'm in a position to do something about it – I've got the skills and a few contacts. I travel about and that's a help. And also because I can afford to . . .'

I could see from his clothes that he wasn't talking about money.

'I can afford not to give up hope, you see. They're not my kids as you say and so it doesn't cost me the same.'

I was angry then and I stood up, John. He'd touched a nerve. Her nerve. Then when I looked at his pale face I felt in sympathy with him again. Because I could see that he was smitten by her – as if she'd laid a hand on him, her inky little thumbprint.

You ought to buy yourself some vests at least, I told him.

I must have interrupted a train of thought. 'What?'

I told him I had to go now. I stepped past but he caught my hand. He did it casually but he held it lightly, with his thumb across the palm.

'Will you leave me your number!'

'Why should I?'

He looked smug then, holding on without any force. He glanced at my belly, my high little bump – like it was there for him for the first time. 'Oh, I thought sometimes you might like to talk.'

I had half dreams about my little girl. Dreams that didn't concern her only people would mention her name. Alex Vosper calling me to the hatch and laughing, his mouth exploding with it – my dead Pearl and crumbs of Jaffa Cake.

So I tucked my head down and ran, through the group in front of the drinks machine – spilling coffee, pushing aside greasy bags of pasty and sugared doughnuts.

'Sorry!' Alex Vosper shouted, desperate now, jumping up from his chair. 'Sorry, John – I just forgot!'

Or a fare would lean from the back and plant his hand on my shoulder. His mouth just behind my ear. 'Hey, so how's your little girl? What is it?'

Like he only wanted to speak her name. I looked in the mirror and I could see how his face was desperate with it. I'd brush his hand away and carry on driving.

'Sorry, pal! Did I say something?'

Dad took the dressing from his ear and there was a dark scar where the tip had been. He'd stop to look at himself in the mirror, touching it gently, frowning at his own reflection.

'Do you reckon it's spoiled your looks, George?' Rosemary asked, stopping behind him.

'Oh, I've no one left to look pretty for, Rosemary!' He watched himself from the side, putting on a stern face. 'Do you think I should claim compensation?'

'You'd only ruin the poor man,' Rosemary said. 'And what else could he do at his age?'

He winked at her. 'Oh, us old boys have a few tricks left, Rosemary!'

Rosemary laughed and gave me a glance as she passed by. Dad saw me through the doorway and put his hand to his chest. He was wearing a bright silk tie I hadn't seen before and I wondered if Marion had bought him it. And then I wondered if Rosemary had.

'So what are you staring at?' Dad asked.

Rosemary laughed on her way to the kitchen. 'You two!'

'So how's the old man?' Bilko asked.

'He's fine. Why?'

'I heard he's been ill, that's all.'

'Who told you that?'

Bilko sipped his coffee and watched the TV in the corner, settling himself. 'I must have heard something . . . Maybe it was Maurice told me.'

'I've already told Maurice there was nothing wrong with him!'

'Oh, you know how news travels in this place!' Bilko said. 'Like hot piss through snow . . . You give him my regards anyway, won't you?'

'Okay . . .' I watched the TV. Film starring Lucille Ball or it was someone who looked like her. 'So how are you and Fiona nowadays?'

'Don't ask!' Bilko said.

'Okay, I won't.'

'She's turning the kids against me now.'

'I don't think so, Bilko.'

'Well, they've been against me for years – since they were born, I think. As soon as they could work things out for themselves they started to turn against me.'

One of the drivers came in and Alex Vosper beckoned him into the back office. I'd heard a couple of jobs come over the radio and I wondered if he was passing me over. 'You ought to stay calm, Bilko. I don't think this is doing you any good, you know.'

He shook his head. I could see he was nearly in tears now. 'I couldn't get used to living on my own, John. Not at my age! I mean can you picture me stuck in a B'n'B somewhere? I wouldn't know what to do with myself . . .'

'It won't come to that, Bilko! Not in a million years.'

'Are you sure? Can you promise me that, John? I mean she's moved me out to the spare room already.'

'I promise, Bilko. I solemnly promise.' I looked over to where Alex was talking to the other driver. 'Bilko . . . Have you got any sweeties for me?'

He looked over at Alex as well. Alex saw it and gazed back at us through the hatch. The other driver left with the slip. 'I can let you have a few,' Bilko said.

'A few? What use is that?'

'Maybe more, then . . . I think you owe me a few anyway, don't you? More than a few.'

'Okay, Bilko. Point taken.'

'Hey, do you really think I can get back with Fiona, John? You must know her by now . . .'

'I'll do everything I can, Bilko. Just say the word and I'm there.'

'So will you be seeing Victor soon?'

'Yeah. That's what I'll do.'

'D'you think you could get me fifty?'

I blessed Bilko's bleeding little heart, then swallowed a couple and then another. I had a fare to the station and caught another on the way back. Then I drove around, listening to the messages over the radio and laughing to myself. I didn't know what was so funny but something was. About halfway through that I thought of seeing Marion and so I drove to the front and parked near the clock. I phoned her flat from one of the boxes but there was no answer, the machine didn't even click in and I wondered if she'd switched it off.

The tide was a mile out and there was a mist on the water. You could see the sandbars at the mouth of the river looking like stranded whales. The gulls were calling and there was bluish, misty sunshine and I started walking about and looked into the place where Marion sometimes had her lunch but she wasn't at the table she liked nor any of the others. I tried her number again from the booth and her machine came on this time but I decided not to leave a message. I thought about waiting there and ordering something but I felt too restless to sit down.

So I walked through the town. The sun was out now but the warmth lasted only until you stepped into the shade. Somebody barged into me and didn't stop and I was still rubbing my shoulder when I saw Tony Gosse and family on the opposite pavement. I might have walked on but Tony's wife Julia had already spotted me then. She smiled and waved, so that I had to step over.

Tony was a couple of yards in front, his hands resting on the handles of his son's chair. Julia wore a long blue coat with a short, matching cloak. The brightness of the material made her face seem tired but only in the second before she smiled. Tony Gosse was dressed in casual but expensive clothes, as if he wanted to be well dressed but not too blatant. He stood upright against the wheelchair's tall back and pushed on the brake with his foot.

I was smiling at them like an idiot then. I could do nothing else whenever I saw them together. But Tony was looking anxious already, frowning down at the boy's narrow scalp.

'You looked lost over there,' Julia said, full of sympathy. I'd always liked Julia. I was never sweet on her but I'd always liked her.

'Lost in a dream,' I told her. 'That's right.'

She had a face that was homely and then pretty – on and

off like a switch. I wondered which side Tony saw and when, if she was stuck in one phase for him. I could feel the way my smile was starting to be fixed.

'I was looking for Marion,' I said, because I couldn't resist. 'You haven't seen her about, have you?'

Tony shook his head. Some time ago he'd decided that I could be unpredictable, so if he was anxious before he'd be panicking now. But he didn't show it and I supposed I should have been impressed. 'I'm afraid not, John. Not for a while now . . .' He turned to his wife. 'You haven't seen her lately, have you, Julia?'

Julia shook her head. I always wondered what she suspected but didn't pursue. Sometimes she had a clever cast to her face, a twist that might have been guile. Other times it seemed like she and the boy were the only ones not to know. And I sometimes wondered about the boy . . . 'I've not seen Marion in ages,' she said, regretfully. 'Neither of you, in fact.'

'Oh, we keep ourselves to ourselves,' I said. 'It's better that way.'

She frowned as if she didn't understand and looked towards Tony. He shrugged and I felt ashamed then – at the stuff I was spouting. I saw then that the boy was watching me from his harness of straps and springs. I smiled and nodded down at him.

'His name is Nat,' Tony said, 'if you're thinking of saying hello.'

'I hadn't forgotten.'

Julia had stepped up to us now and was holding on to the sleeve of Tony's sweater. I could see just from her loose grip that she trusted him completely, and that she was a little afraid of me. I wasn't sure that she even liked Marion either, maybe she sensed a danger in us both. The boy made a noise then and I squatted down so that we were at eye-level. He had twisted in his supports until he was shoulder-on to me and now he started to work his way back. The harness kept him upright but allowed free

70

movement, the springs and straps holding their tension one against the other. He had a hand resting in his lap while the other curled and uncurled at the height of his chest, showing the smooth pink of his palm.

'Hello, Nat,' I said. 'What's new with you?'

He made himself still suddenly, as if something had caught his attention – something frightening or fascinating. It could have been the sound of his own name. He was facing me now, pushing out his pale pebble of a chin. His glossy hair was combed to the side and trimmed carefully around his ears, which were small and perfect. I reached to touch the back of his hand and his skin had a smooth, cool feel like washed stone, as if there was no grain to it. I heard Tony draw in his breath, as if he was about to say something, but then Nat made a grunt of effort and looked at me from his short-lidded eyes. He gave me such a soft, loving look that I could feel my bones turn to water.

Julia was watching us both, smiling down at me.

'I think we should go now,' Tony said, anxious again.

Then they were both watching, waiting to see what I'd do.

I had a couple of drinks in town at a place called the Propeller. It had a nice name but it was one of those theme pubs with nets and brassware. I didn't care what the fuck it was anyway . . . I started thinking about Dad being ill and then Nat in his chair and the woman I'd nearly knocked down and the child who'd stopped crying suddenly and looked at me. Then I started to think about Maurice's dog, wondering if I was the one who'd run it down and I hadn't even noticed. Or I'd run it down and then hidden it from myself, tucked it away somewhere . . .

I went back to the car then and Alex Vosper was asking for me over the radio but I pulled the jack to switch it off. The silence got on my nerves and I turned the radio back on. I took the road to Maurice's and I was already starting to be down. I wondered if they were the same type of pills or another.

Maurice was playing pool with one of the customers while the part-timer looked after the bar. The friend lifted his head and winked at me while Maurice kept his nose over the cue. I thought it was the one who hawked big fluffy animals through the pubs in town and I looked to the bench and saw a pink elephant and a penguin stuffed into a plastic bag.

I stood at the bar and watched the pool game. The part-timer came to stand beside me while Maurice was still frowning in the other direction.

'What's wrong with Maurice?' I asked.

'Oh, he reckons he'd have barred you the other night, only he thought you were too pissed to take it in.'

'I wasn't as bad as that.'

'He's been a bit sensitive ever since that thing with his dog, though.'

'Any ideas on that?' I asked. I could nearly feel my wheels going over it now, as if thinking about it was bringing up the memory.

He looked back at the portrait and shrugged his shoulders. 'Whoever did it is keeping quiet and I'm not sure if I blame them.'

I looked at the dog and it was little Pearl standing there, in a blue denim dress she'd worn for her third birthday party – standing against the grey background and she had the same misty and air-brushed look as Maurice's dog.

The game finished and Maurice came to stand at the bar. The man with the animals was talking to a girl playing one of the machines. She was laughing and keeping her eyes on the screen. Then he started to squeeze a fluffy donkey out of his sack.

'Hello, Maurice. Something the matter?'

'Clowns like you are the matter,' Maurice said. 'I could sell this pub and retire, you know. D'you think anyone else would stand the sight of you?'

'You wouldn't last six months,' I told him. 'Where else would you go?'

'You'd be surprised,' Maurice said. 'You'd be surprised at the openings I'd have.'

He opened the hatch and stepped through to the other side of the bar. He called over the part-timer and they put their heads together and I wondered if they were talking about me. I tried to sit quiet on the stool but couldn't. I looked at the dog again, I'd been afraid to, and it gazed softly back at me from behind the glaze.

'I won't stay,' I told it.

When I got out I was surprised that it was still light because Maurice's always had that atmophere of lateness, the hours changing. A column of oily smoke was lifting over the dyke behind the car park – bending and spinning, barrelling inland with a cargo of smuts. I could smell its rubbery oiliness even in the car. I still wanted to talk to Marion but the fire was troubling me and I didn't know what I'd say anyway and so instead I took the road to the big and small fields, bumping over the potholes filled with grey water. I took the slab bridge and then the path across the field. I could still see the smoke and then it was hidden by the ridge of the dyke.

I parked the car on the grass and got out. A woman stared at me from the door of her caravan and I wondered if I was walking okay, if my flies were open. I couldn't see the smoke now but I could feel it as a tingling in my hands. I reached the dyke and rested for a second, then climbed the slope to the flat top where a narrow path ran along. Children were whooping and shouting on the beach, their voices carrying. The mist had lifted and the river-mouth was made up of lines of small, busy waves moving slantwise towards the sands. A tight flock of little birds flew low over the water and doubled back, like a sock being turned.

The smoke was coming from a hundred yards away

among the dunes, close to the shore but still on what would have been dry sand. The wind had slackened and it looked dark and compact now, busy. I still couldn't see any flames. I had a feeling of dizziness for a second, as if the dyke was much higher than it really was, then I started down the other slope, sliding and stumbling, not able to stop myself until I reached the sand with its litter of driftwood and crumbled polystyrene cups. I put my hands on my knees to catch my breath, staring ahead. There was a strand of dried kelp and mussel-shells, then sloping ribs of pale rock. The water was still out over shiny sands and a child of about three or four, little girl, say, was dashing along its edge kicking up spray. Another child, older, chased behind on a bike, standing up in the pedals and pumping against the resistance of the sand.

Then I heard something or saw it, a movement more than a noise. She would have been only ten feet away but she'd been keeping so still. She must have seen me scramble down the bank and I wondered what sort of idiot I'd looked. She didn't smile for a second but then she managed it, giving her face permission.

'Are they yours?' I asked. I nodded towards the water. I only half meant it – she looked too young.

She blew between her lips, a raspberry nearly. 'Those kids? I wouldn't have them as a prize in a raffle!'

'They must be freezing – splashing about like that!'

'Kids that age don't know the meaning of cold.'

She wore black leggings and a grey sweater of thick, speckled wool. Her hair was in a different style to before, more elaborate or the wind had twisted it that way. I could see the way its darkness was growing out, combating the blond.

'Fiona's missing you,' I told her.

She turned down her lip. 'That would surprise me very much.'

The smoke of the fire was billowing close to the sands;

74

its oily stink carried to us again. 'Oh, Fiona's not so bad,' I told her.

'Are you a friend of hers?'

'More of her old man's.'

'It would need to be one or the other.'

'What d'you mean by that?'

'Nothing.'

I watched the way her hair blew about, exposing her face and then covering it. The smoke twisted in our direction and I could make out the flames – nearly colourless with a dark clot of something at their roots.

'So how's the baby?' I asked.

She stared at me for a second. 'What baby?'

'You had a child with you the other night – a toddler.'

She shook her head. 'Then it was someone else you saw.'

I kept looking at her, couldn't keep my eyes away. 'You must have a double then. They reckon everyone has somewhere, so you must have one just here.'

'If you say so.'

'Oh, I do . . .'

She shrugged, holding herself against the wind. There was a shout from near the water and I saw another gang of children coming from the far end of the sands, from beyond Whiteheads. They were pushing something before them – rolling it with kicks and shoves along the part of the beach where the sand would be damp and firm. It toppled over and they crowded around it, screaming and calling. They set it upright again and sent it trundling on – a fat tyre that came up to the shoulder of the tallest of them. I could understand now the oiliness of the smoke.

'Did they set the fire going?' I asked.

She stared at me. 'There's no harm in that, is there? No harm in a bit of a fire.'

'They could burn themselves, that's all.'

'Not if they know how to respect it!'

'But kids aren't respectful.'

She smiled, looking the other way. I had an idea she was

75

making fun of me, seeing some joke she thought I wouldn't appreciate. I thought how she would be capable of inflicting pain and I started to worry about the child then, seeing its face below the red cap.

'So where do they get the tyres from?' I asked. I had an idea already.

She pointed to her chest. 'Are you asking me or my double?'

'You, I think.'

She nodded down the beach. 'The guy at the breaker's yard throws them out.'

'If the coppers spot smoke like that they'll be along here.'

'How often do they bother with this place?'

The children were dragging the tyre towards the flames now – bumping it over ridges of rock. The pair with the bike had joined in, so that there might have been a dozen of them now – scruffy kids from the site.

'Someone must have given them a light!' I said.

She shook her head. 'I don't know who that could have been.'

Then they gave a cheer, nearly a shriek of joy. The tyre was leaning at an angle in the fire, attacked along one edge by the flames. Flakes of soot were flying like bats and the smoke turned in on itself and then belched out again in a black ball that trailed along the sands for a few yards, then lifted. The kids jumped and screamed, looking from that distance as if they were on top of the fire. The woman was peering at them with a pale, excited face.

'Are you here to keep an eye on them?' I asked. 'Or just to watch the fun?'

'Don't you like children enjoying themselves?'

'Why shouldn't I?'

'You don't strike me as the sort who enjoys their own life much.'

'You'd be surprised what I do.'

'Yeah, I'm sure.'

She started to walk away then, towards the fire. I let her gain a few yards and then followed. She looked back over her shoulder and her face was still intent and excited; I was wishing it was by me.

'Don't you say goodbye to people?'

'Goodbye, then!'

'My name's John – I don't know yours.'

'What's the point if you did?'

'You'd be better with a name. If I wanted to write you a letter, say.'

She smiled then. She was looking my way and then back towards the blaze and the darting children. 'Enid,' she said. 'It's so short you'll forget it.'

'I promise I won't, Enid . . .'

I saw then how she was staring at my hands. I thought of hiding them, tucking them away in my pockets but then I let her look.

'What did you do to yourself?' she asked.

'The funny thing is, I was involved in a fire.'

She stepped closer. 'Can I see?'

She had such a look that I was scared for a second. Then I shrugged and held my hands towards her, palms up. She stared at them as though they were a map she was reading. How to get there. Then she took hold of my wrists and brought them towards her. She leaned and kissed the centre of each palm in turn and I felt first her dry lips and then just a tiny point of damp where the tip of her tongue touched. I could feel their thickened skin start to tingle and warm.

She let them go then, stayed looking at me. The kids were still shrieking behind her.

'Why did you do that, Enid?'

'Are you complaining?'

'No. I just wondered why.'

She put on a sly expression. 'Was it much of a fire – the one you were involved with?'

77

I was uneasy with her and aroused – shifty-footed. I laughed. 'It seemed like that at the time.'

'Were you badly burnt?'

'Not badly – just my hands. I needed a couple of grafts, that's all.'

She gave a short nod, as if she were disappointed in me now. As if I'd claimed too much. The smoke was swinging back towards us, given a twist by the wind so that it spun in the air like a hollow barrel. When it faced us directly I could see the white sky through its centre – a telescope view of nothing.

'Goodbye then,' she said, looking between me and the squalling kids.

'You could kiss me again,' I told her.

She looked capable of it for a second. I thought she might have crossed the space between us and kissed me on the lips. Then she shook her head. 'Once is enough.'

'It was twice.'

'Then that's more than your ration . . .'

'Can I call on you?'

'Why should you do that?'

'To be friends.'

'I don't think that's possible . . .' She nodded towards the blaze. 'You can warm yourself on that instead.'

'I don't think so. I think I've had enough of fires.'

8

A night and a day. Night. The tyre was burning, eaten up by small flames. Its empty hub breathed out a black ball of smoke. Enid stepped past in the long coat in which I'd first seen her. She walked through snapping valves of heat. She was holding the child again and its red cap showed just above her shoulder.

Dad was moving about downstairs. It would have been early morning because of the line of felt-grey where the curtains didn't meet. He trailed from the kitchen to the front room, through to the dining-room and then upstairs again. I heard him murmur to himself as he reached the landing. I could tell that his feet were bare from their hard scuff on the rug.

He stood in the doorway, his yellow pyjamas open on his chest, which made me think of a bird cage, though what bird you'd find there I couldn't have said.

'Can't you sleep, Dad?'

He didn't answer. He was looking cautiously at the light behind the curtains, as if he wasn't sure if it was morning or evening – if what was there would grow stronger or fainter. Then he must have made up his mind.

'Will my daughter come today?'

I sat up in the bed. I could still smell oily smoke, as if a trace of it must have been left on my clothes that I'd let fall beside the bed. 'I'm not sure, Dad. We could phone her later and ask.'

Dad nodded, still standing not a yard from the door. One foot was extended and I could see the shapes of the long, prominent bones. 'Ask her when, if not. Tell her I want to see her . . .' He stopped himself. His eyes were dark and moist, dark-rimmed.

'I'll try to get in touch with her today, Dad.'

'She forgets us!' Dad said. He laughed. 'Poor memory must run in this family!'

He was looking sideways now, listening for something. There was no noise from Rosemary's small room in the attic. He came closer when I turned on the lamp and sat down on the edge of the bed. His weight seemed to make no impression. He gave me a little, disarming smile.

'The fact is, I was thinking about her and I realised that I couldn't remember her name . . . That's why I came to you – I'm relying on you to tell me, John.' He put his hand to his face and smiled into it, like a child caught out.

'It's Marion, Dad. Her name is Marion.'

It seemed a strange word in the circumstances, awkward in my mouth. For a second I even wondered if I'd got it right. Then Dad nodded.

'I'm relieved, son! The worse thought was that you'd tell me and it would still mean nothing.'

'Oh, names are like that, Dad – you can lose them sometimes!'

Dad let his head droop, then he smiled to himself, as if he were recalling something. 'I could remember that other name, you see – that was as clear as day to me!'

'You've lost me now, Dad.'

He glanced up and managed to look like a stranger for a second. 'It was like they'd been changed over in the night, you see – Pearl was close to me and I'd lost my Marion . . . Can you imagine that? As if I had to make a choice between them.'

'Go back to sleep, Dad, You'll feel better then.'

'Oh, sometimes I sleep and things are worse after that! I might start thinking about your mother, for instance. Or Teddy Sandringham. Then that other one will pop into my mind . . .'

'You're upsetting yourself now, Dad!'

'Oh yeah? Well, that's how I know that I'm still alive.'

I put out my hand but he leaned away, shrugging his shoulder under the pyjamas. He blew out a long breath, settling himself. 'Look, I might be a prisoner here but I've friends outside.'

'How are you a prisoner, Dad?'

He brushed it aside, agitated now. 'Oh, I've got people on the outside – friends I can turn to. I've friends in the Labour Party and the Snooker Association – between those two I'll have half the world covered!'

I phoned Dr Spelling's office after breakfast. Her receptionist answered and I made an appointment. I thought of phoning Marion but decided not. I'd be in town later and I could see her then. Rosemary was talking to Dad in the front room and I heard him laugh as I walked out to the car. I felt better then.

I drove the couple of miles to Vic's.

SPARES AT BEST PRICES!
GEAR BOXES AND COMPLETE ENGINES SUPPLIED!
WARNING! DOG LOOSE!
VISITORS MUST REPORT TO OFFICE.

The wire gates were open and I went through into the yard. I'd gone a few feet when Vic's ivory-coloured crossbred bitch leapt up from among the wrecks and started struggling at the end of its wire leash. I'd wound up the window already but I thought that if it managed to break the cable then the force of its leap would carry it through my windscreen. I sounded the horn but Vic would already know that he had an early visitor.

The house itself was nearly surrounded by the stacks of wrecked cars, leaving just a small courtyard of oily gravel. Vic's blue Peugeot estate was parked at the front with the tow-truck beside it. The dog was still yapping but then it settled to growls. Victor came around from the side of the house in red overalls. He had about a week's growth of beard and it made his face look round and dark.

'Your dog doesn't like me, Vic.'

'I don't keep her to like people. When she starts liking people then I'll give her away . . .' Vic said.

Engine-blocks and exhaust-pipes were stacked against the front of the house. There was a leather bench taken from the back of a Rover or similar. The front door was wedged back and there was a light in the hall.

'Got a few minutes?' I asked.

He picked up a cloth from a bench and started to wipe his hands. 'Depends what you're here for, John. I've some things I need to get on with.'

He led me through into the living room. There was a smell of drink and stale cake, as if a birthday party had been held the day before. A radio was playing at the back of the house – a rock station. The mother stayed upstairs most of the time now and I hadn't seen her in the couple of years I'd been back. She'd call down sometimes, with a voice like the wind in a broken pipe.

'She does that to keep herself company,' Vic said, nodding towards the door.

'Who's that?'

'The hound. She gets lonely out here.'

'You should find her a friend then.'

'I tried her with another bitch once. I gave a guy a tow, then sorted him a new alternator. He said he couldn't pay straightaway and a couple of days later he brought me this dog on a piece of rope – some kind of Staffie cross with markings on the brindle. He had this idea they'd get on but we'd had it about a week when she chewed one ear off the thing . . .'

'What did you do then?'

'I took it back to him and asked for cash instead. I told him I didn't deal in livestock.'

I'd been looking about the room. There was a collapsed couch and a big wooden-cased TV on spindle legs. The parts of a carburettor were laid out on the table on sheets of newspaper. I could smell the petrol he'd used to clean it. Vic sat down and started to pull off his boots. You could see where the rug was grimed on a path from the door.

'Bilko said you might help me out,' I told him.

'Well, that's not for him to say, really.'

'He'd help me himself but he's the same problem himself – supply and demand, you see.'

'You're demanding and he isn't supplying,' Vic said.

He disappeared into the back of the house and I heard the water in the pipes as he washed his hands. After about five minutes he came back with a scuffed Adidas holdall. He set it down on the couch and lifted out a sealed plastic bag that was opaque with violet dust. He teased open the knot and started counting out tablets on the surface of a cushion, pushing them about with his fingertip, making rows of ten, counting below his breath with his head to one side.

'I see your dad now and again,' he said.

'Where?'

'Oh, walking around. Taking the air, I suppose. I stopped to say hello the other day but he walked past as if he didn't know me.'

'He'd remember you as a schooboy, Vic.'

'Funny, that's more than I can.'

He started humming to himself, pushing the tablets from one pile to the other like someone working an abacus. Then he scooped them up and funnelled them through his fist into a plastic pouch.

'Anything else?'

'There's a woman lives on the site,' I told him. 'But I haven't got the address. I was wondering if you'd know her.'

'Never trust a woman in a caravan,' Vic said.

'Why not?'

'People say these things, don't they? So what's her name?'

'Enid.'

He shook his head. 'Could be anyone, couldn't it?'

'You do a bit of business that way, don't you?' Supply and the other thing.

He looked careful and shook his head. 'I used to, more like. I try to stay clear of them nowadays – their bloody kids are bad enough!'

I thought of the worn tyre they'd rolled along the beach. 'Do they pester you, Vic?'

'Oh, they chuck stones at the dog – that kind of thing. You know what amuses the little bastards . . . So you're interested in this woman, are you? What's her name again?'

'Enid. I'm trying to find that out, you see – whether to be interested or not.'

He was smirking down at the rug now, paying me back for crossing the line somewhere – invisible line of amphetamine manners. 'What I've heard is that you're knocking off that housekeeper of yours.'

'Whoever's spreading that one is a sick person, Vic.'

He was still amusing himself. 'Oh yeah? Then maybe it's your dad they were talking about . . .'

There was a movement upstairs, a shuffle and scrape on the other side of the ceiling. He gave it a sharp look.

'Sounds like your ma's awake,' I said. 'So I'd better go now. It's been nice to hear the gossip.'

I handed over a couple of notes, then stuffed the plastic bag in my pocket. It had a calming weight.

'Look, don't bother with those caravan bitches,' Vic called as I went out. 'Find somebody with a life.'

I got into town just as Papa Gosse announced the hour. The cracked echo bounced from the hotels along the front, settled like a headache on the empty boating-pond and the bowling-green. It was spitting with rain but I thought the damp might do me good, give me back a sense of proportion.

Marion lived in two rooms and a kitchen above a shop selling junk furniture and white goods. In the summer the owner and his friends sat outside in sagging armchairs but that morning he hadn't bothered to take down the mesh screens. The machines were stacked inside with their backs to the windows, trailing cables and corrugated hoses. Second-hand cycles were chained along the front wall.

I rang her bell and when there was no answer I found her keys on my ring and let myself into the hall. I could hear a conversation in the shop through the partition wall. I climbed to the landing and knocked on the door of the flat, then unlocked the yale. The blinds were still drawn inside and the only light came from the small aquarium in the hall. A little pump was working, leaking bubbles. Tropical fish hung in the water like twists of sweet-wrapping.

'Marion?'

I caught a breath of her scent through the open door of the bedroom. In the lounge the long couch between the windows spilled a slide of cushions and magazines on to the rug. There were the leavings of a meal in tin-foil trays on the low table.

Half a dozen messages were flagged on her answering-machine and I was tempted by that because of the fidgety state I was in. But she would know anyway if the tape had been played. Her stereo-system was in the recess between the chimney-breast and one window – shelves of vinyl below and cassettes and discs above. I started to finger the cassettes, reading her notes on the spines. The dates reached back in different colours of biro – ten years ago, fifteen. I didn't like to think that all that time had passed, not for my sister.

I switched on the deck and slipped in a tape. I settled down at the end of the couch to listen. Marion's teenage voice was thin but held up well, respected itself finally. I put my head back. I could hear the noise from downstairs in the gaps between songs. The phone went and I let it go on to the machine. Baby Gosse's voice. 'Marion . . . ? Catch you later, Marion.'

A noise on the stairs. I hadn't slept but I felt as if I had. Marion came into the room and her hair was tied back and her face was puffy. She stared at me for five seconds and then came over and kissed me on the lips. Then she seemed to recognise her own voice for the first time.

'You can take that off!'

'It's years since I've heard you sing like that, Marion.'

'I don't any more, that's why! God, I ought to get rid of that stuff. I ought to put it out with the rest of the rubbish!'

'Please don't,' I said.

She leaned over and ejected the cassette in the middle of a song, then tossed it on the couch beside me. 'You can take it with you when you leave.'

'Okay. Thanks.'

Then she touched me on the cheek, buffing it with the back of her fingers. I took her hand and kissed it.

'Rosemary says that touching you always gives her a little shock,' Marion said. 'She thinks it's because you're charged up with something.'

'When did she say that?'

'Oh, a while ago. In Maurice's, I think. It was a slow evening and we were talking about you.' She pushed more magazines on to the floor and sat down next to me. 'I worry about you and her, you know.'

'Me and Rosemary? Why?'

'I think Dad's too much for you to bear sometimes. I think he's too much for the both of you . . .'

She leaned closer and took my shoulders, pushing her thumbs into their hollows. I could feel the current she'd mentioned start to ebb away.

We sat in her nest of a kitchen, drinking coffee. She put a gas jet on to take the chill from the air.

'There's a stale smell in here, Marion.'

She rolled her eyes. 'I'll get the air-freshener.'

'What's wrong with opening the window?'

'You try it.'

I fought with the sash. The seal of old paint broke with a crack and I managed to wedge it half-open. A washer-drier was swishing through its cycle in the narrow yard below.

'Have you and Tony had a row?' I asked.

'We've had a row, yeah. What about is personal to us.'

'That's fair enough.'

'I know it's fair.'

'You should give that one up, Marion. You're just going over the same ground with him. You need to make more progress.'

'You mean at my age I shouldn't waste time?'

'If you like.'

'Oh, I don't like. The thing is, the more time you spend the more you have invested.'

I tried to picture Baby Gosse taking his breakfast at the folding table. It would need to be for love.

'You hate his liver and lights anyway,' Marion said.

'But I don't hate you . . . I've heard a rumour that he's calling in his investments. Teddy's already feeling the pinch.'

'I feel sorry for Teddy but Tony's business is his own.'

I got up to lower the sash a little. The rain was getting heavier, splashing off the sill. I wished I hadn't had coffee because my hand was shaking.

'Dad couldn't remember your name this morning. I had to tell him in the end. He was nearly in tears.'

'So am I. I'm in tears as well,' Marion said. 'You'll have to talk to him, John!'

'I talk to him a lot. I live there, you know.'

'You talk about the wrong things then – you don't give him what he needs.'

'So tell me what that is.'

'You know what it is – you need to talk about Pearl!'

She put her hand over mine but I didn't appreciate that, not in the same breath. I pulled it away and she gave me a hurt look. But then all I'd done was protect myself.

'It's her not being there – never being mentioned. That's what's making him forget things,' she said.

'Is that your diagnosis, doctor?'

She was hurt again, her mouth loosening. 'That's what I think, John.'

'D'you want to send him into another spell of depression?'

'What sort of state do you think he's in now? Look, even when you take her away there's still the space she leaves. Then it's that he has to deal with – that's the hole he's slipping into.'

'I came here hoping for some sense, Marion! I wanted to talk things over with you. Reasonably. I wanted us to use sense to deal with Dad's illness.'

'You won't get away with it, you know, John! You think you can but the more you push her away, the harder she'll come back. And you'll change her. She'll be something else then, something to harm you and Dad . . .'

I watched her lips. For a second I could hear nothing. Only their movements showed she was still talking.

'I think you'll do us all damage, Marion. You and that man of yours. I think that's what he wants in the end. I don't think he's even interested in you apart from that.'

'You're starting to be poisoned, John. You're poisoning yourself. You made Anna leave you and now you're starting on us . . .'

'Did he tell you that? Tony?'

'No, John . . .'

'His father stole Dad blind and then Tony waited until Mam was ill and took what was left!'

'Dad was ill himself, John! It was making him ill. He couldn't deal with Mam's illness and running the site as well. And Tony made him a good offer . . . I mean, how much of a future do you think there is in that place?'

'And what was your part in it, Marion? Did you tell him Dad couldn't cope?'

'I could see it was too much for him, John. Do you think I'd just wait for him to go under?'

'So you tipped off Tony, yeah . . . Did he pay you for that, or was it just part of the service?'

Marion was shaking her head. Rain hit the window like a handful of gravel. 'You don't have to say this, John . . . It's doing no good at all!'

But I couldn't stop. 'You've wasted your life on that little shit! D'you think he'll take you with him if he goes? D'you think he'll give up Julia and the kid?'

I must have said more – but you stop listening after a while, even to yourself. I must have been shouting because there was that disturbance in the air, the shushing of it from one wall to the other. I might have read what I was saying from my sister's face – but then she was unfamiliar to me, a stranger nearly.

'You don't have to stay,' she said. 'You don't have to stay another second.'

I don't know where then. I don't know where I went after Marion's flat. I had a couple of drinks but they didn't register – nothing marked their passage. I kept seeing people I thought I knew but I wasn't talkative or they weren't.

Marion's cassette was still in my pocket and I sat in the car near the talking clock and listened to her voice lift and float. You could tell at once that she'd had the gift. Even at that age there was no mistaking.

I went into the office and Alex called me into the back. He was lounging in his swivel-chair as if he was ready for a long conversation. There were a couple of other chairs but he didn't ask me to sit down.

'John, I've had someone on the phone about you – a couple of times now.'

'That's nothing, is it?'

He prodded his chest with his thumb. 'I have to decide if it's nothing, John! I think that's my job if you don't mind.'

'Fair enough,' I said.

I looked into the other room and saw Bilko on the bench. He made the okay signal with his thumb and finger. Or else he meant Alex Vosper was an arsehole.

'A customer told me you were abusive to him,' Terry said. 'He said he thought you might have had something to drink.'

'When was this supposed to have happened?'

'A couple of weeks ago now. He said he didn't inform me at once because he didn't want to get you into trouble.'

'That was big, Alex.'

'Then he said he thought again and he was worried that you might be a danger to other members of the public.'

'I'd be a danger to him,' I said.

'I hope you're not making threats there, John.'

'No.'

'Because this isn't the first time . . . Do you know how many there's been so far? How many complaints you've had against you?'

'No idea, Alex. To tell the truth.'

'Four or five. At least that. There comes a point when I can't ignore these things, John.'

'I can't ignore them either, Alex. But what am I supposed to have done?'

Alex looked up with his round, damp eyes. His skin had an orange colour because of ten thousand cups of dispenser coffee. 'The customer said you made some remarks about his appearance and then took him out of his way.'

'I thought he'd be too pissed to notice, that's all, Alex. That was my only mistake.'

Alex closed his eyes. 'So you know who I mean, do you? He told me he has several witnesses.'

'To what?'

'To whatever you said to him. Did. He says he's sending a letter to the council . . .' He looked up at me. 'You know I'm licensed by the council, don't you, John?'

90

'You'll be okay.'

'Well, I'll make sure that I am . . . What he wants from you is a written apology. And compensation for any mental harm resulting from the abuse.'

'Mental harm?'

'Distress and upset . . .' He glanced towards the open hatch and then bent forward, lowering his voice. 'Look, was he deformed in some way, John? Or disabled?'

'It was his hair that looked funny.'

'His hair? Couldn't you have kept that to yourself? Couldn't you bear to do that?' He started fiddling with his hands, tugging at the fingers and making the joints crack. 'I've been trying to make allowances for you, John. I've been trying very hard.'

'Now what are you talking about, Alex?'

He tucked in his chin. 'To do with what happened. The tragedy you had . . . I always try to bear that in mind.'

He gave me a gentle little smile and started to reach for a biscuit. I had to put my hand on his arm to stop him.

'Just leave those, will you?'

'Sorry, John?'

'Just leave those fucking biscuits alone, will you?'

Alex kept still, staring at the top of his desk. I left him and went into the front office. Bilko was still sitting on the bench, talking to a man with a built-up shoe. He smiled up at me from his chubby, crazed face. ''Lo, John.'

'Hello, Bilko.'

I took hold of the striped mug he was gripping. It was still half-full of lukewarm sweet tea, which was just how he liked it. He held on to it for a second and then let it go. He and the man with the surgical shoe watched, keeping very still, while I flung it underarm through the open hatchway. Trailing tea it must have sailed just over Alex's head. I heard it explode against the back wall.

I kept dipping my fingers into the plastic pouch and fishing out another pill. I could feel them passing down in little, sparkling bursts like indoor fireworks. The radio started to squawk but I turned it off. I pulled the leads from their terminals.

I started talking to this citizen in one of the pubs near the front. I'd forget what I was saying and he'd be smiling at me, offering conditional friendship – that kind of look. It turned out he was in town to see about buying a caravan.

'Don't,' I told him. 'The bottom's dropping out of the market.'

We had about a drink and a half together and then he nudged my arm. 'They start them young here, don't they?' He nodded over to the other side of the room. 'That lass on the pool-table. She can't be much over twelve.'

I looked around and the girl was facing us, holding her cue while a thin, darkish, shrunken-looking man took his shot. He potted a colour and moved to the other side of the table. He wore a black cap over the crown of his head – a cross between a beret and a skull-cap. It had a silky tassel that bounced when he moved. The girl saw me looking then and stared.

'I wouldn't allow my daughter in this place,' my friend said.

I left my drink and walked over to the table. It was divided from the rest of the room by a long upholstered bench and when I passed the end I saw that a couple of children about two years old were wedged in the corner against the wall. They were dressed in the same red winter suits with hoods drawn up tight around their fat over-heated faces. They seemed identical at first but then I saw that one was a little bigger than the other. That one looked to be sleeping while the other stared into the lamp over the table with hypnotised blue-green eyes.

The man in the cap was taking another shot, taking care as he positioned the cue. He wore two silver rings on the hand that made the bridge. The girl's mousy hair was barbered tightly and you might have mistaken her for a

boy except for something feminine about the face, intelli-
gence, say. She wore dark denims and a zipped black
bomber-jacket, scuffed white trainers, and held herself in a
boy's stiff-shouldered way. She was twelve, thirteen –
difficult to say. I had a mental picture of her racing her
bike along the sands, pumping her knees to power the
pedals.

'I saw you near the fire, didn't I?'

She stared at me and then tapped herself on the chest.
The brass toggle of the zipper bounced. 'Me, you mean?'

'That fire on the sands. You were racing about it on
your bike.'

She shook her head. Her hair was fluffing out of the
crop and the feathered ends had a red tint. 'I wasn't at any
fire!'

'I don't mind if you were. There was a woman there as
well. Her name's Enid. I just wondered if you knew her.'

Her father was staring at us over the top of the table
now and she looked towards him. She shook her head.
'Dunno her.'

'She lives on the site, I think. You must have seen her
about . . .'

She went dumb then, closed her face. The man stepped
around the table, still holding his cue. 'You're interested in
my daughter, are you?'

'Not as such. I was asking her something.'

He leaned towards me and I thought there was a smell
about him then – a whiff of paraffin on the folds of his
clothes. 'Directions, you mean? Like the quickest way out
of here?'

One of the infants started to wail then and the noise cut
through the room's smoky hubbub. One of the barmen
was looking towards us, craning his neck over the crowd
at the bar. The girl picked up the crying child and leaned it
over her shoulder, petting it.

'You should finish your game,' I told her father.

He had a slight cast which made it hard to look at him.

Your eyes would slide to one side. 'Not with you standing here,' he said.

The girl joined us again, rubbing the child's back through its quilted jacket. 'He was only talking to me, Dad!'

'He should talk to me first.' He made the same gesture she had of tapping his chest, pushing back his shoulders.

'Do you know someone called Enid?' I asked.

'Enid who?'

'Just Enid – there can't be that many of them around here.'

'There might be bloody thousands!' The girl laughed and he pointed at her. 'Look, don't you start.'

'So you don't know her?' I asked.

'I've already told you I don't!'

He started to flex his shoulders again, bobbing his head like a bantamweight. A woman was waiting to put money into the table.

'Are you finished here?' she asked.

'I am,' I told her. 'I'm finished all right.'

I walked towards the door and looked back only once. I couldn't see the man but the girl was sitting on the bench and holding the infant on her lap – still soothing it, rocking it gently.

9

*He phoned me, John. David Ordish phoned. I
thought he was drunk at first but then I thought he
was in some state like that but not the same. Rapture,
maybe. He started by telling me that he remembered
her always, that he thought and dreamed about her.
That he saw her in babies, in schoolkids. That he
catches a glimpse of her on TV when the camera
shows the crowd. He says old ladies waiting at bus
stops have her face. He said he stops his car to give
them lifts, talks to them. They invite him to their
homes for cups of tea, their sheltered accommoda-
tion. Can you think of anything unhealthier, John?
He told me he has a manner that everybody trusts.
Well, not me, I thought – I'm a thousand miles from
trust.*

*But then his voice turned quiet and I could see why
the old girls confided. He told me it was a necessary
thing he'd taken upon himself – something like a
religious vocation. His duty was to keep her alive and
present – our little dead Pearl. (To say she's dead,
John, does that hurt you?) He talked as if she'd left
behind this hollow shape he could fill out with his
belief.*

*Oh John, I have a horror he'll persuade me! – just
when I'm filled myself, starting to be heavy with
another child. He talks and I listen – barefoot, sitting
on the edge of the bed. His voice is something small
and alive in the earpiece – a devil or a genie. He
phones from a public box and he has to keep feeding*

in coins. I look down into the garden, on to spiky hedges with that pale, glossy green which leaves have only under shallow, grey skies. I listen, while the TV is playing downstairs and the baby floats on her cord, growing a face and fingernails. Then I start to shiver as if I was talking to a lover, because this is like bedroom-talk, seduction. David Ordish whispers his belief in her, the faith he wants me to share. He tells me we must never weaken or fail. We mustn't forget her for a day, a second – her existence depends on our commitment and constant attention. He's insistent, John, with a lover's gift of words. But then if I wanted to reject him, to be cruel, I would only have to say that the opposite was true – that the task, the real work, was to learn how to leave her.

Dad's plate was empty except for a shine of grease. His eyes followed me across the kitchen as far as he could turn his head.

'If you want breakfast here then you'll need to see after it yourself!'

'It's no trouble to make him something,' Rosemary said. 'When everything's ready for it.'

He stared, transferring his anger to her. 'But why should you, Rosemary? Why should you need to do anything twice?'

He stood up and pushed back his chair, moving stiffly as if he was unsure of his balance, the exact placing of his limbs. I lifted the pot from its stand. There was a swill of tea left.

'That'll be stewed,' Rosemary said.

'It'll do for me, Rosemary.'

'That's right – let him suffer!' Dad said.

I poured my tea and took it into the empty front room. The blinds were still drawn and I switched on the lamp above the table. After a second I heard Rosemary's step in the hall.

'No work this morning?' she asked lightly.

'There's a downturn in the cabbing business.'

'Your boss was on the phone yesterday. He was upset over something.'

'I haven't got a boss – I'm completely self-employed.'

'Is that why you made such a noise last night – self-employment?'

'As I came in?'

'And after that.'

She sat down in one of the faded armchairs near the window and I thought it was unusual to see her sit. Dad was still in the kitchen listening to the news on the radio.

'Your father's invited to a dinner and dance,' Rosemary said.

'He's invited to everything and never goes.'

'He says he'll go this time. If I'll go with him.'

'That's okay, isn't it?'

She shook her head. 'I'm not sure that it is okay, John.'

Dad said something over the talk on the radio then, shouted out. He would get enthusiastic.

'Marion will probably go with him if he asks,' I said.

'It's not just a question of someone going with him, John. He wants me to go as his partner, you see.'

'You've danced with him before, Rosemary!'

'I have, yes. But it's different in a public place. People will start to make assumptions.'

'What assumptions?'

'Oh, that we're together. That we're a couple . . . And I'm afraid your father might start to think that as well.'

'He'll be seventy next birthday, Rosemary!'

She shook her head. 'He wants to take back what he's lost, John. A part of it, anyway – a reminder . . . But I can't do that for him! I have to consider myself in the end.'

'I thought you were happy here, Rosemary. I had that impression . . . You wouldn't leave us, would you?' She'd take a cab and then a train. Whiteheads would shrink behind her and she'd light a cigarette, watching the fields outside the tinted windows.

'I might have to, John. If it goes any further. I wouldn't have the heart to turn him down, you see.'

'Do you think he wants to do that – take it further?'

'I don't know . . .' She shook her head. 'You know, sometimes I think I'm as confused as he is.'

'Is he confused then?'

'He stares into space sometimes and I wonder what he's seeing. I daren't think what it could be.'

'He recalls things, Rosemary. People. He loses himself sometimes.'

'Then I don't want to be lost with him.'

I would see people from the cab-office and I'd sound the horn and wave. There were smiles and lifted thumbs, so that word must have got around that I'd had a fight with Alex. I felt sorry about it now, though, not that I'd walked out but that it had taken that shape. I still had the radio in the cab, its torn leads dangling nearly into my lap.

I drove into town and a stocky dark-haired woman was wrestling with a child near the covered market. The little girl kicked her legs in their red tights, flinging off one of her shoes. Enid was standing with her shopping a couple of yards away and she stepped forward and picked up the thrown shoe. The other woman took it with a nod, still occupied struggling with the little girl.

I stopped alongside a line of parked cars and sounded the horn. Both women sent me an identical angry stare but then Enid came towards my open window. She seemed only curious as to why I'd stopped.

'Would you and your friend like a lift?' I asked.

'Why?'

'Save you waiting for a bus, I suppose.'

She shrugged and looked back towards the pavement. 'She's not my friend, but wait a minute.'

She spoke to the other woman, then picked up a couple

of carrier-bags from the pavement. The little girl was still sobbing and hiccuping, squeezing out tears. I leaned back to push open the back door for them.

'There's nothing you can do when she's like this,' the woman said, climbing in first. The girl had gone shy and sullen, hiding her face. 'All you can do is let her wear herself out.'

'Let nature take its course,' I said.

Enid got in and laughed. I liked the light sound of it. We looked at one another in the mirror for a second and then she turned away with a smile. They arranged themselves on the back seat with their shopping and a folded pushchair around their feet.

'So do you have an identical twin?' I asked Enid.

She went wide-eyed and shook her head. 'Not as far as I know!'

'We worked out that you did the other day. I'd just like to know which one I'm talking to.'

She didn't answer, but she looked pleased that I'd challenged her, amused.

'I think if there were two of us we'd suffer twice as much,' the other woman said, the little girl sitting on her lap now, still sniffing, her face pushed into her mother's throat. 'It's lucky you came along, though. She needed something like this to break the spell.'

'What spell?' I asked.

'Oh, kids put themselves under a spell sometimes. They lose track of themselves.'

Enid smiled again and I thought her face looked fuller and smoother, as though she'd put on a couple of pounds or had some decent sleep. 'Are you still cabbying?' she asked. She might have seen the dangling wires.

'Oh, I'm giving that a rest for a while. I'm looking for work that's more fulfilling.'

'Well, the world's your oyster!' the woman said. She laughed as if she knew she'd said something nonsensical and then turned to Enid. 'Don't I know you from somewhere, love?'

'I can't think where,' Enid said.

The other woman tightened her lips and turned her attention back to the little girl.

'So where are you going?' I asked.

'Oh, we're staying on the site.'

'Which one?'

She laughed. 'Is there more than one?'

'Oh, there's another one but it's smaller.'

I stopped at the second gate to Sunnylands and got down to help her with her bags. She shook out the pushchair and settled the child into it.

'Sometimes they're better when they're asleep,' I said.

'That's right. You'll have some yourself, then?'

I shook my head. 'No.'

'Pity. I can see you'd be good with them.' She nodded towards the car, lowering her voice. 'Not like that one.'

'She's okay.'

'I'd stay away from her if I were you.'

'Why?'

'Because she's cruel – I can see it in her face!'

She hooked the bags over the handles of the buggy and wheeled it away.

I got back into the car.

'She was talking about me,' Enid said.

'Saying what a nice person you are.'

'Like hell she was!'

'Why don't you sit in the front?' I asked her. 'I've got a stiff neck and the doctor says I need to be careful.'

She laughed but stayed in her seat. I turned in the entrance and drew out into the road.

'I think you lost a friend there, anyway. Why ask her along and then treat her like that?'

'Like what?'

'Slapping her down when she was trying to start a conversation.'

'Oh, that's the way I am. I feel drawn to people and then I have second thoughts.'

'Is that a warning to me?'

'You can take it that way if you like.'

She had a flirting tone now and I angled my head to catch her eye in the mirror. 'We could have a drink if you like. I've got a bottle of wine in the boot.'

'It'll be warm by now.'

'We could cool it in your bath.'

She laughed. 'D'you think I run to a bath?'

I found the narrow side entrance to the site. The board had come loose from its fixings and was tilting to one side.

WHITEHEADS
CAMPING AND CARAVANNING
DSS WELCOME

'You live in the house, don't you?' Enid asked.

'That's right.'

'Then your name's Whitehead?'

'No, that's just the house.'

'Ah. Is the old guy there your father?'

I thought she might have known that. She and Fiona must have been friendly enough to talk at some point. 'My dad, yeah.'

'He goes walkabout sometimes, doesn't he?'

'What's that mean?'

'He goes walking about the site – poking his nose in, acting like he owns the place.'

'He used to once. Why shouldn't he take an interest in things, anyway?'

'He takes an interest all right . . . Is the woman there your mother?'

I could feel that she was teasing me now. 'She's more my age than Dad's. She keeps the place for us.'

'You mean you men can't look after yourselves?'

'Well, I'm out a lot and Dad's health isn't so good now.'

101

We bumped along the track, towards the back of the site. She started taking her shopping from the floor, setting it on the seat beside her.

'I saw one of your little friends,' I told her.

'Who's my friend?'

'The girl on the pushbike. The one who looks a bit boyish . . . She was with her dad in town.'

'Did you talk to them?'

'We had a bit of a chat.'

'What about?'

'Ah, nothing much. This and that.'

She was watching me again. I could feel her attention at the back of my neck. 'They're nothing to do with me really,' she said. 'I keep an eye on the kids sometimes, just to give them a break.'

'You're a good neighbour then.'

'That's right.' She reached forward and took hold of my shoulder. 'Hey, thanks for the lift, anyway . . . This is as far as you need come.'

'I thought we were sharing a bottle?'

She peered out, squinting a little. Then she nodded as if she were resigned. 'Okay.'

I wondered what she thought she was resigning herself to. I had an interest in that. We passed the place where I'd seen her double and closer to the dyke was a white tourer with a sheet of green tarpaulin fixed to the roof with ties. The tarpaulin lifted a foot when the wind got under it.

'Is that where you live?'

'You don't have to come in. Not if you don't like.'

'It's all right. I was only asking . . .'

I let the water run. There was hardly room to lean the bottle in the shallow sink. Enid was kneeling before the oil-fire, trying to light the burner with a match. There was already a sweet smell of the paraffin in the air.

'You won't need that for much longer,' I said.

'Why?'

102

'Well, summer's on the way . . . Even around here.'

She managed to start a ring of flame. 'I like to keep a fire going anyway – I'm the cold-blooded type, you see.'

'I wouldn't have taken you for that.'

She shrugged and adjusted the height of the wick.

'Smoke?' I asked.

'Okay . . . Thanks.'

I had three left in the packet and I passed one over and flicked at my lighter. She stared at the flame for a while before she met it with the cigarette.

'Something the matter?'

She shook her head. 'Why do you ask?'

'You had a serious look there. Like you had something on your mind.'

'Is my mind supposed to be empty? Is that how you like your women?'

'Are you my woman then?'

She frowned and then smiled. 'I let myself in for that, didn't I?'

She sat opposite me on the other low bunk. The heater was filling the cabin with oily warmth. 'It's stuffy in here,' I said.

She sighed and got up to open a window on its latch. 'Any more complaints?'

'Not so far . . . So where are the glasses?'

She went to one of the cupboards and reached down a wine-glass and a schooner. The schooner had a little etched crown on the side and I thought it might have been taken from Maurice's. He was always complaining about the number of glasses that disappeared. She passed me a tin-opener with a corkscrew attachment. 'You'll have to do your best with that, I afraid.'

I pulled the cork and poured. I'd bought the bottle at the supermarket in town, meaning to drink it on the sands somewhere. The wine tasted thin but then you felt the glow.

'I could get to like this,' Enid said. 'Where's it from?'

I looked at the label. 'Australia.'

'All that way and it ends up in this place!' She took another swallow.

'Don't stint yourself,' I told her. 'I could always go out for another.'

She shivered, as though the heat was working through. 'I don't want to make a habit of it.'

I leaned back and started looking about, seeing the neatness of the place that had more to do with the absence of things than their order. 'So how do you manage with a kid in here?'

She put down her glass. 'What are you talking about?'

'I was just wondering how you manage – in a place this size, I mean.'

She pushed the bottle back towards me. Wine slopped up the side. 'You can take this cheap piss with you!'

I grabbed the neck and stood up. The air near the ceiling was a mix of wine-fumes and paraffin. 'Look, I'm sorry. You can forget I said that if you like.'

'Can't you control your mouth?' she asked. She looked up at me and then did some movement with her face and her lips looked soft and unhappy, slackened by the wine. 'Okay, stay for a while if you want. Don't give me any more of that, though . . .'

'Okay.'

I sat down, beside her this time. She was breathing through her half-open mouth, not looking at me, and I didn't know when we kissed – couldn't draw a line between kissing and not kissing. It felt like we were fighting until we found some particular angle, got under our own defences. I stroked her face and then she was giving attention to my hands, working at them with her tongue and lips, sighing, so that I could feel the tingle of the damaged skin. She was in my arms for a second and then another – the same second over again. Then something fell and wine was dripping from the edge of the table.

I put the glass right and got up to find a cloth. She was watching me.

'D'you think that was a mistake?' she asked.

'No.'

'Are you sure?'

I wiped the sill, then took hold of her arms. They were cool at first and then the warm blood lifted to my grip.

'Is it still too hot in here?' she asked, teasing.

'I'm getting used to it.'

The wind was blowing outside, pressing at the caravan so that there was a feel of strain and small adjustments, then a release.

'D'you want to stay, John?'

'Of course I do.'

'Give me a hand then . . .'

I helped her to fold away the table and push the bunks together. I kept touching her arms, her face, the bare skin showing above the waistband of her skirt when she leaned to pick something up.

'Do you feel I'm forward?' she said.

'No.'

'I thought we might as well be comfortable . . . Shall I close the curtains?'

'If you like.'

'Are you feeling shy?'

'No.'

I lifted myself away to look at her. My arms were trembling. We were twins joined at the belly. Enid's face was beautiful and blank, turning to the side. We kissed in paraffin-scented dimness and our breath wrapped around us and her pinpoints of nails were along my back, cruel and caring, humorous. She smiled and shifted herself. I started to roll, striking my head against the strut of the folded table. She pressed her weight on me and I could feel a slight quivering. I couldn't stop myself from shouting and she put her hand over my mouth . . .

'Can't you sleep?' she asked.

'No.'

'Why can't you?'

'It's too early in the day for me.'

'It's not so early now . . .'

'Sleeping's not something I'm good at anyway.'

'Since when?'

'A few years now, I suppose.'

'Maybe it's to do with all that crap you swallow – all those pills.'

'How do you know about that?'

'Oh, I know the signs.'

'Clever little miss, aren't you?'

I kissed her again and our skins kept sticking and unsticking. The blanket was prickling my side and I pulled it away.

'I'm cold,' she said.

I looked towards the glow of the fire. 'You're joking! It's like a bloody palm-house in here!'

'That's the way I like it – I'm a lizard woman, you know. A salamander.' She pinched my side, hard enough to make me gasp. 'What do you do when you can't sleep?'

'Play with myself.'

'What do you do after that?'

'Think, I suppose.'

'About what?'

'Oh, all sorts of things. Anything that comes to mind . . .'

'There's no one you think about especially?'

'You're very interested in my thoughts, aren't you?'

'I'm curious, that's all . . .' She turned on her elbow to watch me. I liked the way she did that – with her face so calm and attentive. 'Would you like me to put you to sleep, John?' she asked.

'Isn't that what they do to dogs?'.

She laughed. 'Oh, it works on people too.'

I closed my eyes and I could feel her breath against my

106

face. She was making little kisses and endearments, planting them in my ear. After a few seconds I lost track of what she was saying and just listened to the sound of her voice. Then I wasn't sure if she was speaking at all or if it was something else that was going through me like a tremor – something set moving and then speeding quickly beyond hearing . . .

She wasn't there. I separated my clothes from the tangle of bedding and put them on. It was already dark and I wiped the mist from a window and looked out. Lights were on in the windows of the caravan opposite. I looked in the tiny cubicle of the shower and there was a yellow bar of soap and a drip gathering on the fitting.

'Enid?'

I found the switch and turned on the light. It was unshaded and savage between the white walls. There wasn't the space to withdraw yourself, hide. The coil of the heater was still glowing and I went to turn it down but then didn't trust myself and left it alone. I rinsed my face in the little sink. A pink towel lolled from a shelf in the cupboard. I tugged at it and something that was caught in the folds tumbled on to the floor. I picked it up and spread it between my hands. It was a child's white vest, tiny, with press-studs at the shoulders and where it fastened below the crotch – so small that I thought it would fit only a newborn baby. It had the stiff feel of much-washed cotton.

I put it back. I felt afraid of Enid for a second, of what she might do or say if she opened the door. I could feel the heat of the fire like something toxic. There was an inch of wine left in the bottle and I dosed myself with it. The cheap metallic taste braced me. I wondered if she kept the fire burning like that always, like the lamp in a church. But I could hardly smell the fumes now, as if I'd lost my sensitivity to them, gone native. I found one shoe and then the other and as I laced them I heard paraffin drip from the tank into the reservoir below the wick.

The door was unlocked and I went outside. The wind was gusting, stripping the warmth from the folds of my clothes. The sea made a very low sound that I could feel through the soles of my shoes rather than hear, as if the turf had a slow tremble to it, a creep underfoot. I passed by the back of a caravan and saw a shadow in the window, heard the chime of a cup. Drops of rain or blown spray struck my face as I went towards the dyke. My muscles were still loose with sleep and I stumbled a couple of times as I climbed the slope. The grass and low shrubs had a sour smell. I reached the top and saw that the tide was in among the rocks. Its movement generated a low light so that it seemed brighter than the sky. Further out, it had a shiny, muscular look like slabs of raw, dark meat.

I wasn't dressed for the wind and I started to shiver. The wind was making me weep. I could see the luminous trail from the chimney of the OKO plant, broadening as it passed overhead. A woman was sitting on the bench a dozen feet away.

'Is that you, Enid?'

She stood up and turned towards me. She wore her dark coat with bands of shiny trim. I couldn't quite make out her face, only that she was smiling. The wind had made her hair a nest.

'That's my mother's bench,' I told her.

'Oh?' She turned back to look at it, then felt along the inscription.

'That's her name,' I said. 'Lilian. In delectable memory.'

'Why delectable?'

'I don't know. I suppose that's the way Dad felt about her.'

'Ah . . . Did she like this spot?'

'She used to come here when it was fine. She asked for her ashes to be scattered just below.'

I pointed down the far slope. There was a sucking scramble of loose stones. I wanted to touch her but I couldn't close the distance. I had the funny feeling she

108

might not have been the same person. 'You told me there wasn't a child,' I said.

'Did I? Oh.'

'I found some clothes – kid's clothes. A baby's.'

She stepped towards me. 'You'll always find something you don't need to – you're that type . . . Do you really think you should take an interest in this?'

'I wondered why you lied about it. It does you no good, anyway – you ought to give it up.'

She laughed. 'Like smoking, you mean?'

She came closer and I thought I could make out the tight little space between her eyebrows where the lies were generated – a gland that was out of control.

'So have you one left?' she asked. 'A cigarette?'

I took out the packet. There was just one and I passed it over.

'And a light, please?'

I struck the lighter and shielded it with my hand. The blue flame with its yellow margin made the darkness more visible. Enid's lit face was so intent that I felt a need to accommodate her, make allowances. She stepped back and drew on the cigarette.

'You could give me the lighter as well,' she said.

'Why?'

She shrugged. 'Just for something of yours to keep . . . I'll give you a kiss as fair exchange.'

I gave it to her and she dropped it into her pocket. She drew on the cigarette, then took it from her mouth and I kissed her, searching with my tongue. She shifted herself and then held me close, one hand at the back of my neck, the other below and working. Nothing I'd felt before had been so painful, so personal. I caught her hand and forced it away, like someone taking a leech from their side. She let the burning end fall and stood back, watching me, waiting.

10

I didn't go near the site, even driving the long way around
when I had to go into town. I took warm baths, three or
four a day, because the tepid water drew some of the heat
that had sealed itself below the burnt skin. Dad would
come up the stairs to complain at the time I was taking.

'Why are you hiding away in there? This cleanliness isn't
like you!'

I listened to the drag of his breath outside the door and
pushed myself deeper. But he must have heard the splash
as I submerged because he started to rap with his knuckles
at the panel.

'Why won't you wish us goodnight like a civilised
person? Are you going to show your face at all tonight?'

'You know what my face looks like, Dad!'

'Too right, I do! The one you show me, that is . . .'
Building to a tirade now. He tried the handle, leaning his
weight against it. I could see the door straining against its
little brass bolt. Then I heard Rosemary call up from the
hall.

'Will you leave him, George!'

Dad gave a sour laugh. 'To his own devices, you mean?
A lot of good that would do him!'

'At least to bathe himself.'

'Well, it seems you've a defender in this house, son! God
knows you need one . . .'

I heard him go down, mutter something to Rosemary at
the foot of the stairs. The burn started to sting again as
soon as I climbed out of the bath so I took the packet of
paracetamol from the cabinet and swallowed six or eight,

sitting on the edge of the bath and washing them down with water from the cold tap. I looked at myself in the mirror over the handbasin and I could see the pale crater of the wound and then a spreading area of inflammation – just above my left hip, where the flesh was pale and flabby. I squeezed the last from a tube of antiseptic cream and spread it carefully with a fingertip, then put on a plaster. The burn itched like something that was burrowing into my skin. I thought of a crab, burying itself in sand.

I bought ointment and fresh dressings in town and lifted up my shirt and applied them sitting in the car. Papa Gosse called the time and I put the engine into gear. Five o'clock. The mist from the estuary had changed to rain and the town was filled with shoppers in coloured waterproofs and carrying umbrellas. I saw Enid in any woman with a child in a buggy or sling. Her head was down against the rain and she would lift it and smile, like she had done before she stubbed her cigarette on me. I remembered that she had kept my lighter and thought how I'd hold out my hand for it and she'd understand. She would place it in my palm carefully, watching me – frowning. The child would turn its smooth face towards me.

I parked in the market car park and walked to the multiscreen. I had a drink in the bar, then bought a ticket to one of the films. I dozed in the seat and woke and watched the big faces for a minute without knowing what they were. When I looked around the place was nearly empty and for a second I felt the panic I thought Dad must have felt when he had come shivering to my room. My side was itching under the new dressing and I wondered if it had become infected and I was in a fever. But then when I stood up to leave I felt steady in the darkness.

I drove out towards Whiteheads and the site, saw Bilko's Orion that must have been coming from Maurice's because he and Fi lived over towards Hooperstown. He lifted his hand to me and sounded the horn as he passed.

He'd slowed and I suppose he might have wanted me to stop but I drove on. Then when I came to the turning for the pub I took the left, bumping down the lane with its splattered white board. FUNCTION ROOMS. EVENTS A SPECIALITY.

Maurice was busy with a customer and he didn't look up as I crossed the room. Then he sidled over with his face kept straight and I wondered what Bilko had been telling him.

'Someone was looking for you,' he said.

'Oh? Who's that?'

'Your sister's friend – Rosemary. She phoned about an hour ago. I think she'd already tried your office but . . .'

'But I'm not there any more. Thanks, Maurice.'

I phoned home from the back bar. An old woman and a gent watched me from the bench.

'Your father's had a little accident,' Rosemary said.

I thought of his ear but that had happened already. It had made a connection between Dad and accidents, disasters. It had cleared a path for them. 'What happened, Rosemary?'

Someone opened the door to look in and I had to struggle to hear over the chat and music from the other side. 'Tony Gosse phoned from the Assembly Rooms to say he thought your dad's car had taken a knock. He said George seemed unhurt but there was a bit of a dent in the front wing.'

'Dad was driving the car?'

'That's right . . . he took himself off to the dinner-dance. I tried to stop him but he wouldn't listen.'

'And you wouldn't go with him?'

'I'd already been through that with him, John. He asked me again and when I said no he just walked out to the car.'

'Christ, Rosemary!'

'Are you blaming me, John?'

'You must know him by now! You know the way he behaves.'

'Okay, I do. But knowing how to stop him is a different matter.' She sighed. 'Look, I'm stranded here without the car, John . . .'

'Okay. I'll go there now, Rosemary.'

'You could pick me up if you want and we'll go together.'

'It's okay . . . I'll do it myself.' I was angry with her though I didn't know what she could have done. I knew I was being unfair but I wanted to give myself that luxury. I was putting down the phone and I heard her voice in the earpiece.

'Rosemary?'

'Are you sure, John? Can I trust you to do that?'

It was about ten thirty when I reached the Assembly Rooms and parked in the narrow street behind. I looked for Dad's car but couldn't see it. Music from the band was sounding through the vents in the hall's tall back windows. I walked around to the main entrance and a couple of tables had been set across the foyer to prevent access to the lower halls but leave the staircase and the rest of the floors open. Bilko was sitting on a stacking chair wearing a hired jacket and dickie. The jacket was too tight and made him look slope-shouldered and paunchy. He must have been tippling from something because he was smiling and red-cheeked.

'Your dad passed this way an hour ago, John!'

'Was he okay?'

Bilko winked and pointed to the doors set with stained glass that gave entrance to the hall. 'Tony Gosse came out and took him through there. I haven't seen either of them since.'

One of the other doormen came through with a pile of sandwiches wrapped in paper tissues. He dropped them on

114

to the table and Bilko took one, cocking his elbow. 'You're not going to spoil his fun, are you, John?'

The other man sniggered, a floppy white-bread sandwich halfway to his mouth. 'Is that the old guy who was through earlier? You're his cab, are you?'

'I'm his son.'

He watched me, stuffing in the sandwich.

I went through. The band was playing at the far end of the hall, on stage under the spread of gilded organ-pipes. The music sounded lost in the big marbled space and then shrill as I went closer, crashing from the hard surfaces. A few elderly couples were dancing the waltz and a crowd had gathered in one corner near a table set with drinks – my father's generation with a sprinkling of respectful youngsters. The men were in evening dress or dark suits while the women wore coloured ball-gowns and carried little glittery bags on their arms. I spotted Alice Sandringham, standing close to the group but separate from them, carrying a stemmed glass in her gloved hand.

'Hello, Alice.' I kissed her powdered cheek.

'You'll be looking for your dad, I expect . . .' she said.

'Does it show?'

She looked at my shoes and then at my face. 'You don't look like you're here for the ball, anyway . . . Last thing I saw of George he was on his way downstairs with my husband. Teddy had his arm around your dad's shoulders and I don't know if he was cuddling him or keeping him out of mischief . . .'

'A bit of both I'd say, Alice. Aren't you joining them?'

She shook her head. 'Oh, I join in so much and then I prefer my own company.'

'I'd better see how Dad's doing then. I'll be seeing you later.'

She pulled a face. 'Oh, if I decide to stay, you might . . .'

I went downstairs. Waiters were clearing the long tables, working their way through a mess of plates and soiled napkins. Others in tight steward's uniform were taking up

115

the chairs in twos and carrying them through the open rear
doors. There was a high table where special guests would
have sat and I wondered if my father had been among
them. A pair of microphones on stands were canted
towards the middle seats so there must have been speeches.
A stout man with thinning red hair was still in his seat,
leaning back and smoking a cigarette with his waistcoat
unbuttoned.

Then Baby Gosse opened one of the doors at the side,
keeping one hand on the brass scroll of the handle and
beckoning me with the other.

'I was told you were in the building, John. It looks like
your father had a bit of a knock on the way here.'

'Knock?'

'To his car, I mean. He seems a hundred per cent,
himself: I'm not even sure he knew that he'd done it . . .'
He laughed. 'Trouble is that since my father died there's
no one left in this town who dares to question him about
anything. Not me, anyway . . .'

He smiled as if he'd meant to pay a compliment. He was
in his shirtsleeves with his necktie undone and hanging to
the side. His chest was swelling the starched white cotton
and his face had a gloss of perspiration, as if he'd been
exerting himself.

'Is Marion here?' I asked.

He stared, shook his head. 'No, and I wish I wasn't.'

I walked behind him along a corridor of coloured
marble. The dusty high windows must have looked out at
street-level because they were guarded with grilles. Baby
Gosse pushed back a door and then stepped aside. The
room seemed full of smoke but then I saw it was mainly
the blue tints of the marble. A pair of crystal electroliers
were set over the long green of a snooker-table and, in a
stained overall, Victor was playing my father who wore a
white dress shirt with the cuffs undone and turned back. I
saw how the back of the collar was worn through to its
lining.

116

'Your boy's here, George!' Tony announced.

Dad leaned over the table, frowning. Victor was smoking in the way he had with the cigarette in the exact centre of his lips and he took it out to grin at me. Teddy Sandringham sat in a chair against the back wall, still in full dinner dress with his shoes gleaming and a dickie tight against his thin throat. There were a couple of other men I didn't know – one of them in police uniform although he'd removed the cap and jacket.

'My what?' Dad enquired quietly. The rest of the room was looking between us.

I tried to make a joke of it. 'Don't you know me, Dad?'

He lowered his eyes to the table – checking the alignment of his cue and the ball. 'Oh, I know you well enough . . .'

He played with a push of his elbow. The contact was dull and the balls cannoned without result. He was left leaning against the apron and I saw his legs tremble as he pushed himself upright. The lace of one of his patent shoes was undone and trailing.

Tony Gosse sent me a look from the tail of his eye and stepped forward. 'Can I help you there, George?'

'I'm okay . . .'

'Your lad's come to take you home,' Teddy said from his chair. 'I wish I'd a son to drive me about.'

Dad looked over at him coolly and I noticed that his eyes were small with drink. Teddy was holding a little silver flask in one hand and I wondered if he'd been sharing that. 'If I wanted a lift then I'd call a cab,' Dad announced. 'Besides, we haven't finished the game, have we, Vic?'

Victor grinned and stepped round the table. 'I'd have thought you'd had enough of it now, George! You've been on your feet for the best part of an hour!'

'I knew your mother, you bloody little pup!' Dad said. 'She'd a hard face and a soft arse.' He laughed and glanced round the room with a look of who's next? There was a speck of blood in the corner of one eye now and the lower lid looked swollen, almost as if he'd taken a punch.

'Rosemary was worried about you,' I said. 'She called me at the office.'

He put on a puzzled look. 'And who is Rosemary?'

'Mrs Shand, if you prefer.'

'Oh, I do . . . Let's call her that in future.'

Victor took his shot, potted a red and a couple of colours, then left an easy one. I think Dad might have been able to clear the table but he only stared at it, leaning on his cue, as if he couldn't summon the concentration now.

'I think you ought to come home, Dad,' I said.

He thought about it and then gave a nod. 'I suppose the pleasure's gone anyway . . . I lost the joy of it the second you walked through that door.'

Victor hefted his cue and laid it lengthwise on the table. Dad looked unsteady for a second and I offered him my hand but he slipped past it and caught at Tony Gosse, putting his arms around him. Tony looked surprised and bashful and started patting Dad's back in a clumsy way. Dad was leaning against him, as if he meant to rest his head on his shoulder.

'You're a good boy,' Dad said. 'I won't say you're like your father because no one is.'

'That's an act I don't try to follow, George,' Baby Gosse said.

Dad stepped back, still smiling at him and gripping his upper arms. 'I meant it about the cab, you know, Tony! If I'm too arseholed to drive myself then I'll pay someone to do it . . .'

Baby Gosse looked over Dad's shoulder at me.

'Get him one!' I said. 'Give him his own way because that's what he's used to.'

Tony nodded. 'See to it, will you, Vic?'

Teddy laughed from his chair. He'd just taken a swallow from his flask and the silver stopper was hinged back. 'Listen to the old sod – he'd sooner pay than ride free!'

Dad smiled at him, delighted. 'Paying for it can be cheaper in the long run!'

'Well, don't I know it,' Teddy said sadly.

He got up stiffly and brought Dad's jacket from the back of a chair. Dad looked at it and then sniffed and slipped in one arm. He let Teddy ease and pat it on to his shoulders. I felt sorry for Teddy until I saw the foxy and malicious look he sent towards Tony Gosse, as if he'd beaten him for possession of my father. He stepped back and looked around the room. 'So did you have a coat with you, George? I'm fucked if I can recall . . .'

'No need for coats where I'm going,' Dad said.

Teddy stared at him then, troubled. 'Where's that, George – fucking Honolulu?'

A fire-door let out on to steps in a well between iron railings. We were at the far side of the building now and I could see Dad's bull-nosed Rover parked against the other kerb. There was a lamp opposite and the scrape on the front wing showed up silver.

'Did you hit something, Dad?' I asked.

He half turned. 'Did I what?'

'Only the car looks like you had a knock.'

'If I did then I'll take care of it.'

Tony Gosse stepped towards us, still in his shirtsleeves. He smiled at me. 'Everything under control, John?'

'That's right, Tony. Thanks for keeping the old sod civilised.'

He laughed, trying to include Dad in it. 'Vic says the cab's on its way.'

Dad sniffed and turned his back on us, peering towards the corner. Loops of coloured light were shining along the front. I knew that it must be low tide because of the mealy smell from exposed shoals on the estuary. Tony Gosse stepped close and nudged my arm.

'I reckon it's the stink that keeps people away, John. They'll stand for anything except a bad smell.'

119

'Nothing you can do about that, Tony. Unless you tow the place to somewhere else.'

'Or move ourselves, John. We could always do that.'

'I heard you were thinking of that. Some people might be sorry to see you go.'

'Not you, though?'

'I wasn't thinking of myself, no.'

He sighed, looking nervously towards my father as if he thought he might step out into the road. A car rounded the corner then, swinging out and then its lights sweeping towards us. Teddy had his hand on Dad's shoulder. 'So here comes the bloody US cavalry!' he called.

Dad smiled back at the building. The windows were open on the dance floor and we could hear the music of the conga. 'They're all pissed up there, Teddy! You'd better go and rescue Alice.'

'Oh, sober or drunk she'll take care of herself,' Teddy said.

The cab parked a couple of spaces behind Dad's Rover. The driver flashed his lights and then waited. I didn't recognise him or the car. Tony leaned towards me again and I could smell the wine on his breath. 'What I do really depends on Marion, you see, and she's a mystery to me lately!'

'She needs you to make a choice, I think.'

'Oh, I don't know if that's what she wants at all. I don't think she's even sure. Three-quarters of what she thinks is a mystery to me. I just have to work with the rest . . .' He turned to Teddy. 'Is it three-quarters of an iceberg that's under water, Teddy?'

'No fucking idea,' Teddy said, scowling.

The cabby sounded his horn. I touched Dad's sleeve but he flinched away, twitching his shoulders.

'C'mon, Dad!'

He turned to me at the kerb, one patent foot forward. 'You couldn't take care of *her*, could you?'

'Who's that, Dad?' Although I knew.

He shook his head, not facing me but watching the lights along the front. 'You want to treat me like a bloody kid but you couldn't take care of our little Pearl!'

The driver was waiting for him, dangling his arm out of the window with a cigarette between the fingers. He flicked at it and dislodged burning ash.

'You'd better go now, Dad,' I said.

The TV was on downstairs – turned loud to suit Dad's hearing. I lay on my bed and listened to the buzz of it through the floor while I waited for some sleeping-pills to take effect. The TV meant that Rosemary was getting him settled at last, calmed. But I didn't want to know now, I didn't want to intervene . . .

When I was nearly asleep I thought about Enid, picturing her with a smooth, calm smile that filled her face. The child floated before her, weightless so that she didn't need to support it. It was wrapped tightly in a white shawl and crying, wriggling as if it were trying to free itself. Then it stopped and the quiet was worse than the noise it had made. The little mouth was open and silent, dumb . . . Enid was trying to touch the child but it kept floating weightlessly out of her grasp, bobbing in the currents. She wanted to comfort it but it was too late. Months had passed, years . . .

I sat up and my head broke through a red net. It was still dark but there was a glow to it – the colour I'd thought was behind my eyelids. Someone was there and I squinted at her.

'Rosemary?' My voice was to the side of me somewhere. I cleared my throat. 'Is there something wrong, Rosemary?'

She was standing at the window in her gown, lifting a corner of the curtains. 'I think something's burning on the site – I think one of the caravans might have gone up!'

I rolled out of bed before she had a chance to turn away.

If she saw the dressing on my side she didn't comment. I pulled on my trousers and went to stand beside her. I could see nothing but then I made out the path of the Course by its cover of white mist. There was a trembling red glow beyond the fence at the back of the garden, a reflection on cloud.

Rosemary waited outside while I dressed. I nearly lost my balance and had to lean against the door frame.

'Are you all right?' she asked.

'Is Dad awake?'

She shook her head. 'I put a tablet in his rum. He'd roam about half the night otherwise . . .' She stared at me. 'So, what happened to you, John?'

'Nothing happened.'

I went downstairs and I could hear her coming down behind me.

'What's the time?'

'Oh . . . five in the morning.'

I drew the bolts on the back door and went out. Running towards the back gate, I thought I could taste smoke mixed with the mist. I crossed the little bridge and the Course was passing invisible along its channel. I thought Rosemary might follow but when I looked back I couldn't see her. Probably she wouldn't leave Dad on his own.

The gate was standing open so that she might have been there before me. The long grass of the field was slippery with dew. I could see a spinning blue light now and a dog was barking. When I got nearer I heard the throb of the pumps. Then a curl of flame lifted into the air like a tall question-mark, sparking reflection on the sides and roofs of the caravans. It sank quickly but left a white shape in front of my eyes. The shining mist that gathered and floated might have been smoke.

A police squad-car was parked among the long grass with its doors left open and the headlights on, shining towards the blaze. Black streams of smoke welled from the windows of the burning caravan and joined in a twisting rope over its roof. It seemed flat in the light of the lamps, hard-edged. The fire-engine faced the dyke so that its lights washed up the slope and lit the gorse and shocks of coarse grass. I saw how the caravan was leaning to one side as if it might tip over any second. A pair of firemen in yellow jackets were directing the thick jet from a hose through its broken back window and the cabin rocked under its force and water poured out over the threshold of the open door. From a distance of fifty feet I could feel the stray drops striking my face. I went closer and noticed other people for the first time – standing in groups above their long shadows. A pair of coppers were keeping them at a distance from the fire. I nearly tripped over the lead of a dog and its owner smiled at me from his round, excited face.

'They've got somebody in the ambulance now.'

He pushed out his hand with the fingers spread, as if he were warming it at the fire. The dog started to bark and people in the crowd were calling to one another, already starting to drift away. The heavy metallic taste of the smoke was at the back of my throat, as if it had turned to something foul. Another rush of orange-white flame lit up backs and turning faces, hung in the air for a second, then collapsed back into the caravan's windows and door like something being sucked into a vacuum. I felt its heat on my face and hands.

A clear band of daylight was showing over the top of the dyke now. The firemen had stepped back and a hose was being trained on the fire from the back of the tender, isolating it in a shining fall of water. I spotted the ambulance and headed towards it. Its back doors were open and a young girl in her vest and pants stood close to them, rubbing her face and eyes with the heels of her hands. Her bare legs were splashed with drying red mud up to the knees. A tall copper – older than the others and bareheaded – bent to talk into her ear and his hair was turned blue-white by the lamps. He took a gentle hold of her wrists, tugging them down. Her face was smeared with tears and soot and it was because of her cropped and feathered hair that I saw it was the girl who had been playing pool with her father.

I went closer. The back of the ambulance was filled with white light and it made me think of a small side chapel of a church lit by candles. The girl's skinny father sat on the bunk at one side in muddy denims and a soaked black T-shirt. His hands gripped his thighs, the thumbs digging deep. He wasn't wearing his cap and I might not have known him except for his silver rings. A medic squatted at the side of the other bunk, unrolling what looked like a broad sheet of clear plastic and packing it around a shape, a figure – working swiftly and urgently, the folds of plastic shining silver as they thickened. A bare foot was pushing over the edge of the bunk and I saw it clench suddenly, curl on itself nearly like a hand would.

The older copper had his arm around the girl's shoulders. Her face was tight and dull, the eyes slitted. I wanted to speak to her but didn't. It would only have been a question. The motor of the ambulance was already running and I caught sight of Enid's narrow foot again, noticing a smear of soot along the sole. I couldn't take my eyes from it until the driver came round to close the doors. The girl started to wail and the copper was leading her away, his head close to hers, gripping her bare shoulders as if he thought she would fall. The water from the hoses was still drumming on the caravan's roof but the fire seemed to be out, drawn back inside. Steam was lifting now that the smoke had died down and there was the smell of heated metal. It was getting light and the caravan was surrounded by the pool made by the hoses. Rosemary was standing on the edge of it and she nodded, as if she was only acknowledging me, then stared at the caravan again.

11

They lived in the wildwood, in the Christmas-tree forest. John would read the child a story – sitting on his lap while the twigs tapped on the window and the rooms were warm and sweet-smelling from the woodstove. While his wife sat before her VDU he would read the child tales from the world beyond the forest, outside the little circle of their lives. The woodsman and his Pearl. The child's hair was against his cheek, clove-scented from the bath. Then as he turned a page she went slack and heavy.

'She's asleep. I'll put her to bed.'

Anna smiled at the screen. The woodsman's clever and charming wife. 'Are you sure you're okay with her, John?'

'What d'you mean?'

She frowned. She had a dozen invoices to finish – big breadwinner Anna. And he'd been difficult ever since the accident. Being at home with an arm in plaster was making him short with her and the girl. You had to be constantly on your guard, as she said to Mr Natta in the wages section – anything seemed to start him off. Like now. And sometimes he would talk in his sleep – just nonsense as they do. But then she woke up once and heard him sob. Just one sob in the Christmas-tree forest.

'Can you manage with her on the stairs – that's all I meant!'

'I can carry my own daughter, thanks.'

He carried Pearl up the wooden hill, one arm in its

plaster so that holding her was awkward, into the pine smells of her little room. He pressed the switch on the cord of the half-moon lamp. A bough against her window, tap-tap, like a friendly word. The shy creatures of the forest were settling in their burrows and mossy nests. He let her slip into the bed, under the woollen waves. She curled her legs beneath her and settled. Settled and sighed. Listening to her dreamy sigh the woodsman could feel himself begin to weep or nearly. Looking at her sweet tousle-head in the light of the lamp, he could feel himself nearly in tears.

Though why should he weep? What excuse was there in the story-book cottage?

'St Martin's Hospital!' she said, bright and brisk.

'There was a fire last night. On one of the caravan sites. A woman called Enid was hurt.' I couldn't say burned.

'Yes? Do you have a surname, sir?'

'I'm sorry. I'm not sure of her full name. She must have been admitted late last night . . . This morning, really – five or six in the morning, say.'

'Wait a moment . . .' Slipping away as she said it. I looked in the mirror above the hall table and Rosemary was watching from the door of the front room. She rolled her eyes away from me and went back inside. Dad was still sleeping.

'Hello? Yes . . . A Miss E. Sharpe was admitted at six thirty. Would that be her?'

I looked on the table for a pen but I couldn't see one. I had to say the name to myself, fix it. *Sharpe*. 'Could you tell me how she is?'

'Are you a relative, sir?'

'A friend . . . I live close by.'

'Wait a moment . . .' I looked for Rosemary but she was gone. I heard my father moving upstairs then, the scud of his bare feet across the landing to the bathroom. He'd slept late while I hadn't slept at all. I couldn't remember sleeping.

'Sir . . . ?'

'Hello?'

'I've rung the ward and she's quite stable. She's in a little bit of pain but they're dealing with that. She swallowed some smoke and that's the problem at the moment, apparently. She's in Winstanley, which is our casualty ward, but when she's recovered from that she'll probably be transferred to our burns unit.'

'I know it,' I said. 'How badly was she burnt?' I could say it now, as if I'd swallowed something myself. I still had the taste of the fire in my mouth.

'She has some second-degree burns to her hands and face. She seems to have escaped the fire fairly quickly.'

'Was anyone else involved?'

'In the fire? I don't think so . . .'

'Was anyone admitted with her. A child, say?'

'Let's see . . . No, the next admission was after seven o'clock. An elderly man . . . Was a child living in the caravan, sir?'

My hand started to tingle and feel numb. I had to push the phone tight against my cheek to stop it falling. 'I thought there might have been. I was just asking . . .'

'We've no record of a child that morning. What age would they have been?'

'A year . . . Eighteen months. I'm not sure.'

'Boy or a girl?'

'I'm sorry, I don't know.'

'So you're saying there was a child in the caravan at the time of the fire?'

'I'm trying to find that out, you see.'

Another pause while she spoke to someone off the phone. She must have covered the mouthpiece with her hand because I could hear the voices only as a shudder in the earpiece. 'Hello?'

'I'm sorry, sir . . . I don't think I can help you any

further. You could try the police if you're concerned about it . . . Or the fire-brigade would have a record of anyone involved—'

'Can I come to see her? Enid?'

She sighed as if she was in a difficulty. 'I'm afraid we're not allowing visits from non-family at the moment. She'll still be under sedation, I think . . . You could phone tonight or tomorrow and I'll be able to tell you if there's any change. I'm afraid that's all I can say at the moment . . .'

A bell was ringing and all the time I could hear other lines, voices.

Something shone in front of me – the handle of a spoon? A fork. I picked it up from the sludge of mud and broken glass, cleaned one side of it with a finger. It had been bent by the heat, turned back on itself. I dropped it again and it made a little splash. There was a litter of scorched wood, damp rags of carpet. The firemen must have hacked away the furniture and fittings, then dragged them outside to be doused by the hoses. The shell of the paraffin-fire sat like a black bird-cage a distance away in a pool of grey water.

The door of the caravan had been torn from its frail hinges and lay on its face a dozen yards away. The blank doorway was crossed with broad yellow tapes that breathed in the gusts – darkness behind, then, when I stepped closer, I could see that a little light was admitted by the broken windows. I tugged down one of the tapes and looked inside. The air still had a faint sweetness like scorched pie-crust. I pulled back my head, then looked again and saw how the smoke had left the walls and ceiling a smooth sooty-black, like the inside of a camera, and I recalled then how she'd kept my lighter, closed it in her fist. I leaned forward, trying to see into the cabin's blind corners. The top of a table hinged down from the far wall. Burnt ends of timber leant in the corner. I stepped back and a gust whistled in the grille of the paraffin-fire.

An elderly woman was watching me.

'Are you thinking that you know me?' she asked.

'Sorry, Ma?'

She held the collar of her coat tight to her old throat. 'I sometimes remind people of their mothers, which is funny because I've no children of my own – never wanted the trouble they bring, you see.'

'No one would blame you there, Ma.'

She pointed to the caravan across the way. 'I live just there, so I'd a good view of everything!' She laughed, wrinkling her face. 'With the mob there was I could have sold tickets!'

'Did you know her, then? The woman who lived there?'

She frowned. The sun came out and made the lines swarm on her face. 'Why should I know her?'

'If you were a neighbour, I thought.'

'Oh, people come and go and they're not worth troubling over. And the sorts you get here now would cut your throat if you looked at them . . .'

'You stay here though, Ma.'

She looked disgusted at herself. 'We came and stuck, you see. That was one of the mistakes we made . . .' She looked at me again, peering one-eyed like a bird. 'You're George Drean's lad, aren't you?'

'That's right – John.'

'Oh, I know your name all right! But you don't look well, love – a youngster like you should be in the pink.'

'I'm all right. I'm fine, Ma.'

She pointed her finger. 'You were a cheeky little get, anyway! I needed to give you a clip once and you cried like hell. You went running home and your dad came over to talk to me and we ended up laughing over it . . .' She wiped her lip. 'Your mother's dead now, isn't she?'

'That's right. Ma . . . A couple of years ago now.'

I stepped across the mud, wanting to go. I still felt sickly because of the smell of burning and an empty stomach. She shook her head. 'She was a fine, big woman. I'm glad it was your dad came to see me and not her . . .' She squinted at me. 'You know I keep seeing you as a boy and then as you are now, like there's one standing behind the other. I notice more than I should, you know.'

'D'you, Ma?'

She nodded towards the burnt caravan. 'She was a pretty girl – a bit tarty though. I don't know why they do that to themselves . . .'

I looked back. 'You did know her then?'

'I didn't say I knew her . . . What would she have to say to an old boiler like me, anyway?' She laughed to herself, standing on the fringe of the mud in loose slippers. A crêpe bandage showed palely below one stocking.

'Did you ever see her and a child together?' I asked. 'A toddler, say?'

There was effort on her face, like she was developing something behind her eyes. Grey film with pictures forming. 'Oh, younger than that! Nothing more than a baby, I'd say. A sweet little thing but then they all are.'

'Thanks, Ma.'

I went into town. The speaking clock called ten or eleven and I thought of seeing Marion. I parked down the street from her door and then walked back. The owner of the shop and a friend were sitting in scruffy armchairs outside, taking the air.

'She's not there any more,' he told me when I rang the bell.

'What?'

He looked at me as if he thought I ought to know. 'She's been trying to let the place out and I think she must have found somebody because they were here with a van yesterday, carrying stuff inside.'

'Are you sure?'

I must have had my mouth open because the friend

started to snigger. 'Think so,' the owner said. 'I'll tell her you were looking for her if I see her.'

'Thanks.'

He laid his head to one side. 'You're her brother, aren't you?'

'That's right. Her brother.' I found her key and slipped it in the lock but it wouldn't turn.

'They changed the locks last night,' the owner said. 'She sold us a few bits of furniture the other day and we've still got to collect them.'

The friend laughed. 'We should have got in while we could, Trev.'

'Oh, I'll find a way,' Trev said. 'There's always a way through.'

I drove through town, then stopped outside the Circle Mart and went inside for a bottle. I was just paying when I saw a warden through the window and dashed out.

She tapped her watch at me and I opened the car door which I'd left unlocked.

'Waiting restricted to four minutes,' she said.

'I KNOW!'

I'd leaned forward out of the door and maybe she thought I was going to hit her, because she stepped back and stared at me. She had a pale oldish face under her cap.

'Sorry,' I told her.

'You ought to calm down,' she said.

'I could do that, yeah. But not much point, is there?'

She put her pen back in her pocket. 'You might live longer.'

I got inside the car and Bilko was looking at me through the other window. I opened the door for him. ''Lo, Bilko.'

He settled down in the seat. He must have just had his lunch because he brushed crumbs of dry pastry from his front and on to the rug. 'You're a silly bastard, aren't you, John?'

'I'm not in the mood for all that now, Bilko.'

131

'Pardon me . . .' He started fiddling with the torn leads of the radio that were still dangling from the dash. 'Alex wants to talk to you.'

'Fuck Alex.'

'He said he was pissing himself when you started on him. He thought you were going for his throat!'

'I'm not even thinking about that now, Bilko.'

'You need to earn a living though, John . . . Or will the old man provide?'

'Look, don't you start as well!' Tugging it into a joke but meaning it.

'Okay, John. Fair enough . . . Hey, I heard there was a fire round your end last night.'

'Bit of one, yeah.'

'Bad one, I heard. That little lass that worked with Fi was hurt, wasn't she?'

'Who told you that?'

He thought back. 'Alex did. One of the drivers heard it from somebody . . . So is she bad?'

'She was burnt, Bilko.'

He started to be careful now, looking at me with a moon face. 'Pity . . . Hope it didn't spoil her looks.'

I passed Dad in the hall and he turned away his eyes, as if I left a bad smell he was too polite to mention. He played snooker incessantly, not asking Rosemary to join him. The rumble and clack of the balls was monotonous. I phoned the hospital again and there was no change. Rosemary coughed in the kitchen against the noise of the twin-tub. A drying day and later she'd peg out the clothes in the garden. Lying on my bed with the curtains open, I could see the warning lights on the top of the OKO chimney and its trail of white smoke. I drank the heel of the bottle and I could feel it warming me but there was always somewhere cold, it just moved around inside me.

I slept. I must have been tired from the other night.

I'd already heard Rosemary on the stairs. She settled on the edge of the bed in the dark. Dark Mrs Shand.

'What's the time, Rosemary?'

'Nearly nine. You missed dinner but I thought I'd let you sleep.'

'Good, because I wouldn't have been hungry.'

'You should keep that door locked if you don't want visitors,' she said.

'Oh, you're always welcome, Rosemary. Would you like a cigarette?'

She held out a packet. 'I've brought my own today.'

'Okay . . . Thanks.' I took one, then reached for the cord of the light.

'Leave it, John – I can see well enough like this.'

'You're like a cat then, Mrs Shand. A very nice cat.' I sat back against the end of the bed and she lit the cigarette for me. 'Is Dad in bed?'

'He's asleep in front of the TV. I think he wore himself out with all that snooker.'

'It's an interest for him.'

'I think he hates us both now,' Rosemary said.

'Not you! You're only getting the sidewash.'

'It'd be easier if he did, John. In a way it would. I'm scared to death he'll do something, you see.'

I stared at her. 'What kind of thing?'

She blew out smoke. 'Oh, I don't know . . . I keep expecting him to make some kind of declaration.'

'Oh, Rosemary!'

'D'you think he will, John? D'you think that's what's on his mind . . . You see, I think I'd have to go if he did that.'

'Where would you go, though?'

As if I couldn't believe there was anywhere else. I could already feel the empty house around me, Dad sleeping with his injured breath – a catch between the in-breath and the out that I never heard before. As if he stopped for thought, considered it.

'Oh, there's always somewhere in my line of work –

some old boy or girl who needs their meals and a bit of company. But could you look after him, John? I mean, the way he is at the moment . . . I suppose Marion would help with that.'

'Marion might have her own plans,' I said. 'I haven't spoken to her lately.'

'You Dreans! You keep each other at arm's-length and I have to make sense of it.'

'You don't though, Rosemary.'

She looked my way in the dark. I wondered if she'd been crying and that was why she didn't want the light on. 'So what was that thing on your side, John – a burn?'

'You've sharp eyes, Mrs Shand.'

'Oh, I need them in this place . . . Are you starting that again – that business of fires?'

'I promise you I'm not, Rosemary.'

'Then I'll need to take your word on it – I can't keep watch on George and you as well.'

I listened to the house. On windy nights it had a way of making little sounds that were comfortable, like the sighs of a settling dog. Or it was Rosemary that made me feel that way. 'That's right, Mrs Shand – you're not our keeper.'

'So, did you know her, John? The woman who was involved?'

'Involved is a good word, Rosemary. Oh, we'd talked a couple of times. Chatted.'

'But you looked to me as if you might have known her well.'

'When did I look like that?'

'After the fire. You looked like you'd had a loss.'

'Haven't you enough to think about with Dad?' I knew she could be insistent and that made me nervous.

'You said a child might have been living there. In the caravan. I heard you say that on the phone . . .'

'Then you shouldn't have listened.'

'Oh, I think I've a right to do that, John. I have in this

house. A child being involved makes me worry about you, you see . . .'

I heard a door slam downstairs that meant Dad must have woken. 'I thought there might have been a child . . . It seems I was mistaken.'

'But you don't really believe that?'

'Oh, what I believe can't be trusted, Rosemary. What I believe doesn't change a thing.'

12

I went to the hospital yesterday, John. For my scan. Do you remember when we went together? I know you do. Do you remember the little shining head, the fishbone spine? The Indian woman at the desk smiled and gave me directions, leaning over the desk and pointing. Of course I'd been before but that was a while ago.

Seven years? Eight? I followed the signs along green corridors. ULTRASOUND»› A waiting room and then a receptionist behind a partition. I gave my name. The seats were uncomfortable but there were only a couple of people before me – a slow time of the year for pregnancies, I suppose. I crossed my legs and the baby gave one of its half-turns, shifting its balance. It must be the size of a hampster now – a sweet little rat.

Half an hour. Children were running in the corridor. I could hear their shouts and the scuff of their shoes. Then one of them started to cry and a man stood up and went out. He came back with a black-haired little girl and sat her in his lap. She stared over his shoulder at me with her brown eyes and I smiled but she wouldn't. I put my hand on my belly and she stared at it, as though I'd done something that made her distrust me. Then the door to the examination room opened and the doctor let out a slight, pale woman and called my name. As the woman passed I could see she was in tears and that made me feel shivery and fated.

The doctor had a dark, trimmed beard, just a touch above stubble. His skin was a very warm, smooth brown. He showed me to a couch with a cover of absorbent paper. Now could you get up there, please. Smiling and apologetic. I had to climb up and then roll on to my back and I found myself blushing at the sight I must have made.

'The other lady looked upset,' I said.

The doctor rinsed his hands over a tiny aluminium sink. 'Oh, but that was tears of joy, you see! They've been trying for a child for over five years and seeing it on the screen was too much for her suddenly.' He smiled at me. 'We get the odd one like that. This is your second, isn't it?'

'That's right.'

He looked at his notes again, turning pages. 'So, no problems with the first . . . ?'

'Nothing medical,' I said.

He frowned and then smiled again and the little beard made a bar across the tip of his chin. I wondered where he was from. Sri Lanka? Mauritius? Somewhere with warm seas and warm rain. 'Now if you could just show me your belly . . .'

I tugged up my smock. I was still at the stage where it could be fat or a beer-gut, the navel not extruded. I wanted it to grow so that I would be unmistakably pregnant. The navel to be pressed out into a little dome. The doctor squeezed a fat white tube in his fist and trailed transparent gel down the centre-line of my belly. He smoothed it across with his palm and it felt clammy at first but then took the warmth of my skin.

'This is just to get a better contact, really . . . It'd be cheaper to use margarine but some people might object.'

He smiled at me and I had to give a little laugh. I felt angry with him for a second. So what's wrong

138

with margarine? He was still smiling, holding the terminal over my shining belly.

'Tell me if it's uncomfortable . . . I need to press quite firmly to get a good contact, you see . . .'

He slid the handpiece through the gel, across and then lengthways. It wasn't unpleasant – almost like a massage. I turned my head and watched the picture change on a six-inch screen – fragile shapes of light that seemed to turn themselves inside out. Head, belly, the fishbone spine, swivelling sticks of limbs and then the strong clench of the little heart.

'All seems to be as it should . . . I'll take a few measurements to see exactly how things are coming along.'

He swung the chair closer to the machine and froze the picture with a touch on the keyboard. I saw a circle drawn around the dark shape of the skull, then the spoke of a diameter. He clicked a mouse and figures appeared in the bottom corner. 'That's fine . . . Your dates seem about right, I'd say.' He smiled. 'Just in time for the fireworks, ay?'

'Oh, I'm not one for loud bangs,' I said.

He measured the length of a thigh-bone, clicked. The shapes on the screen came to life again. He moved the instrument across, delving. 'Would you like to know the sex?'

'No. I think I'll keep that for a surprise, doctor!'

He nodded but I could see that he would have liked me to know. He was still gazing at the screen, at the heart and the secretive little head, the puzzle-piece of the hips.

Downstairs I squeezed into one of the booths. Gerald was on a job out of town and I dialled the number of his mobile. I got only the trill of the tone and then the operator came in and said he wasn't responding. I opened my book then and dialled the number written crosswise across the page.

'David?'

'Is that you, Anna?' He sounded so pleased that I was fearful.

'I wasn't sure that you'd be in . . . Is this a slow time of year for security?'

'Oh, there's troughs and peaks. Like any business.'

'Do criminals take a break in the summer?'

He laughed. 'It's not so much that – a lot of people take a break from worrying about them.'

I joined in, glad that we'd found something we could laugh about. 'Oh, I find that cheering, David!'

'So where are you, Anna?' he asked.

'I'm in a booth at the hospital.'

'You're not ill, I hope!'

'Not ill, no. I came for a scan . . . Or I brought my belly in for one.'

He was concerned now. The way he drew in his breath told me. And I was so pleased that some kind of chemical was released by my heart. I could feel it passing through my veins, warming me. That he should stop his breath for my child's sake.

'No problems, I hope?'

'No . . . She looks fine.'

A nurse was pushing a trolley full of magazines and papers in racks and I was so pleased she stepped firmly and delicately across the blue and red tiles.

'She?' he asked.

'I didn't want him to tell me. But then I saw the screen and I know what to look for.'

'A girl then?' He was so intent, so serious.

I phoned St Martin's again.

'She's awake now but she still doesn't feel up to visitors.'

'Why?'

She drew in her breath. 'Well, I'm not sure why, sir. She

may be still in a little bit of shock . . . We just have to respect her wishes, don't we?'

'Her family though . . . Wouldn't they like to see her?'

'I think she might be separated from her family . . . She might have fallen out with them in the past.' She made a little click in her throat. 'She certainly doesn't want to see them now.'

'Will she be okay?'

'We think so.'

I put the phone down and it rang, jumped in my hand nearly.

'Hello?'

'John . . . ? Fiona.'

'Something the matter, Fi?'

'One of the customers at the cafe just phoned and said Teddy was throwing a fit . . . I thought I'd better get over there fast.'

'I'm surprised you're not there anyway, Fi.'

'You're out of touch, aren't you, John? Can you get here and give me a lift? My car's in the garage and Frank's already gone to work . . .' She meant Bilko. I think she was the only one who gave him his right name. Maybe his mother had.

Fi and Bilko had one of the new bungalows at Hooperstown. She was already standing at the side of the road, holding a magazine over her head to shield herself from the drizzle. I stopped about twenty feet away and she started running along the slope of the verge, gimp-footed to keep her balance.

I pushed open the passenger door and she climbed inside. She was without her make-up and her face looked as if a layer had been removed.

'Are you all right, Fi?'

She shook her head. 'If I was I'd be the only one around here.' She stared at me and I looked away, letting out the

141

clutch. I wondered what Bilko had told her, wondered if they still spoke.

'So why aren't you at the cafe, Fi?'

'Well, Teddy came to me a week ago and said he had to let me go. He was nearly in tears.'

'Why did he have to?'

'Because Tony Gosse pulled the plug on him.'

'Tony's got no right,' I said.

She nodded, tucking in her chin. 'Do you know anything about it, John? About him selling up?'

'We're not the best of friends, Fi.'

'I know that. I wondered if Marion had told you something.'

My sister, with a phone line to the great. 'I don't know what's going on, Fi. I don't even ask . . . So why's Teddy so upset?'

'Oh, some people came around for their slice of the assets. Tony bought most of the equipment a couple of years ago, you see, and he was renting it back.'

'And now Tony's sold it on?'

She shrugged. 'That's what must have happened.'

I found the side entrance for Sunnylands and drove along one of the avenues. A few of the caravans were already occupied with awnings erected outside. A white five-ton van was parked behind the cafe with its rear doors open and I spotted Teddy sitting with his head in his hands on the low wall at the side. A man in painter's overalls was perched beside him with an arm draped around his shoulders. I stopped the car and when Teddy looked up he had a bloody cut across the bridge of his nose.

I let Fiona out and followed as she ran across the yard.

'What happened to you, Teddy?' she called.

'He fell and hurt himself,' the other man said.

She glared at him. 'Was I asking you?'

He gave me a look and then shrugged and shifted a yard away. Fiona was on Teddy's other side now, holding his hand and rubbing his back. He looked pale and shaken but closer-to the damage to his nose was more of a graze than a cut. He stared at me, then swallowed and nodded over to the van. 'Go and take a look, John!'

I walked over to the van. For a second I could see nothing in the back but darkness but then I made out the square bulk of a deep-frier, the grill-pans and the range on its side, the fan of the dismantled ventilator.

The driver had climbed down and was standing beside me now. 'You're not here to cause trouble, are you?'

'Where are you going with these?'

'Oh, we might have a buyer for one or two items – the rest will go to auction. There's always plenty of interest in used catering equipment.' He nodded towards Teddy and Fiona. 'Your friend over there doesn't seem to understand that.'

'Was it you that pushed him?'

He shook his head. 'He was running about like a lunatic and then he slipped. There was something on the floor and he went arse-over.' He put his hand on my shoulder. He had a rosy, concerned face. 'Look, could you take him home or somewhere? I don't want him upsetting himself any more.'

The cafe's fire-door had been wedged open and a man in jeans and a soiled sweat-shirt stepped out carrying a bulging sack in each hand. You could see the edges of things, the handles. Teddy tried to struggle up but Fiona kept him down, leaning her weight on his shoulders.

'Look, it brings me no joy to see people in a state like that,' the driver said. 'Specially at his age.'

I went back to Teddy and sat down on his other side. The painter had disappeared. Teddy's hands were white and trembling on his thighs and they seemed to remind me of something. Then I thought of the fluttering hands of the hairdresser after he had drawn blood from Dad's ear.

'There's not much point in staying here, Teddy,' Fiona was saying into his ear. 'I'll phone Alice and tell her to expect you home.'

Teddy shook his head. 'No, I'm not leaving! I'll take my last breath here if I need to!'

Fiona kissed him on the forehead and then the temple, talking into his ear. She must have said the right thing because he nodded and stood up. His white shirt had come loose from his waistband and he tried to tuck it in. Then the van started up and drew away. He followed it with his eyes. I could hear the crash and slither of the stacked equipment.

As we drove into town Teddy bent forward and sent a fast stream of vomit past his knees.

'I won't say better out than in,' Fiona said quietly. I looked in the mirror and she had her arm around Teddy's shoulders. 'Are you all right, Teddy?'

Teddy mumbled something.

'I'll take care of him now, Fi,' I said.

'Are you sure?'

'Look, I'm his godson, aren't I? I'll take you to the cab-office if you want.'

'That place,' Fiona said.

'It's up to you, Fi.'

'Okay.'

I double-parked across the road from the office. A couple of drivers were leaning against the wall to the side, smoking and sipping coffee. One of them lifted his cup and grinned as I got out to open Fiona's door. I saw the mess on her shoes and the hem of her coat.

'You ask Alex to get off his arse and find some water for you, Fi . . . Look, I'll treat you to a lift home if Bilko's not there.'

She gave me her over-the-counter stare. 'It's okay – I'm still allowed my own money.'

'Okay, Fi. Sorry.'

She kissed Teddy on the forehead and then eased herself out. Teddy was leaning back with his eyes closed, hardly breathing. His face was like a map of a flat place with a few minor roads.

144

'Sure you're all right, Teddy?'.

'I'm fine,' he said without opening his eyes.

He lived in a quiet street on the other side of town. I knew the house by its square-trimmed hedge. They'd lived there for about twenty years now and it was the only place in the street that looked especially cared-for. Dad had said they'd sold a bigger property when they'd given up trying for children. Teddy sat up as I parked outside and started adjusting his tie.

'Look, I'm sorry about the rug, son . . .'

'Forget it, Teddy! It's not the first time that's happened.'

'It is for me.'

Alice opened the front door. Fi must have phoned from the cab-office to tell her to expect us. She smiled as we came through the gate, then let her jaw drop when she saw the damage to Teddy's nose.

'Who did that to him?'

'He fell, so they said.'

'I'm still here, you know!' Teddy complained.

Alice ignored him. 'Isn't he like a child, John? Getting into trouble over a few pots and pans.'

'That equipment was worth thousands,' Teddy said.

Alice nodded and sighed. 'Then that's more than you've ever been.'

She took hold of his arm and pushed him towards the open door. He held back for a second and then went inside.

'Well, that's the end of him, I think,' Alice said.

'Oh, he'll get over it!'

She shook her head. 'No, all he had left was that place! Without that to keep him sane he'll go the way of the rest of them.'

I wondered if she meant Dad – there was no one else that would have suited, unless she was including me. Then I thought of the night in the Assembly Rooms, how Teddy had helped Dad on with his coat and lovingly smoothed it over his shoulders.

145

'Look, I could bring Dad down sometimes. They could sit in your front room and put the world to rights, Alice.'

She looked back into the house. I could see Teddy making his way slowly up the flight of stairs, holding on to the banister as if he needed to pull himself up. It gave me a shock because he always seemed so sure-footed and dapper. Or maybe that was already in the past.

Alice faced me again, frowning. 'But Teddy and your father never got on all that well, you see, John. Not really . . .'

'No?'

She shook her head. 'Not while they were younger anyway. Your dad and Johnny Gosse were very close and then when Teddy came along it seemed to put his nose out of joint.' She allowed herself a smile. 'Teddy could always charm people, you see. He was always good for that.'

'Johnny Gosse has been dead a few years now,' I told her. 'So it's time they kissed and made up.'

She gave me a sweet elderly smile. 'There was something to do with your mother, as well. Between her and Teddy . . . Oh, I'm not saying that there was anything wrong with it. He was all talk like that and I suppose your mother didn't take him seriously, either. Then I think she started to despise him for it – that he kept everything on that level.'

'What level, Alice?'

'Oh, you could see the way they were together – the smiles on their faces. Like the cat that got the milk! But that was all it was for Teddy – all smiles and no substance.'

I looked up at the house. He would be undressing, folding his splattered clothes. 'What about Dad? What did he think of it?'

She looked mischievous, much younger for a second. 'George? Oh, he knew enough about Teddy not to be worried. I think he even might have felt sorry for your mother . . .'

146

'Look, I'd better go now, Alice.'

She put her hand on my arm, as if she wouldn't let me. 'Am I talking too much, John?' She stared up at me and smiled. 'But how is he? How is George?'

'I won't pretend that he's well, Alice.'

She looked comfortable with that, nodding. 'Oh, at least he has you and Marion. And that woman of his . . .'

'Rosemary,' I said.

'That's right.' She tugged at me, lifting herself, and kissed me on the cheek. Her breath had a sweetish powdery smell as if she'd just chewed a freshener. 'And you look after yourself, John.'

'Right, I'll do that, Alice.'

She nodded, as if that was the promise she'd wanted of me, already moving towards her door.

There was a pub nearby. A place I didn't like but I wasn't feeling particular. I thought the barman was someone I'd gone to school with but we didn't talk. You could just hear the talking clock from there, coming in through a window open at the top. Twelve. One. Two old girls playing dominoes, sipping glasses of Guinness. I phoned the hospital again but the exchange was busy and I listened to this little tune while I waited. When someone answered I put the phone down.

I drove with the window wide open to clear my head. You climbed a long hill and then there was scrubby land and then St Martin's. I turned at the sign for the clinic and there was the old wing with new buildings of two and three storeys around which I knew my way from my half-dozen visits as an out-patient. The grounds were fringed with shrubs and young firs so that there was the antiseptic smell of pine in the air. It made me shiver as I got out of the car.

A woman looked up from behind the desk and smiled, leaning towards me with her hands clasped. I noticed a thin gold ring with a little blue stone. I gave her a nod as I walked by.

'Sir . . . ?' she called to my back.

I expected her to call again but she might have picked up the phone and told security. A porter was pushing a trolley out from one of the lifts. Glass jars in racks rattled and collided. I held back the door for him and he nodded to me but didn't speak. I stepped inside and pushed the button for two floors above. Mosely and Winstanley wards. An announcement came to an end as I was stepping out of the lift and I wondered if it had concerned me.

I pushed open a pair of rubberised double doors and stepped inside. The air was full of noises which hardly broke the quiet – words, a whispering of fans, the squeak of rubber wheels. There were about a dozen beds, some of them curtained off. A nurse was walking away from me, rushing, skidding her heels across the tiled floors. There was a heavy grey light spread like a mist over everything equally.

I parted one of the curtains. Someone asleep, curled at the top of the bed, little. Thin white hair on the white pillow so it wasn't a child. Two empty beds then and machinery on a trolley, its wires hanging. Enid was on the other side of that and I thought she was dead at first because I couldn't hear her breathe. She looked dead-white anyway, the same colour as the dressings on her head and hands. Her head and one side of her face were bandaged. I might not have known her except her eyes, which had the same look I remembered.

'Enid?'

She said something I didn't catch. I went closer.

She started shaking her head, pressing back against the pillow. She was sitting up slightly. 'Will you go? Go . . .'

'Look, can I just sit with you, Enid? Talk for a couple of minutes?'

'No . . .'

'Just for a while. I'll just sit here, keep you company. We don't have to talk if you don't want . . .'

I looked for a chair but there wasn't one. The man in the next bed had a tube up one nostril and he was staring at me, as if he were afraid of what I might do.

'Could you go?' Enid asked. She glanced down the ward as if she expected help from there. Both of her bandaged hands were on the covers.

A nurse shook my shoulder. I wasn't sure how long I'd been standing there. 'Are you the one they made an announcement about?'.

'I must be.'

'You know you're not supposed to be here, don't you? Patients have a right to their privacy if they want it.'

She had a cap that looked impossible. A lace thing on the top of her head that made me smile. Another nurse coming towards us wore the same thing. Enid had closed her eyes now but the man in the other bed was still staring as if he were outraged.

'But you thought you'd sneak in anyway,' the nurse said. She still had her hand on my arm.

'Is she asleep?' I asked.

She nodded. 'The more rest she gets the quicker she'll be out of here.'

'I'd have liked to have talked to her.'

'Oh, you're lucky you got this far!' She nodded towards Enid. 'Is she your girlfriend?'

'Yes.' It didn't seem an exact lie.

'Did you have a row over something?'

I watched Enid's face. There was the yellow line of an eye. 'Sort of.'

'That has nothing to do with her being in this condition, has it?'

'That's the trouble – I don't even know.'

13

I don't think Dad even knew that I'd given up the job. Or he did know and didn't care. I wondered what else went on in his mind but snooker. He'd lean over the table, frowning and resting his weight on his cue – as if he were making a calculation. It scared me to think what the result might be. He watched Rosemary and spoke to her politely, carefully, hiding his intentions.

I phoned the hospital every other day or so, as often as I could take. They might have known me by now, known my history as a patient. A steady improvement but still no visiting. The ward sister was kind – a voice of tea and biscuits. Warmish weeks of mid-May, after the bank holiday. Pinpricks of fine rain, then sun. The mud and standing water around Enid's caravan dried to a crust marked by shoeprints and tracks of birds.

A mouthful of wine and the sun came out and put white caps on the waves. I walked at the edge of the water and it ran over the soles of my shoes, then drew back. Little birds flew in a tight bunch fast over the tops of the waves. Another swallow of Australian red and the burn on my side started to itch but I thought it was healing now, sealing the last of its heat under new skin. I sat down in the damp sand. When I'd had enough of the wine I threw the bottle towards the water, watched it up-end and spin, trail the last of the sweetish muck. A green splash where it fell and there was someone pushing a bike near the water, between lines of stranded weed.

'Hello?'

She squinted because the sun was behind me. Her feathered hair looked as dry as straw.

'You know me, don't you?'

Shook her head, leaning on the curved-back handlebars. She wore a red and white striped top and worn-out denims. I pointed at her boy's bike.

'You'll ruin your gears like that. Once the sand gets in it'll chew them away.'

She shrugged, peered around. She might have been hoping to see someone. 'Doesn't matter . . . My dad'll fix it up.'

'Is he good with bikes, your dad?'

'He's all right.'

'You're lucky if he's all right . . . So have you been to see your friend?' I asked.

'What friend?' She tried to look dim for a second, foolish. But her eyes were too sharp.

'The one in the hospital. Enid, isn't it? Have you been to see her yet?'

She shook her head. 'Don't know her.'

'She lived in the caravan that burnt out. I saw you standing next to the ambulance and your dad was inside.'

'We just went to see. Dad said he'd go with her 'cause no one else knew her . . .'

'I'd like to see your dad.'

'What for?'

'Oh, to tell him what you've just told me. See if he has the same story.'

I saw her lip turn and I wished I hadn't had the drink then because it had made me clumsy.

'So what's your name?' I asked.

'Nothing.'

'It can't be nothing. You must be more than that . . .'

She lifted one shoulder like a bird pretending an injury and started to walk away, towards the lines of sloping rocks and the dyke. The gears of the bike clicked as she pushed it along.

152

'Hey, can I come?'

She ignored me and walked on, heading down the beach, away from Whiteheads and towards Victor's yard and the marshy ground where the sea sometimes seeped through the dyke. I followed a couple of yards behind. She started trudging through the drier sand but I thought there was a chance she would any second break into a run.

'So how old are you?' I called.

I thought she wasn't going to answer again but then she looked back at me over her shoulder. 'Sixteen.'

'That's handy, because I'm sixteen myself.'

She waited a second. 'Twelve.'

'Then you haven't a worry in the world, love!'

She shrugged again. I was catching her up now.

'What's your dad called?'

'I call him Dad.'

'You're not forthcoming, are you? You're not very informative.'

We were walking alongside but she still wouldn't look at me. We came to the steps of railway sleepers and infill.

'Do you like to play pool?' I asked.

She looked at me from the tail of her eye. I could see that she was interested. 'S'okay . . . D'you?'

'Not pool much, no. Not as such. I play snooker with my dad sometimes. We've got a table at home.'

She stopped with her foot on a step. 'A full-size?'

'Two-thirds sort of. You can still have a proper game, though . . . Ever played it?'

'Dad takes me to a club sometimes. He used to work there.'

'In town? Is it the Roses?'

She shrugged. 'Someplace. Dunno . . .' She started climbing, dragging the bike alongside her in the smooth drag beside the steps. I put a hand on its saddle to help her but she jerked it away. 'Don't touch my bike!'

'Okay . . . Okay.'

We were on the tarmac track along the top then. She put

153

her foot on one of the pedals and bowled it along, so that I had to break into a trot.

'Hey!'

She looked back at me, scornful, then trailed a toe to slow herself. 'So why do you want to see my dad?'

'I want to ask him about Enid.'

'He won't tell you anything!'

'No harm in asking then . . .'

She shrugged again, then kicked her leg over the crossbar and started cycling, slow at first, then picking up speed. When she was twenty feet ahead she looked over her shoulder, then rang her creaking bell and steered down the landward slope of the dyke, standing back on the pedals and freewheeling. She hit the level ground and started pushing at the pedals again, heading for a group of caravans.

I watched her and then let myself down the slope. A grey horse was tethered near the foot and the ground was mined with its droppings. The girl had disappeared now but I could see a trail through the longish grass. A couple of women talking at a standpipe looked my way and I nodded but they carried on staring. I might have looked like a policeman or a murderer, I'd lost track of myself lately. Then I heard a whirring noise and the girl swooped across my path and stopped dead with a squeak of her brakes.

'Dad said he'll see you but he hasn't got long.'

'Leads a busy life, does he? That's good . . .'

She pushed the bike ahead of me again, keeping her head down, not acknowledging me. 'My dad's called Ray,' she said, like a sacrifice to forestall further questions.

'Ray. I'll remember that . . .' I was getting my breath back. 'So is it far now?'

She pointed and I heard a thin rattle and saw a child's plastic windmill pinned to the top of a post. Its red and green sails were catching the wind, spinning it to flame colour. Behind it a patched grey tarpaulin strained against

154

its ropes. The girl dropped her bike into the grass suddenly and ran towards it, calling out as she ducked inside.

'*Daaaad!*'

The little windmill scuttered. A noise that made me want to pee. After half a minute he looked out at me, holding on to the edge of canvas like a door he could slam. He wore his dark cap with the tassle and looked more himself under it, not frail as he'd seemed in the back of the ambulance. He pushed out his chin with its sprinkle of beard.

'Yeah?'

'I wanted to talk to you, Ray.'

'About my girl?'

'About Enid.'

He gave me another look, then nodded. There was something well-knit and alert about him. 'Come on inside, then!'

He turned back and I followed, ducking under the flap. I could see then that the tarpaulin spanned the space between two caravans set at a square angle – one a thirty-footer and the other smaller, barely more than a trailer. A trestle table and four or five stacking chairs stood on the trampled grass and there was a mess of parts on the table – little wheels and cogs, dismantled bearings and black coils of chain, all set in smears of oil on the bare surface. The stripped frames of cycles were stacked between the table legs and to one side. There was no sign of the girl now.

I nodded at the table. 'Do you sell these in town, is that it? Do them up and sell 'em on?'

He gave his head a shake. 'You chase my daughter home and you want to know my business! You don't know where to stop, d'you?'

'I didn't chase her. We walked all the way.'

'Well, she looked bloody terrified! I could have the police on you, you know!'

'You won't though, will you?'

155

He shrugged just like the girl had done. 'You'll find out . . . So what did you want to ask me?'

'Have you known Enid for long, Ray?'

'Knowing my name doesn't give you any rights,' he said. 'Hers neither.'

'Well, my name's John.' I pointed towards the flapping canvas, in the direction of the house. 'I live at the house.'

'That place?'

'That place, yeah . . . So are you a friend of the family?'

I thought he had a dog's face then – a sharp, terrier expression. 'Whose family?'

'Enid and the kid, I meant.'

He shook his head, smiling as if it were laughable. 'There is no kid!'

'I saw her with one. Other people have as well.'

'Doesn't mean anything, does it? She babysat for people – for us sometimes. We'd shove her a couple of quid. It might even have been one of ours you saw . . .'

'How old are they?'

He looked sly again. 'You reckon you've seen them – work it out for yourself!'

He sat down on one of the chairs and rested one leg on the other. He didn't offer me a seat. His eyes flickered at something over my shoulder and I turned and saw a woman's face at the window of the larger caravan before she ducked out of sight. I could smell paraffin now and there was some in a bowl on the table-top. He must have been using it to clean the parts.

'D'you use that stuff for heating as well?'

He wouldn't look that way. 'What stuff?'

'Paraffin. Enid did and I think that might have caused the fire.'

He shook his head. 'She was always careful with it.'

'It goes up in a second.'

'You seem to know a lot, so you tell me.'

'Look, Ray, I just want to find out about this.'

156

'There's nothing to find. So you're wasting your time and mine.'

I heard a noise to the side and spotted the girl then, peering at us from around the back of the trailer. She looked back at me from one blue eye. 'Have you seen Enid since then, Ray?' I asked. 'At the hospital, say?'

'She doesn't want visitors, so I've been told.'

'She must have a family, though?'

He pulled a face. 'Not necessarily.'

'I'd have thought it was necessary.'

The girl strolled out from cover and stood behind her father's chair. She put her hand on his shoulder and I thought they had a resemblance that wasn't obvious. You saw it but then struggled to find it again. Ray put down what he had been playing with – a little toothed wheel.

'Look, can you go now, John, whoever you are . . . ? I don't want to spoil your fun but could you leave us in fucking peace?'

14

The woodsman watched from the gate while their car disappeared – Anna's little mouse of a Fiat nosing down the road and into the wildwood, hidden by the mossy boughs for a minute and then emerging into the valley where the winds blew fierce through the gap in the hills, climbing past plantations of dwarf-conifers towards the pass. He turned back to the silent house.

That night he said, 'I could look after her next week. What's the point of laying out forty quid for childcare when only one of us is earning?'

'You've got a problem with that, haven't you?' Anna said. 'Me bringing home the money?'

'Not at all.'

She laughed. She had no idea how her laughter hurt him. 'Liar!'

'I just want to do something, that's all. While I'm laid up I may as well be useful, save us a bit.'

'But what about Pearl? She needs to see other children . . .'

'She won't mind being around her dad for a while, will she? What am I – a bloody ogre?'

'You just hate being on your own, don't you? That's what this is all about!'

He had to laugh at the way she saw through him. He took her hand. 'Partly, yeah. I can't go on watching that shite on the box all day. Trying to read.'

'What about your arm, though? You know what a handful she can be!'

'I can still walk, can't I? I can still get about. What's she going to do – run away from me?'

There was a tightness in the healed skin of my hands. I didn't know what it promised – rain, was it? I checked my wallet and I had the price of one more tankful of petrol. I used the garage at the Circle Mart, then drove back to the site and parked within sight of Ray's caravan. I could see his tarpaulin filling with wind, breathing out again. The girl came from somewhere on her bike and circled the car twice, then sounded her bell at me and pushed away, standing up on the pedals. She would have been used to me by then. When I closed my eyes I could see shapes and little animals, gemstones in orange and purple. I could have slept but Rosemary called me.

'John . . . John!'

She was reaching through the open window, shaking me.

'What's wrong, Rosemary?'

'Oh, John . . . I can't find your father!'

It seemed like a joke for a second. 'What d'you mean you can't find him?'

She stood back, looking angry now. 'Just what I said! I thought he was in the garden but when I went out there I couldn't see him!'

I pushed back the passenger door for her and scooped rubbish from the seat. 'He hasn't gone upstairs for a nap, has he?'

She put her hand to her face. 'D'you think I haven't looked there, John?'

'Why should he have walked off, though?'

'Oh, I don't know . . . Why are you sitting here, John?'

'Oh, no reason.' I took a last look at Ray's shelter. 'Let's see if we can see him. How long d'you think he's been gone?'

160

'It could have been a couple of hours.'

'You mean you haven't seen him in a couple of hours?'

She didn't answer and so I left it. I bumped along the tarmac track, splashed through the pools that seemed to stay there through half the summer.

'We had a bit of a row,' she told me.

'Ah, so what about?'

'I turned him down, John . . .'

'Oh, Rosemary!'

'I always thought it would happen, you see, and I had all these answers ready. Things about the difference in our ages, about staying friends, that we were better off the way we were . . .' She laughed. 'You can imagine, can't you?'

'I can, Rosemary.'

'Then when it came to it I knew none of it would do. I knew I just had to be definite.' She turned the other way, still looking for him.

'And he took offence?'

'I wasn't sure if he had or not . . . We spent the rest of the morning avoiding each other and so I was quite relieved when I heard him go out the back.'

'And you thought you'd leave him to it?'

She stared at me again. 'We've hardly seen you the last few days, John! Marion neither . . .'

'Okay. I'm sorry about that, Rosemary. I'm sorry if you haven't.'

'It's my job, though . . . I should have done it better.'

'You're here to look after the house, Rosemary – not keep an eye on him. God knows I should be doing that myself.'

'I managed to reach Marion on her mobile number. She was out of town but she says she's on her way back.'

I dropped Rosemary off at the house, in case Dad should wander back, then I drove back across the site towards the dyke and Mam's bench. I was almost certain that he would be there but when I climbed the slope there was a litter of cigarette ends and a couple of crumpled cans of drink around the base but no sign of Dad.

I looked along the beach. The tide was going out and someone was digging for worms in the flat sand, dumping shovelfuls and then kicking them with his heels before he sifted through them. The sun made a cold dazzle in the water and I felt afraid then. I looked at my watch and thought that Rosemary might have already called the police.

I drove on to the B-road that led past Sunnylands. There was a phone-box near one of the entrances and I stopped to phone home.

'Rosemary?'

'Have you found him, John?'

'No. Not yet. I just wanted to make sure that he hadn't come back.'

'I keep hearing noises in the house and running upstairs. I'm starting to think he might be hiding somewhere, John, listening to me . . .'

'Any sign of Marion yet?'

'She phoned me and said she was on her way.'

'Okay . . . So you stay calm, Rosemary! We need somebody to do that.'

Another mile towards town, past the turning for Maurice's, I spotted Dad walking along the narrow path that ran along the top of the verge on the other side of the road. He looked tired and he was leaning carefully forwards as if he was having trouble keeping his balance. I could see what an effort he was making to put one foot in front of the other.

I kept pace and called through the open window at him. Either he didn't hear or he decided to ignore me because he kept his face to the front. He had on brown slacks and the old blue V-necked sweater he'd wear for days around the house.

'Dad!'

162

He looked my way and stopped for a second, one foot pushed forward. Then he started walking again. I was hogging the middle of the road and a car overtook on the inside and sounded its horn. Dad started to frown as if all the noise disturbed him.

I drew a few yards ahead and parked half on the verge. By the time I'd crossed the road he was plodding patiently up to me. His face looked pale and wind-chapped and he sent me a puzzled look, as if he couldn't account for my presence.

There wasn't room for us both on the path and so I fell into step just behind him. 'Can I give you a lift, Dad?'

He sniffed and wiped his top lip, then gave a suspicious glance over his shoulder. 'Where to?'

'Anywhere. Home, if you like . . .'

He stumbled over a hole in the tarmac and I put my hand on his arm. He stopped and looked down at it. 'I was looking for little Pearl . . . I thought she might have come this way.'

He turned again and I could see the waxy, yellowish folds of his ear. 'She wouldn't come here, Dad. Not now.'

'Oh . . . ? Why wouldn't she?' As if he knew the answer but he had to have it from me.

'Because she's dead, Dad.'

Another car on the road. He gave a little shiver, as if he were shaking off a cold. 'We may as well go home then.'

Tony Gosse's car was there when I parked in the yard. Not the specially adapted estate he used for taking his son to school and hospital but the slim silver Opel saloon he used as a run-about. I peered through the reflections in the windscreen and saw Tony staring back. He started to get out and I looked past him for Marion because I thought they would have come together. There was no sign of her.

Dad was drowsy now, as if the couple of miles' walk had begun to tell. Tony got on his other side and helped me guide him through the door.

'Where's Marion?' I asked. I was almost angry with him for touching my father.

'She's looking around the site with Rosemary. She thought someone might have invited him in.'

'Into their caravan? I hadn't thought of that . . .'

I let Dad down into his chair near the snooker-table. He stared ahead of him for a second and then sniffed. His nostrils still looked scornful but there was a softer look to his eyes. Baby Gosse was looking about the room in a way that made me notice the mismatched chairs and the places on the rug where the scuffed boards showed through. Rosemary was always warning me that Dad might trip and break a bone. I thought that it was probably the first time since he was a child that Tony had been inside the house.

'So thanks for your interest,' I said.

He looked back at me. A mild look was all he could manage. He had the beginnings of a beard and his collar was grubby.

'You look like you've been sleeping in that car,' I told him.

'That and a flea-pit hotel. I've been on the move lately, John.'

'With Marion?'

He looked down at Dad and I could see Dad's eyelids drooping. 'With Marion, yes.'

My sister and Rosemary came back a few minutes later. Marion rushed to Dad who was half-asleep and kissed him on the cheek. He nuzzled the side of her face, drowsy, murmuring. 'Marion . . .'

She let him slip back, but stayed bending over the armchair, looking into his face. 'Where did you go, Dad?'

He slid his eyes towards me. 'Oh, nowhere special, love . . . Just a walk.'

'You should tell us, Dad! You should have told Rosemary where you were going.'

'Does it matter now?' I asked, wanting to defend him. She shook her head as if she thought I was being irresponsible. 'Okay, we'll talk about it later, shall we, John?'

She sent Tony a smile and he smiled back, leaning with his arms folded against the edge of the pool-table. I looked over to Rosemary for support but she was standing near the door as if she were afraid that Dad might start to abuse her. But then his eyes were closed anyway . . .

Marion stepped forward and kissed me on the cheek. 'Thanks for finding him, John.'

'He was no trouble,' I said.

She nodded. She had a little blue bruise below her temple and I wondered how she had done it. 'So whereabouts was he?'

'Taking a stroll like he said, that's all.'

She clicked her tongue. 'I thought I wouldn't get any sense from you, either . . .' She looked towards Tony again. 'You may as well go, Tony. None of this will mean much to you.'

Tony laughed, including me and Rosemary in it. I couldn't stand the way he could be likeable. 'If he wants to go walkabout then why shouldn't he? He kept himself in harness for long enough.'

Marion shook her head. 'You don't know anything about it, Tony.'

'That's right, I don't.' He nodded to us again and then kissed her on the forehead. I noticed how she closed her eyes, as if she didn't wish to acknowledge it.

15

Dad slept for fifteen hours and then played himself back into existence on the snooker-table. He positioned his cue, making a bridge with his thumb hooked back. His face was full of frowns and puckers. Then he smiled and sent the white on a slanting, silent run across the cloth.

'I can't be expected to . . .' Rosemary said in the kitchen. 'How can I tell him to do one thing and not the other? I can't be at his heels all day like a *dog*.'

'No one expects you to,' I told her. 'You can't be his keeper.'

'So who will be, then? You?'

I trailed Dad across the garden. A couple of yards behind. He glanced back at me, then kicked his foot to free it of the long grass.

'Are you following me?'

'I'm just going the same way, Dad.'

He laughed to himself. 'And which way is that?'

'You're making life hard for Rosemary,' I told him. 'She keeps expecting that you'll run off again.'

'Oh, is that what I did – like a boy to the circus?'

'You know how she is, Dad. This sort of thing will only worry her.'

He nodded, looking shrewd and calm after a long stint on the snooker-table, drawn in on himself. 'Well, I've a great respect for Rosemary – more, obviously, than she has for me . . .'

'She's every respect for you, Dad.'

'She only thinks I've gone soft in the head, is that it? Is that what Dr Spelling told her?'

'The doctor thinks you should take better care of yourself, that's all.'

'Or someone else will do it for me?'

'If you put us in that position, Dad.'

He watched me carefully for a while, like I was an animal that might possibly bite. Then he cleared his throat and straightened himself, one hand fingering the buttons on the front of his plaid shirt. He frowned, looking towards the house.

'Something the matter?' I asked.

He started to smile, as if he'd recalled something that pleased him. 'I've a photograph of them, you know – on this very spot!' He laughed and shook his head. 'All I need to do is find it . . .'

'Who, Dad? Who are you talking about?'

'Your mother and little Pearl! Our Pearl in your mother's arms . . .' He turned and pointed to Marion's window. The tip of his finger trembled in a circle. 'It must have been from up there with my old Pentax. I called out to them and they both looked up towards me. I'd never seen your mother looking prettier . . .'

'So when was this, Dad?'

'Oh, years back now . . .' He laughed and looked at me fondly. 'Your mother had a lovely smile in those days, you know. Radiant. Men would stop to look after her in the street. It made me angry and proud at the same time . . . It must have been the early morning because the light caught the child's face just right. And you know the sort of skin they have at that age – like there's a lamp behind it.'

'I know, Dad . . . So how old would she have been? How old was Pearl?'

'Just a baby. A toddler, say. Your mother smiled and I snapped them both.' He grinned like a younger man and then looked shrewd again, lifting his finger to me. 'You can't fail with that particular lens, you see, John. F.8. A little care with the exposure and you're home and dry . . .'

I left him and went back into the house. My sister and Rosemary were talking in the kitchen and then Rosemary came to the door. 'Is he okay?'

'Dad?' As if I were surprised that she'd asked. 'He's taking the air out there. He'll be fine.'

'He should take the air in here,' Marion said, 'where we can keep an eye on him.'

'Don't worry, Marion – it's all under control.'

'Then it's the only thing that is,' Marion said.

She wore a glossy orange blouse that drew the light from the tall window. I saw her little mobile phone on the edge of the table and snatched it up.

'Hey!' She made a grab for it from her seat but I held it to my chest.

'Can I borrow this for a minute?'

'What's wrong with your phone?'

'I don't want to use it with you ladies earwigging.'

I went up to my room and stood near the window where the signal would be clear. Dad was still standing thoughtfully in the long grass. I thought how I should cut it but the Flymo needed a new blade and it was gone too far for the hand-mower.

I punched from memory the number of the hospital, then asked for the extension for the ward.

'Winstanley?'

'Enid Sharpe. Is she any better?'

'Is it the prowler again?' She had started giving me points for persistence.

'That's right, sister.'

'Nurse,' she corrected. 'But you see you're too late now because she's discharged herself—'

'She's left the hospital?'

'Oh, we'd have liked to have kept her a few days longer,

but anyway she seemed to be making a quicker recovery then we thought. She said she had friends to go to.'

'The friends who were visiting her?'

'I suppose they were the same. She'll be attending as an out-patient in another hospital – for further minor treatment to her burns.'

'Which hospital?'

She cleared her throat and I could hear the noises of the ward – the squeal of rubber wheels and a door closing.

'You can't tell me that, can you, nurse?'

The celluloid windmill scraped and rattled against its post – spinning in the breeze that started at that hour, fraying into a broken star of green, red and orange. I spotted something lying in the grass and picked it up. It was a child's blue leather shoe, embroidered with a design of flowers across the toe.

I looked around for the girl and just then her name came back to me: Rhona. The sun was already dropping behind the nearest row of caravans and washing was blowing and cracking on a line, dancing above its long shadows. I stepped under the awning and I could smell the trapped scent of the trodden grass. One of the stacking chairs lay on its back and the trestle table carried its cycle parts and oil-smears. Then I heard a noise from the larger of the two caravans – the thin fret of a child's voice. It carried on for a minute, lifting and falling. Then it stopped. I left the silence alone for a few seconds and then rapped my knuckles against the door, holding the shoe in my other hand.

'Ray?'

Someone was listening and I rapped again.

'Wait!' the woman shouted.

She sounded harassed, as if I'd provided the last straw. I heard her moving about inside, putting something down on a table. The awning filled with wind and went slack. I kept my foot on the step while a bolt was withdrawn and she showed herself through the gap of the door.

She looked younger than Ray although her dark hair had a touch of grey. She had a soft largeness and wore a black, velvety dress with coloured panels. Her pale skin looked as if it would hold the print of a thumb.

'Ray's not here . . .'

'Okay . . . Can I speak to you then?'

An infant was pushing against her leg, looking past its shelter. A little boy from his clothes, though I couldn't be sure . . . Snot pushed down from his nose and his eyes looked gummy.

I showed her the shoe. 'I found this in the grass.'

She took it and nodded. 'It belongs to the other one. We had a search for that. They've gone now anyway.'

'Ray and the child?'

She nodded. 'My girl as well. We thought this one was too poorly . . .'

'Where have they gone?'

She didn't answer, because she thought I'd no right to ask. The child was still staring, mesmerised with terror at the sight of me.

'Can I come in?'

'Why?'

'I could just go away,' I said. 'But where will that get us?'

She watched me for a second, then looked back into the caravan, as if she were checking that the place was presentable. 'Okay . . . Just for a minute.'

I stepped up into the same oily warmth I remembered from Enid's 'van. The little boy twisted away from us, acting bashful now, wiping his nose with the back of a hand. Ray's wife held the little shoe in her hands, turning it.

'Kids are murder on shoes,' I said. 'You can never keep up with them.'

171

She pointed to the boy. 'It's a size too big for him. The other always had bigger feet.'

'Because they're not twins. Not even brothers.'

'I shouldn't have let you in, should I? When you could be anyone.'

'You've seen me before though, when you looked out of your window . . . My name's John, what's yours?'

She hesitated. 'Valerie . . . Ray's told me about you, anyway.'

'Warned you off, you mean?'

She shrugged. 'Not exactly. I think he felt sorry for you, only . . .'

'He thought I could make life awkward.'

She sat down and the child snuggled between her open knees. 'He knew she wanted a bit of space, you see. A breather.'

'So he's taken them somewhere? Enid and her little boy?'

'You're no fool, are you?'

'I reckon Ray thought otherwise.'

She shrugged. 'He finds it easier to lie sometimes – like the rest of the human race.'

She was crying then – the shine of it on her cheek. It was a surprise to me but then I caught the distress she was in like a breath. She pressed her face against the little boy's hair, so that he struggled against her.

'I didn't want him to go – I told Ray that I didn't . . . Enid's my friend but I worry about him, you see – about what could happen.'

'About the boy? She might hurt him, you mean.'

'I think about what happened before . . . What nearly happened.'

'But you were looking after him then, so it didn't.'

She was struggling with herself, swallowing. I stepped and put my hand on her arm. I could feel the jolt of her sobs. The little boy squirmed against her. 'She knew it was coming. She could feel herself building up to it. And there was nothing she could do about it.'

'So she passed him to you? But why did she lie about him, Valerie? Why did she hide him from me like that?'

'Oh, she's got a history of it, you see – of fires.' She grinned at me, as if she'd decided to be mischievous. Her eyes were still glittering. 'D'you think she's fit to bring up a child?'

I had to look down at the head of the boy pushing against her side, the curl of hair at his perfect little scalp. 'I don't know,' I said.

'I think you do know. She was scared he'd be taken away from her – that's why she kept him hidden like some pet she wasn't supposed to have. She didn't want social services sniffing around.'

'What about her family?'

'Her family are long gone. She's a mother and brother in the West Country but I think that's far enough away for safety.'

'Where's Ray taken her?'

'To a friend's house. To some place a friend of ours has bought . . . We're going to live there soon, anyway. He's coming back for us.'

'Anywhere but here, eh, Valerie?'

She managed to smile then, resting her hand on the boy's head. 'That's right – anywhere but this bloody place!'

16

Comfort spreads from the baby, John – this placid-
ness like I'm a cow on the hillside, chewing my cud.
And I'm doing fine. But then David Ordish sinks like
a stone into the centre of me, until he's in my womb
as well – a little voodoo doll floating alongside the
other!

He keeps phoning. When can we meet? When and
where? When Gerald kisses me I think of what this
David says, hear his tone of gentle firmness. I don't
like to think of him talking that way to anyone else!
He mentions God and I want to smile. It seems so
ridiculous over the phone. My faith, he says, I take
strength from my faith, and I have to stop myself
from laughing – at this little pale-haired man and his
God!

It might help you, he says, to come to terms. But
what terms am I coming to? With what? I sit on the
edge of the bed with his firm, tender, ridiculous voice
in my ear. I take the phone away a couple of inches so
that I can hear his whisper buzzing close to my ear, a
captive whisper that's all my own – his soft voice with
its security salesman's tricks and phrases.

Then he asks after you, John, in a way that makes
me think he really cares. I don't know, I say. I don't
know how he is – I've no idea. How can you not? he
asks and seems concerned for your welfare, the
condition of your soul. He thinks that I'm shallow,
I'm sure, for letting things slide between us. Losing
touch. It makes me smile that he's so earnest, but I'm

afraid as well. A light, pregnant person like myself has
no defence against it.

You should never lose hope, he told me. Hope is
eternal. But losing hope is my achievement – my
masterpiece nearly! Strangling hope every time at
birth. Stopping it before it gets that far even. Taking
precautions. And you'll know yourself how impossi-
ble it seems at first, how there are so many things that
keep you wanting and wishing – little strings and
hooks to catch at you. Pictures in the mind's eye. I
suspect that you never did quite get the hang of it,
John.

Not you.

David listened quietly when I said this. As if I was
raving, he let me finish.

There's somewhere I'd like to take you, he said.

A letter for Rosemary by the afternoon post – from
Winnipeg, Manitoba, with a stamp of a lady aviator. I
picked it from the mat and carried it upstairs to her. She
was sitting at her small desk below the skylight set in the
slope of the ceiling. Her desk was a knee-hole dressing-
table from which she'd removed the shaped mirror. The
mirror leaned in an angle of the wall and showed me
myself holding the blue-edged envelope.

'Letter for you . . .' I thought that I should have left it
for her to find.

She marked the page of a book and closed it. She liked
anything with a solution. Then looked at me over her
shoulder. 'Are you my postman, John?'

I leaned across the room to drop the letter carefully on
the edge of her bed, on the faded pink towelling counter-
pane that had probably been a purchase of my mother's. 'I
thought it might be urgent.'

She shook her head. 'You were surprised to see a letter
for me and you wanted to know what it was.'

I stayed near the door, half in the room and half out, as

she would herself stand sometimes. 'D'you think I'm being nosey, Rosemary?'

'Oh, no more then you should be, I suppose.' She got up from her chair. 'It'll be another letter from Mark.'

I was lost for a second, then I recalled. 'Your son?'

'That's right . . . He wrote to me a couple of weeks ago and I sent him a letter back. My husband died a while ago, and Mark managed to find me.'

'How?'

'Oh, I'm not sure how! He wasn't forthcoming about that. He's in Canada at the moment and so I suppose he used someone – a tracing agency.'

'A detective, you mean?'

'Oh, nothing like that! I think most of it can be done over the phone nowadays. I'm sure my husband could have found me except he knew that I'd made up my mind.'

'But now he's dead . . .'

She nodded. 'More than a year ago . . . Mark said it was due to an aneurysm – a stroke. While he was getting on a train to go to work.'

'I'm sorry.'

'So am I, which is surprising . . . I was sorry and I wanted to tell someone about it. So I told your father.'

'Ah.'

'I suppose I knew what might happen but I needed someone to share the news with. And I thought it might help him break his silence. Because he's been very silent, John.'

'You could have talked to me.'

'I thought of that as well. Only you've been busy with something else lately. Someone.'

'Someone, yeah.'

The skylight was open on its ratchet and I could smell the slates drying after a shower of rain. I wondered if Dad was still asleep because he would wake about this time, sit up stiffly in the bed and massage his temples.

'So, how's that going?' Rosemary asked.

'Oh, all I'm doing is waiting.'

She sat on the side of her bed and picked up the letter, examining it. 'So is my son. Waiting for an answer . . .' She stared at the postmark. 'He seems to have moved since he last wrote.'

'What does he do?'

'For a living, you mean? He makes people laugh.'

'He's a comic?'

'That's right, John – I've a comedian in the family . . . He's on tour at the moment. Apparently he's in demand over there.'

'Will he come to see you when he's finished?'

She shook her head. 'I think the idea is that I join him over there. He said he'd send me a ticket – return if I like.'

'So will you go?' And will you come back if you do? I could have asked.

She twitched her shoulders. 'I don't know. Sometimes it's too late for these things. Don't you think that, John?'

'I'm not sure if it is, Rosemary. I'm not sure if there's a time like that.'

'You're brave then.'

'I might have to go away myself, you see. Just for a few days.'

'To see your friend?'

'I'm hoping that I might, yeah.'

'Well, live in hope, John.' She listened, looking down at the rug between her stockinged feet. 'It sounds like your father's finished his nap.'

I parked down the street from the cab-office and walked back. I had the radio under my arm with its leads and connections dangling. The TV was playing on its shelf in the waiting room and a driver and a couple of fares were sitting on the long bench opposite. I thought one was the man who I'd seen selling soft toys in Maurice's bar. I could feel their eyes on my back as I went to the hatch.

Alex was working at the timesheets, or pretending to. I

was sure that he must have seen me walking through the open door. I put the radio down on the counter of the hatch.

'That's yours, Alex. I might be going away soon so I thought I'd better settle up with you.'

He looked at it as if he expected me to snatch it back any second, then nodded. 'Thanks . . . I'd given that one up to tell you the truth, John. But thanks anyway.'

'Sorry for the delay, Al. Sorry I nearly scalped you with that mug, as well.'

He shrugged his fat shoulder. 'All in the line of business, John. All in a day's work.' There was a crumb in the corner of his mouth and he looked down at the open packet of biscuits. 'Want one?'

'No thanks. Thanks all the same . . .' I glanced at the timesheets spread across his desk. Little corrections and an hour he'd snatch back. Three kids and a time-share. He couldn't help himself. 'Bilko in today?' I asked.

'Oh, he's taken a few days off to sort things out with Fiona. They've left the kids with her sister and gone off to the Canaries. Taken a chalet on Fuerteventura.'

'Very nice. I hope that gives him some credit with her.'

'Dunno there, John. Fiona can be a hard person to please and she's worse since she lost that job of hers.'

'They'll swim not sink, Alex. Don't you worry.'

'Hope so . . .' He pulled a face again, then took hold of the radio and dragged it below the counter. 'So how's your old man keeping?'

'Oh, he went through a bad patch but he's getting stronger.'

He nodded but still looked doubtful. 'Well, that's good at his age. I've heard his old pal isn't a hundred per cent nowadays.'

'Teddy? I'm on my way there as it happens.'

'Well, give him my best,' Alex said. 'Tell him he still owes me a fare from that Assembly Rooms do.'

I went outside and there was the same warden as before hovering around the car. She closed her notebook.

'I've no money anyway,' I told her.

'You shouldn't be on the road then.'

'That's right, love, I shouldn't be.' She had the same pale face with a trace of liner around the eyes that made her look paler still. 'Hey, you need a holiday,' I told her. 'I've heard the Canaries are very nice.'

She laughed. 'Oh, chance would be a fine thing . . . All we can afford is a week in a bloody caravan.'

I started getting in the car. 'Not around here, I hope?'

'Anywhere but this place!'

'That's right, love. Anywhere but here.'

Alice led me upstairs, into a lavender-scented room. Teddy was sitting up in bed, reading a newspaper. When he saw me he folded it and put it down.

''Lo, Teddy!'

He smiled and one side of his face lagged behind the other, like it was slow to see the joke. Alice left us and went downstairs, became noisily busy in the back of the house.

'So how's retirement suiting you?' I asked.

He rolled his eyes. 'Retirement? Feels like bloody imprisonment to me . . . Alice insists that I stay in bed but it's just to keep me out of the way, that's all. I could run a mile if she'd let me! I could run and never stop . . .'

'You rest if it's called for, Teddy.'

He shook his head, disgusted with the idea. His moustache looked white as bone. 'A rest is the last thing I want. If I keep on resting I'll just bloody stop!'

'Has Dr Spelling seen you lately?'

He glared at the door which Alice had left half open. 'Those two are in bloody collusion! I have to be careful what I say. She spends more time talking to Alice than she does to me. Can that be right, John . . . ?'

'No, it can't,' I said, knowing the only way was to agree. 'Dad was asking after you,' I told him.

He put his head to one side, as if he were listening to something – an angel speaking in his ear. 'He shouldn't then. We both need a break from that.'

'A break from what, Teddy?'

He worked his head. 'Oh, from the bloody double-act we make of ourselves!'

'Are you joking now, Teddy?'

He stared at me, then started to look anxious, watching my face. 'Look, if I say anything you don't like just tell me to shut up, will you? With the rest of them I don't mind but I swore on the Bible to look after you, you know.'

'I know that, Teddy.'

'In the eyes of God and man, though I couldn't give two fucks about God, you understand . . .'

'We can look out for one another, Teddy – that's the way.'

He shook his head, because that was too easy. 'I might have run off with your mother, you know – you don't know how close I came to that! I might have left you without her, you see . . .'

'Okay, stop now, Teddy! Stop where you are!'

He nodded. 'That's right, son – it's what you leave out that counts!'

I rubbed his shoulder. I could feel the sharp corners of bone that had been underneath his dapper and well-pressed clothes. 'Are you sure you're okay, Teddy?'

'I promised to look after you and now you're doing it to me!'

'I'm only looking you over.'

'I was no good for Alice, you know. Or I was good in the wrong places – not where she wanted it.'

I listened to the clatter she was making downstairs, the shudder of her energetic footsteps. 'You're talking a load of rubbish now, Teddy!'

'Oh, there was bugger-all they could do about it in those

days. I told her we should adopt but it wasn't what she wanted . . .' He shook his head. 'Firing blanks – that's the way some people express it.'

'Then you have to feel sorry for them, Teddy.'

He struggled to sit higher in the bed. His nose was swollen above the feathery moustache. 'We've never got over what happened to little Pearl, you know.'

'I know, Teddy. I know that.'

He cleared his throat. 'I was wondering for a while if we'd caused it . . . If we'd brought it about.'

'How could you have done that?'

'If we were loving her like our child and that wasn't meant to happen . . . I was wondering that.'

There was a draught from the chimney – nothing serious but a draught. I felt like telling him to fasten the top button of his jacket. 'I lost her, Teddy – it was as simple as that. I was supposed to be taking care of her but that wasn't what I did.'

He was smiling, just as if he hadn't heard. 'Me and Alice talk about her and it's like she's there before us. It's like this sweetness we both feel.'

'Sweetness, Teddy?'

'That's right – like someone's stirred a spoonful of sugar into us.' He looked up, humorous. 'Hey, that's a funny thing for an old cunt to say . . .'

17

Two of next door's children – sisters, eight and ten –
were playing on their front path as I stepped out of
the house. I smiled at them and waved but they only
nodded back, as their parents do – to acknowledge
me and no more. It has to do with Gerald's divorce,
which seems to involve the whole street. David's car
had a scratch along its wing and I wondered why he
didn't get it repaired – you'd have thought image was
important in the security business. He smiled as if
he'd sensed the thought and leaned over to push open
the door. The radio was playing and the air inside had
a scent of pine-freshener. I got inside and fumbled for
the clip of the seat belt and he found it for me.

Ever the gent.

He looked out at the girls who were watching us. I
could see that it bothered him. 'I could have arranged
to meet you in town instead,' he said.

'Am I supposed to make a secret of this?'

'Only if you want to.'

His lips were fullish but tight and his eyes were
elsewhere mostly. Not on my face, anyway. Then
when he looked at me directly they became sharply
focused. What colour? That sort of flat blue-grey –
the shade I remember plasticine always ending up as –
a final colour. But then I'm not particular about eyes,
not an eye person.

He looked past me at the house. 'You've done well
for yourself.'

'Gerald's done well for me. You see, I decided that

*what I really wanted was to be taken care of – I'd
reached the stage where I could admit that to myself.'*

*'Well, we could all do with some of that,' he said.
'I wanted a lot of it.'*

*He laughed as he does when he's feeling nervous or
out of his depth. I can read him already, you see. His
laugh will start to irritate me or I'll get to like it – it's
too early to say. Would he ask me to call him Dave or
Davey? I wondered. I hoped not – David was the
only thing bearable.*

*He drove fast but without the flashiness to attract
attention. When we nearly clipped the wing of a
delivery van he gave the driver a blank stare which
reminded me of the day he came to the cottage.*

*'Do you ever see the other copper – the one that
came with you?'*

*'Carmichael? No . . . He's still in the force as far as
I know. He moved to a different division just before I
quit.'*

'I didn't like him.'

'Well, you wouldn't in the circumstances.'

*'I wouldn't have whatever they were . . . I didn't
like you much, either.'*

*He smiled again and gave a shrug. All in the line of
duty. Sometimes his copper's status seemed to hang
about him like a smell of old fish about a kitchen. We
were still on the outskirts of town but then this place
is all outskirts, all suburb. There was a playground
where I stopped to watch the children sometimes on
my way back from the shopping centre and it was
swarming with them now because of half-term and
the spring sunshine. David kept silent and turned up
the radio as soon as we'd reached the open road.*

'Don't you want to talk?' I asked.

*That shrug and smile. 'So what would you like to
talk about, Anna?'*

'Christ! You're as bad as Gerald . . .'

184

He drove faster, until I tugged his sleeve.

'Hey, could you ease down a bit, David? I'm worrying for two, you know.'

He dropped back to around fifty-five. There was higher ground ahead – not hills exactly but a dull purplish ridge. The road was heating in the sun so that the view kept shimmering, like water coming to the boil. I could feel my heart being slowed by the drag of the baby's, its flywheel to my engine.

'You thought he'd done something, didn't you?'

He turned down the volume, just when it was a song I liked. 'Who?'

'You know. Pearl's father. John. You were soft with him for a while and then you started.'

'That was just something we had to cover – it wasn't personal.'

'You mean the father's always a suspect?'

'In some cases, yes. I wouldn't say always.'

'What a world you must live in!'

He looked smug for a second, pleased with himself. 'I'm out of it now, remember.'

The fields on either side were lower than the road as if we were driving along a raised causeway. The land was folded so that the ditches cut back on themselves.

'Should I call you David or Dave?' I asked.

'Whichever you prefer.'

'What does your girlfriend call you?'

'I haven't a girlfriend at the moment.'

'Then what does your mother call you?'

'She's dead, actually.'

The 'actually' did it for me, killed any interest I might have had in the subject. 'Then David it'll have to be.'

He smiled as if he'd won. The way he shaped his lips made me think of the other copper, Carmichael –

*as if that one were contained within him somewhere
and the smile let him out.*

*'He never seemed like a father to me,' he said after
a second.*

'Who's that?' I couldn't think, didn't want to.

'John.'

'What do you mean?'

'He didn't seem the type for it, I suppose.'

'Is there a type?'

*'I reckon so, yeah. I'm not one myself and so I
should know.'*

'And John wasn't either?'

'That was the thing that struck me about him.'

*'You and Carmichael, you mean? Tell me, do all
coppers think alike, or is that just an ugly rumour?'*

*He drew in his lips and started to watch me then,
like a fish he thought might be slipping the line. Then
the baby started to move in my belly. It felt
wonderful, with feathery little ticklings.*

*'We had a procedure,' David Ordish said, 'a road
we had to follow.'*

*'A road. Right . . . Is that where we're going then –
to the cottage?'*

Marion told the dead rat joke, the snake in the trombone.
Then she was singing to a rhythm-box and a new guitarist.
The guitarist looked about twenty-two or three. After a
couple of songs she had the audience calling out and
cheering. The bar had an extra couple of staff as well as
the part-timer.

Maurice looked the length of the bar and over at the
stage – heavy-eyed with one hand spread in spillage.

'What d'you think of the act tonight?' I asked, teasing
him.

He shook his head and turned away for a second, his
white acrylic shirt sticking to his fat side. 'Oh, she'll get

what she wants in the end, John. Maybe that's the worst you can wish on anyone.'

Marion stepped over in the interval while her guitarist queued for drinks leaving his guitar in its satin-lined case like a corpse displayed in its coffin. Maurice nodded towards him. 'A new man in your life, Marion?'

She lowered her lids. 'He's good – I'm giving him a trial. I'm getting sick of tapes and boxes.'

'He keeps looking at your backside, that's all,' Maurice said.

'Oh, I'll forgive him for that at my age.'

I leaned towards her on my stool, noticing that she'd barely acknowledged me yet. 'So where's the boyfriend tonight?'

She gave me a stare and Maurice turned away. 'He said he might be along to give me a lift home.'

'When you're finished here, you mean?'

She didn't answer but glanced at Maurice, careful of his feelings. The guitarist came over with the drinks. He seemed even younger off-stage. He smiled, then looked between us in an anxious way.

'Don't worry – we're always like this,' Marion said. 'Like cats in a bloody sack . . . Phil, this is my brother John.'

We shook hands. 'I knew you were something,' he said. 'I could see the resemblance from over there.'

'You're another little liar,' Marion told him without a smile.

He stared at her, then looked to me for help. But Marion was tugging at my sleeve already. We took our drinks about a yard down the bar, out of earshot in the din of music and chat.

'I'll be staying at home tonight,' Marion said.

'Good for you . . .'

'What I mean is that Tony will be with me.'

'D'you need my permission for that?'

'I was just giving you the information.'

'Okay . . . I expect Dad'll be asleep when you get back anyway. So don't let me disturb you.' I noticed she was wearing a gold chain I hadn't seen before, with a little pendant of clear stone. 'So tell me what you get from it, Marion. From you and Tony, I mean.'

Like it was her little habit.

She looked at the empty square of the stage. Maurice had turned on the lamp above the pool-table again and most of the interest was on that now. 'Oh, let me think . . . He's kind to me, for a start. Some men are, you know – some men are kind to women.'

'And that's enough for you?'

'But you shouldn't underestimate it, John! He gives me little gifts and then he'll give me himself. Do you think I should turn that down?'

'It doesn't come free though, sis.'

'Is it Julia and the boy you mean?'

'Something like that, yeah.'

'Oh, I'll just have to take that on, John. That's all I can do. Because if he decides to then I have to as well. If he makes that choice then I can't be the one to get cold feet . . .'

I couldn't look at her. Not at that second, anyway. 'So where are you thinking of going?'

'Tony's talking about France. He's got some business over there we might be able to step into. A bar in one of the tourist spots.'

'When?'

'I'm not sure when. It might be soon. Might be a year away.'

Might be never, I thought. Her guitarist was hovering near our table again, pretending to watch the pool game but glancing over at her. 'I think it's time we all got away from this place, Marion.'

'That's right. But Dad'd never leave. It's a pity Rose-mary couldn't see her way there . . .'

'To marry him, you mean? Were you behind that?'

She looked shocked. 'I promise you I wasn't! Cross my heart.'

I was still watching her. 'You think it'd be an idea, though.'

'It'd settle them both, wouldn't it?'

'Take him off our hands, you mean? Not much fun for her, though.'

'She'd be the lady of the house,' Marion said. 'Of Whiteheads.'

'That place is half-rotten anyway.'

'They could sell it . . . It'd make a little nursing-home or something like that. Tony was saying how the site would make an eight-hole golf-course.'

'Is he thinking of buying it himself?'

'He's getting rid of his investments – you know that.'

'That's right. He got rid of Teddy near enough.'

'He'll see Teddy all right, don't worry about that.'

The part-timer came around, collecting glasses. 'Dad says he has a photograph,' I said.

'Oh yeah? One that you didn't burn?'

'A photograph of Mam and little Pearl. He said he took it when Mam was younger . . . when she still had her looks.'

'You know that isn't possible, John. Mam was already ill when she was born.'

'It's possible for him, Marion. And I think that's enough.'

'Poor Dad!' she said.

I put my hand on her arm. 'Dad's fine, Marion. He isn't poor at all.'

She sat closer to me, holding my hand. I looked towards the bar and saw Ray there, talking to Maurice who was sitting bulkily on a tall stool. Ray said something into his ear and he smiled and nodded. Ray was dressed in a wrinkled grey T-shirt and shorts but he still had on his black cap with the tassel that bounced as he spoke.

'Who are you looking at?' Marion asked.

'Oh, there's a child out there, Marion.'

She stared at me. 'Outside here, you mean?'

'Not here, I expect . . . A child I need to see. To make sure he's all right, that he's fine.'

I could see from her face the way her heart sank. 'What child?'

'One I thought I'd lost but I think I might find him soon.'

'Who, John?' Quietly now, carefully.

'Just a child, Marion. A little boy.'

The dog with a limp, the nun in the helicopter. Marion told her stories, working the crowd, then sang another couple of numbers. The guitarist was watching her every move with lust and adoration. I went over to the bar again and she glanced my way, as if she thought I might escape her. Which I would. A gang from the OKO plant pushed laughing through the side door from the car park, then stopped in front of the stage. I couldn't see Ray now and I made my way over to Maurice who was chatting to the part-timer.

'What did he tell you, Maurice?' I asked.

He looked at me as if he meant to ask who.

'That little feller. Ray. What did he say?'

'Oh, Him? He was asking if I was interested in a dog. Apparently Vic's got one a customer gave him. A Dobermann cross, he reckons. A bitch.'

'I think I've heard that one before, Maurice. So he sent the other feller to tell you?'

'He just dropped in for a tin of tobacco and thought he'd pass on the news . . . D'you know him, John?'

'A little bit, Maurice. Will you be taking the dog then?'

'I'm tempted, you know. The place isn't the same without one.' He looked up at the portrait of his dead dog above the optics. 'I don't know though, John. I don't think I could ever trust another dog . . .'

'Well, try, Maurice – try your hardest!'

I could feel my head clearing as I crossed the Course, then cut through the site to Whiteheads. I took the gravel road and drove around the front of the house. The lights were on in the living room but the other rooms seemed to be in darkness. I wondered if Dad was already asleep but then when I got out of the car I could see him moving in his stiff way round the snooker-table while a slighter person waited behind him in the corner of the room, standing with their back to the jumping light from the trophy-cabinet. I took it for Rosemary but that was only for a second. Then Dad bent to take a shot and I could see the girl's smooth face over the length of the table.

I let myself in – quietly, I thought, but I must have made a noise because Dad came to the door. He was holding his cue and smiling. He looked very pleased with himself.

'She's already better than you'll ever be!' he told me with satisfaction.

'Who's that, Dad?' Although I already knew.

As I stepped into the room Rhona sent the green to the top pocket. It did the thing of hitting both sides before spinning in. Wiped its feet. The white came off the cushion towards the middle of the table and stopped dead, perfect for the straggler of the half-dozen reds. She stood up with a quiet look towards us and Dad started to laugh, hissing between his teeth.

'And she won't even tell me who taught her to play!'

Rhona kept her blank, astute look on them. 'We'll have to go now, anyway.'

'Who's we?' I asked.

She pointed her thumb at me, the same gesture her father used. 'My dad wants to talk to you.'

I saw the disappointment on my father's face, that the game might have to end. 'Where's Rosemary?' I asked.

He sniggered again. 'Oh, I sent her to her room. I told her I had no further use for her services.'

Rhona laughed – a child's sharp laugh – and it struck me

that she might actually like him. 'She'll take you at your word one day, Dad,' I warned him.

He still looked pleased. 'Oh, what if she does! We're alone in this world from start to finish.'

'Marion will be back soon,' I told him, 'to keep you company.'

'With that little friend of hers?'

'Who's that, Dad?'

'Do you think I don't know he'll be sneaking in here as soon as I'm asleep?'

'You should phone the police, Dad. Tell them there's an intruder.'

He smirked, contemplating it. 'No, I couldn't shame your sister like that.'

'She'd wring your neck, that's why.'

'I'm ready to go any time,' Dad said. 'And one method is as good as another.'

They played on and he couldn't keep the smile from his face when Rhona sent down the black. He struck the heel of his cue on the rug to show his appreciation. 'You're a bloody miracle, you are! If you're ever looking for a manager . . .'

She lay down her cue on the table. 'My dad's my manager.'

'Well, that's how it should be! How old are you again?'

'Twelve.' She looked over at me, impatient with him now. It must have been already midnight.

Dad shook his head. 'Well, you can't say fairer than twelve.'

She took her jacket from the arm of a chair and put it on with a flourish of the red lining. She zipped it, then waited with her hands in the deep pockets.

'You'll have children of your own one day, Rhona! But I'll warn you now that they'll always disappoint you,' Dad said.

She shook her head. 'Oh, I'm never having kids – fuck that!'

Dad laughed, then turned back to me. 'Well you'd better hurry, John! Just in case you miss something . . .'

18

His girl knew the forest with a deeper knowledge than his own. It made him proud and afraid, startled by the way she would know the call of a bird or recognise without fear the cry of one of the heavy, awkward beasts. She would whisper a name before he spoke it, identify the shape of leaves that slipped edge-on like playing cards, the stands of toadstool and the smell of the dry dust of their spores. Was he leading her, or she him?

He held her little, wise hand on the old tracks. They crossed the boundaries of vanished farms, lost paddocks – from the time before the trees had swallowed them. They heard a scramble among the roots and followed that as well, her feet padding. They tracked the flight of a bird through the branches. The journey had been long, taking them miles from their home on the fringe of the wood. His pack was already heavy on his shoulders.

'One good thing about your mam is she always makes enough sandwiches!'

They ate with their backs against the mossy stump of a wall. He delved into the bag – ham and pickle on brown bread, a flask of tea with a dot of whisky to help him with the pain of his arm that still troubled. Where the spinning blade had cut. Fanta for the girl. If he turned to his left he could see the empty windows of an old homestead, look up into the boughs and spaces of white air in place of the fallen roof.

'Who lived here, Dad?' Her own voice sounded funny.

'No idea. Seven dwarfs, I expect . . .' He settled his back against the stone. A swig of whiskied tea.

Little Pearl wandered through the old rooms. She saw the sooty brickwork of the hearth – a hook for the pot set in the deep arch. The breeze down the chimney was an old man's sigh. Chilly, as if something was dead and gone. She could see her own breath, rising.

She ran outside, across the collapsed floor. 'Dad!'

He was asleep, his head tipped back against the base of the wall. A pulse was beating steady in his throat. His arm was sprawled out, where he had hurt it, and the bandage was dirty, fraying at the ends. His hand looked yellow where it pushed through.

'Dad?'

She touched him on the face but he only murmured and twitched. She was afraid of him now – the different person he turned into when he slept. The one, if you weren't careful, he might wake up as. She held the can of Fanta – a slop in the bottom – and he shifted again, taking himself deeper into sleep. She saw the rash of dark hairs under his chin.

The crashing of a beast. They had found a place where one had lain, its sharp smell like burnt hair. She looked around and she could see where the roof of the house had fallen, the bright mould eating its timbers.

'Dad?'

Scared. She felt a scrape of blood on her cheek where a thorn had dragged earlier. He was too fast asleep to hear now, or she spoke too quietly. His head was turned but she knew that his face would already have changed. She stepped back and her shoes made sucking noises in the softness. A breeze was coming to her through the channels of the trees – like a song, a march you had to follow.

'Was he all right?' Rhona asked in the car.

'Dad? That's as good as I've seen him in a while, so thanks.'

'He told me he had an angel on his shoulder and she sometimes helped him and sometimes put him off his stroke.'

'Did he? Well, I think I know that angel.'

I took the lower road for quickness, crossing the Course on its bridge of concrete slabs that rocked under the weight of the car. On the other side the weedy margins were littered with stripped hulks of cars and vans and we passed the black shell of Enid's caravan. I looked over at the girl and either she hadn't seen it or it was familiar to her and not worth a glance.

The gates of Vic's yard were open and lit by the lamp on its tall pole. DOG LOOSE! I heard the thump and blare of music and then the ivory mongrel's yaps. The lights of the house shone between the aisles of rusting vehicles and as soon as I stopped the car Rhona was out and running towards them, as if she'd delivered me and a weight had been lifted. I followed behind. The downstairs windows had been thrown open and music was coming from fat speakers mounted on the sills. A refrigerator stood guard in the middle of the yard, trailing a length of yellow extension cable. Victor and Ray were sitting companion-like on a low couch backed against the wall.

Vic pointed to the fridge. 'Help yourself there, John!'

Inside were a couple of cardboard pallets of lager, chicken drumsticks, chipolatas, finger-food on trays. I rummaged for a can. 'So am I late for the party, Vic?'

He slipped his arm around Ray's shoulders. 'Ah, I'm just seeing off a couple of friends, John – sending them on the road . . .'

'I didn't know that you two were an item,' I said.

197

Vic planted a kiss on the other man's cheek. 'I can't keep away from the riff-raff in my business.'

Ray nodded. 'He finds treasure in the trash, you see. That's one of his talents.'

Rhona was playing with a thin liver-coloured young dog. Dobermann cross or similar, snapping her fingers at it. The dog leaped and snuffled and for a second they both had the same intent look, peering into one another's faces. Then Vic's hound started to howl again and I watched the way the other dog crouched and pinned back its ears.

'Is that the dog you're offering Maurice?'.

Vic shrugged. 'If he's interested at all . . . He's still wrapped up in the other one though, the one that was killed.'

'I think he's coming round a bit,' I said.

'I've heard he was more upset about the dog than when his missis left him,' Vic said. 'That's a funny thing, isn't it?'

'Marion says that'.

'Then it might have been her I heard it from . . .' The dog put its nose to his open hand and he pushed it away gently. 'Ray found this one for me. I'd told him it'd bring a smile to the old fart's face.'

'You find dogs?' I asked Ray.

'Oh, I've a method with them. Dogs aren't a problem.'

Rhona was punching her hands to the music, lifting her feet slowly in their high-laced boots. The dog skittered around her on its puppyish paws. Vic went to the fridge and helped himself to a chicken drumstick. He took a bite and wiped his chin with his fingers, nodded at Ray and me.

'You two have a chat. Don't mind us.'

We walked between the rows of scrapped cars, breathing the smell of oily gravel that the warmth of the air had brought out. Vic's dog started its racket again.

'I'd like to show you something first,' Ray said. He was without his tasselled cap and he kept smoothing back his hair.

'Okay.'

The dog was tethered to the bumper of the rust-red shell of a Commer van. We went a yard closer and it charged in a slide of gravel until it was brought up short by the leash, choking, its paws scrambling in the air. I stopped but Ray tapped me on the shoulder and stepped forward.

'It'll lay your arm open!' I warned.

He looked back, smiling. 'Oh, not me.'

The ground around the dog was littered with bone fragments and sawn hanks of timber, their ends made feathery by chewing. A plastic washing-up bowl was smeared with dried blood and another was half-filled with pinkish water. Ray went closer and the dog set its legs wide and looked towards him as if it couldn't fathom his foolishness. It leapt forward again and the wire leash made a thrum as it came into tension. The choke-collar was biting into the flesh of its throat.

Ray sat on his heels then about a yard away and started a mewling noise between his lips. The dog stayed with its legs wide-planted but rolled its head slightly, to one side and then the other. It was like the movement of a fish sick in the water.

'I'm the only friend you'll ever need,' Ray told it. 'Remember that, won't you?'

He came forward slightly, then crouched down again, just out of reach this time. The dog was pressing forward so that the taut cable made little low sounds. I thought about what might happen if it broke. The music from the house had turned quieter and slower, a kissy sort of tune. Ray leaned towards the dog and his scalp caught the light and flashed like a signal. The dog was standing nearly upright now, held by the tension of the leash, Ray's face an inch away from its teeth.

Then it seemed to fall into him, into his arms, its paws against his chest and its head working between them. Ray rocked back, off balance for a second, and I heard him laugh as he turned his face away from its wet snout. He wiped his lips with his sleeve and leaned forward again, so

199

that his nose was close to the dome of the dog's skull. For a second he looked like a man comforting a child, soothing it back into sleep after a dream. I listened to his low voice as he spoke to it, whispering close to its ear. Then the dog was in his arms and he was folding it away, easing it into a smaller space. The leash was slack and trailing.

He looked back at me, to make sure that I'd seen. The animal was a dead weight so that he had to lay it down gently on its side. I heard how the air left its chest in a sigh. Ray stood with a click of his knees and brushed himself down. The front of his blue party shirt was dark with drool. 'So . . .'

'Who taught you that?' I asked.

'A friend of mine. Somebody I was put away with.'

'Because I met someone who could do that with people. It worked with me, anyway.'

'Then we mean the same person . . . She told me her father showed her the knack of it before he left – a parting present. He was a greyhound trainer, she said. That's all you're left with from some people – a bit of education.'

'And that's how you found the dog for Maurice?'

'I hardly needed to with that one. It took to Rhona straightaway, you see. I reckon she's got the touch as well but she was born with it.'

'She worked something on my dad, that's for certain. I've never seen him so happy to lose . . . So it's tonight you're leaving, is it?'

'Oh, we've left already. I just came back for Val and a few of the sticks . . . She told me you'd been to see her.'

'It wasn't her I was looking for. Not you either.'

'Oh, I know that.'

'So where are you going, Ray?'

'You'll find out, if you like . . .' He looked back towards the house. There was still music, but you could hardly hear it now. It just washed forward when the breeze came our way. 'I think I should go back and help Val with the packing.'

'Doesn't she like a party?'

'She's the quiet sort – not like me and the girl. With the boy we've got to see yet . . .'

'And the other one?'

'Oh, that's a different story. Enid wanted to take him with her and so I took them there first. It broke Val's heart to see him go. I suppose she was still worried that something could happen.'

'Aren't you?'

He looked down at the sleeping dog. It seemed small and slack, its back legs trailing and a shiver in one. 'Oh, I'm worried but what else is there? Take him into care? She reckons she's got over that anyway.'

'Setting fires?'

'She says so. She says that one did it for her.'

'Like a last cigarette?'

He smiled. I could still smell the dog on him.

'You could have told me before,' I said. 'About the child.'

'Oh, I couldn't trust you for her – she had to decide to do that. We'll take you to her, anyway. If that's what you'd like . . .'

Tony Gosse's Opel saloon was parked on the verge just before the turning circle, its windows clouded. I parked a yard in front, then let myself in by the back gate. The security light was on above the back door and I stopped to read my watch.

It had just turned two and the house was dark except for the flicker of the faulty tube in the trophy-cabinet. It looked bright and astonishing, exploding silently over Dad's cups and figures. I climbed to the landing and tapped gently on the door of Marion's room. I listened to the heavy silence behind and in a second I could hear her breath or his, I couldn't distinguish.

Dad's door was open a couple of inches because Rosemary always left it like that. I pushed it back and went inside. I could see the flashing red and blue lights on the chimney of the OKO plant through the gap at the top of the curtains. To warn low aircraft. Then I was standing over him and he opened his eyes. I could feel it more than see it. His attention and invisible smile. As if I were there and then not for him. I leaned over and kissed him on the forehead, left a trace of my moisture there.

I found a plastic bag in my room, Circle Mart, and filled it with a shirt and shorts, soap and a disposable razor from the edge of the basin, the towel from the ring. The bed was still unmade from the night before and I plumped the pillow and tidied it, not wanting to leave it to Rosemary. The room had a closed-in smell and I worked the latch to open the window a few inches.

Rosemary was standing on the stairs to the top of the house when I came out of my room. I saw first the bright end of her cigarette.

'Can I take a drag of that, Rosemary?'

She came down the other couple of steps in the greyish robe she wore, which might have been another colour by day. She held out the cigarette and I took it from her fingers. There was the smoker's tremor to them.

'A thief in the night,' she said.

I coughed with the dry smoke, looked back towards Dad's room. 'That's right, Rosemary – I was stealing kisses!'

She nodded at the plastic bag. It could have held anything but I suppose she'd read the situation. 'So, are you going for long?'

'I'd thought of asking you the same question, Rosemary.'

She took the cigarette back and shook her head. 'Oh, I'll stay here. If my boy wants to visit then he knows where to find me.'

'You're a sweetheart, Rosemary.'

'Is that right? You can kiss me then, like you did your dad.'

Careful with the cigarette she leaned forward and I kissed her on the forehead, then the cheek. She closed her eyes, took another lungful. 'So mind you don't get your fingers burned, John.'

'Oh, I think I could handle that, Mrs Shand.'

'Well, I hope so.' She held up the cigarette. 'This is my last one, you know.'

'Why, Rosemary?'

'They say that kissing a woman who smokes is like kissing an ashtray. I don't want my son to have to do that.'

'I can tell you that's not true,' I said.

'So, get out of this house now, anyway. I hope you haven't left your room in a condition.'

'I tidied it a bit.'

'Well, I know your tidiness . . .'

There must have been rain inland because the Course was loud in its runnel, generating nearly a hum. I could feel its charge in the air as I crossed the footbridge. I looked back at the house and a mist covered it, keeping tight to the brickwork and then coming off the roof in wisps like pale dust.

I walked through the long grass at the back of the fields and then found the path. The air was already losing its darkness and a couple of horses tethered near the ditch were ghostlike as I walked by, perfect grey against the grasses and dark hedge. I cut between shuttered caravans towards the back of the site. Curtains were closed behind the beaded windows and there was the bark of a dog from one. Washing was still pegged to a line, heavy with damp. I saw Ray waiting on the concrete base of one of the standpipes. He wore a zipped jacket together with his black cap – like someone dressed for a journey.

'Have you come to help?'

'I told you I would.'

'Oh, it's easy to change your mind.'

He led the way. I saw the black Bedford van that Victor

203

had loaned them and then their canvas awning lit from inside. It looked like a struggle was going on – long shadows of legs and arms. Then Ray caught up a little body and swung it above his head. The boy wailed and struck at him with his fist, screaming, beside himself.

Val stepped out with the girl beside her. She nodded at me but didn't speak and maybe she still didn't trust me. She took the boy from Ray to cuddle him. I looked up and saw the day was nearly here with a bright star hanging low over the dyke.

We sipped coffee from mugs, standing under the awning. The table had been taken from its trestles and thrown out into the grass along with the junk of cycle-parts. Valerie was checking suitcases and cardboard boxes sealed with string and tape. She had the boy with her, not letting him out of her sight. I could feel her anxiety and it made me anxious as well.

Ray was watching her. 'We don't need to take everything Val – just what we really need.'

She shook her head, disgusted with him. 'You've no idea what we need! You never will have!' She took me in with it as well. 'So, are you two going to help or stand and watch me?'

We loaded the van, putting the mattresses in first to make seats and padding, then filling the space near the walls with the cases and boxes. The interior still had the smell of Vic's yard – oil and rust, atoms of dog turd. I fumbled a roll of bedding and it spilled on to the wet grass. Ray came from behind and scooped it up. He bundled it into the back, then stood back to take breath. The little boy was awake again now and Rhona was playing with him, chasing him through the grass, then catching him up, tumbling him. Valerie pointed at her. 'He'll be soaked to the skin by the time you've finished! Give your dad a hand, will you?'

Ray shook his head. 'No need. That might be it, I reckon.'

Val looked back at the caravans. 'I'd better check inside before we go.'

'Check what? Half what we have is rubbish anyway. Let's leave the place as we found it, shall we?'

'A tip, you mean?'

'That's right.'

He felt through his pockets and tugged out a pair of keys clipped to a length of plated chain. He swung them to make a hum in the air and then let go. They flew shining towards the dyke and fell into shadow.

19

You shouldn't come here, John. You shouldn't see the place. Well . . . you know how you left it.

I could see the black scab on the hillside as we came out of the fold of woods and David drove carefully between the plantations of new pines. He'd turned the music down close to silence, or else my ears had gone that way. I could hear the blood in them and only that, so that when he spoke it was like a tissue that had grown over them was torn.

'Have you been here lately?' he asked.

'Never.' I hoped that was definite enough.

'Not since the fire?'

'That's right.'

We went closer. David Ordish slowed and turned into the little gravel drive where we used to leave our cars. He switched off the engine and waited for me to speak first, in the hiss of faint music.

But I wouldn't play that game.

'I would have turned back any time you'd asked, you know. I could turn back now,' he said.

I reached to my side to unclip my seat belt and found he'd already done it. I felt angry then, as if he'd touched me against my will. I was too tense, I suppose. I looked to where the house had stood and I could see only air.

'Anyway, I'd like to stretch my legs,' I told him.

'Sure?'

'Don't ask me that again – not while we're here.'

I got out of the car and saw part of the fence lying

*in long grass – black along some of its edges where
the fire touched it. Shiny, flakey, like black crocodile-
skin.*

'He made a good job of it,' I said.

'He was quite thorough, yes. They often are.'

'Who's they?'

'Arsonists. Setters of fires. Not that I'm claiming he
was habitual . . . They like to work to a method, you
see – that seems to be part of the attraction . . . People
think it's only destruction but really it's about
control.'

I stepped over the scorched timbers into what was
left of the garden. 'He wanted to destroy this place,
all right.'

'Control of the past, you see. Control of the future.
An act like this brings them into their hands – like it's
a black box they seal them into.'

'Did you go on a course or something?'

'Spending most of my day in the car gives me a lot
of time to think. Sometimes I don't like the conclu-
sions but that's a thing I have to get used to.'

'So you drive up here to think?'

'It's a bit out of the way but now and again I like to
make the trip. I've other interests in the area.'

'Selling the yokels security?'

He bent down to massage his knees. He'd been at
the wheel for nearly three hours. 'Rural crime is a big
concern now – stones, peat, bits of hardware. Half the
countryside seems to end up in some garden centre.'

I walked away, through brown weeds that seemed
to draw nourishment from the debris, and stepped on
to a cracked concrete slab. It was carbonised and
glinting. I wondered if it were part of the foundations,
the base of the outhouse where we kept the logs. I'd
forgotten the way the house faced exactly . . . The
slab had a hollow sound under my heels, as if there
was a space below.

'Are you all right?' David asked. He was gentle now, concerned, and I wondered how I could take that.

'Oh yes . . . It might sound funny now but what I remember best is how cold this place always was, even on a summer evening. None of the doors fitted properly and it never seemed to warm up until the heating had been on for days at a time . . . Pearl seemed to have the same cold all winter – I was forever wiping her snotty little nose. I remember it had only just cleared up when she went away.'

He followed me, keeping patiently behind. 'Is that what you say?' he asked. 'That she went away?'

He had his look of a creeping priest. 'Oh, that's the way I explain it to myself, I suppose. A sort of shorthand if you like – short and sweet . . . Short, anyway.'

One strange thing was a wire fence halfway through the lot at the back, where we had the rockery. It was new and the open mesh was nearly the same colour as the air, so that it jumped into sight just before I reached it – like a grid had been laid over my view of the hillside. I suppose the local farmer had taken the opportunity to shift a boundary. I was still looking when David Ordish took hold of the top strand of wire, so that the back of his hand was nearly before my face. I decided then that I didn't like his pale skin with all the colour gathered into dark little freckles. There's something harmful in freckled men.

'It's funny but I had a feeling the woodsman would still be here,' I said.

He leaned forward to look at my face. 'What's that?'

'Oh, we had a woodsman in the back garden – one of those windmills on a stand working a man with a wooden axe. Pearl had been on at us to buy her a kitten but when we took her to buy one she saw that

209

working outside the shop and wanted it instead. We were both a bit relieved . . .'

'A lot less trouble than a cat, I'd think.'

'That's right . . . But the funny thing is I'd thought it might have been the one thing to survive – like his child's toy they always show you after an air-crash . . .'

David sighed and put his cheek against mine – cold against cold. Then he reached his arms around and spread both hands gently on the rise of my belly. I felt as if I'd known about this for a while – not so much expected it as already seen it as a fact, something I would have to deal with when the time came. Because it felt more intimate than a kiss, more intrusive than actual sex. It assumed more than I wanted to share.

He spoke into my ear. 'You would tell me, wouldn't you, Anna?'

I was stiff against him, upright. The neutral way of staying that is worse than walking away. But where could I go anyway? 'Tell you what, David?'

'You would tell me if something had happened, wouldn't you? You wouldn't keep it secret from me now?'

The breeze blew from down the hill and I could smell the young pines – their young confused sappy smell, half bleach and half mother's milk. 'It's too simple for you, isn't it, David?'

His hands felt like the wings of a bird, feathers brushing my skin. 'What is?'

'That she could be lost and never found. That she'd be gone forever.'

There was a warmth between our faces, heat generated by their contact. This went on despite me – senseless chemistry. 'Oh, I'll never think that, Anna . . . Not as long as I live.'

I had to smile and he must have felt it against his cheek – its mocking intent. Which was why he drew

210

back. Just then an energetic little mouse of a car came
out of the woods towards us, grinding its gears as it
climbed the hill. A young woman or a busy matron.

'He did this as soon as you let him go,' I said.

'So does that mean I was responsible?'

'I was staying with friends. He must have made
sure the place was empty . . . I hope he did.'

'He could have been hoping that she'd come back.
He still had his keys. He'd unlock the door and she'd
be waiting. He might have convinced himself of
that . . .'

I gripped his wrists with my hands. I've always
been strong and I knew I could squeeze hard enough
to hurt. 'And are you convinced, David? That she's
still waiting somewhere – in somebody's house, say.
Somebody's room.'

He shook his head. 'I won't be distracted by that
kind of thing. By hopes and long-shots. What I do is
collect information – everything that seems relevant. I
try to work in a step-by-step way.'

'And where do you end up?'

He brushed my cheek again, a trace of bristle
despite his careful shaving. 'Here. I end up here.'

The car drove by without stopping.

Ray and Rhona slept in the back while, with the dozing
child on her lap, Valerie kept company with me in the
front.

'You're too tired to drive yourself,' Valerie said. 'I know
that look.'

'I'll be okay in a while.'

'I'll take over from the ferry,' she said. 'I used to drive
about everywhere before Rhona was born. I drove for a
coach company at one time . . .'

'Whereabouts?'

'Isle of Wight. Taking the tourists around. I used to
make fifty quid a trip in tips.'

'Is that where you're from?'

'My folks are from there.'

'So what happened after Rhona came?'

'Oh, I was busy with that and Ray took over. I let him take over the rest of it as well. I thought I was doing enough, you see. I'm starting to get back a bit of it now – control over my own life, I mean.'

'Have you told him that?'

She took a look over her shoulder. 'Oh, I think I'll surprise him with it. When the time comes.'

The road ran along the bank of the estuary now. The water was low, leaving mud-flats cut by deep gullies. The line of feeding birds at the water's edge looked like a white hem on a grey skirt. One of the ferries was already beating towards the terminal – side-on against the current and looking like it would be swept past but then getting nearer, heading for its berth and trailed by a mob of hysterical gulls.

I joined the end of the queue of vehicles and Ray woke and went to the booth while I stepped out to buy cigarettes from the machine. There were about a dozen cars and a couple of lorries before the gate. When Ray came back with the tickets I asked something I hadn't before because I'd thought the reply wouldn't be worth having. But there was a truthful feel in the air now, us being near water and departure.

'Is the other boy yours, Ray?'

He laughed and shook his head. It could have been something he regretted. 'Enid brought him to us to look after. She thought she couldn't do it herself.'

'Why?'

'You can ask that when you see her.'

'Okay, I will.'

He dragged at my arm so that I had to look into his narrow, dark face. There was a small upright scar under one eye that I hadn't noticed before. 'You be careful with her, won't you? I don't want her to get this far and then some man takes her back to square one. You be careful for your own sake, as well . . .'

The ferry was backing open-ended towards its ramp. The drivers started their engines and the front of the queue crawled forward a couple of yards. I climbed back inside. Rhona was making faces at the boy, making him squeal and laugh. Ray jumped up and closed the double doors after himself. He perched on one of the mattresses with his hands loose between his knees, watching with a mild, smoker's look.

'You'll get used to us in the next couple of days, John,' Valerie said.

'It takes as long as that, does it?'

'We thought you might want to stay a night when we got there.'

'That's his choice,' Ray said. 'You shouldn't act as matchmaker.'

Rhona sniggered and kissed the boy on his pudgy cheek – a smacking kiss. We'd reached the ramp now and I drove up on to the deck of the ferry. I could faintly hear the talking clock, its blurred rasp coming back to us off the water. I thought of Dad and pictured the expressions that might pass over his face when Rosemary told him I was gone. They would end with the one with his mouth turned down which showed that he didn't expect any more, this was how things had always promised to turn out.

My appetite still hadn't surfaced and so I stayed on deck while Ray and family went down into the lounge. The tops of the sandbanks were visible as a smoothness in the water. The boat swung close to the unfinished ends of the chain-bridge and I could see how the exposed metal had been eaten to red ruin by the salt air.

'Was there a fire on the bridge?' Rhona asked, appearing at my elbow.

'No . . . All that happened was they ran out of money. Rust did the rest.'

'Auntie Enid used to start fires,' she said.

'Is that what you call her?'

'I call her that sometimes but she's our friend really.'

'When did you meet?'

'Dad met her when he was in the hospital. He went a bit mad once but he's better now. That was before Colin was born and I was about six. He used to scare me.'

'But he doesn't now?'

She shook her head. 'Mam can handle him better now and that work he does with the bikes calms him down. He likes to play pool as well. Snooker when he can . . .'

'Is he good?'

She thought about it seriously. 'He's okay. He could be a lot better if he settled to practise.'

'But he taught you to play?'

She shook her head. 'He showed me the game and I taught myself. He used to work behind the bar in this club in town. We'd go in together when it was quiet . . . I could hardly reach the table then but I got a bit taller and I started to beat him.'

'I'll bet he didn't like that.'

'Oh, he didn't at first. But then I'd beat other people and he started to be proud of me.'

'Well, you keep on with it, Rhona.'

The boat sounded its whistle. A flock of herring-gulls lifted from the bridge and went screaming about the sky – heavy, vindictive birds. The ferry's sister-ship was circling on a contrary tide about a half-mile away, leaning so that one side was low in the water. You could make out the passengers against its rails and the slack motion of the paddle.

Rhona took her hands down from her ears. 'Do you like Enid?'

'I do, yeah. Of course I do.'

'But you haven't seen her since the fire?'

'Only in the hospital, and she was still . . . upset then. Do you think she's changed much, Rhona?'

She looked at the birds that were settling again. You

could see how they'd cover the bridge with their drop-pings, turn it to a reef of guano. 'She'll be better soon. Now she's taken little Sol back.'

'Sol? That's a good name for a little one! Is it short for something?'

She shook her head and stepped back from the rail, as if she'd lost interest or recalled something she'd been asked to do. The boat was turning its long curve to avoid the shoals and you could see clear across the river, towards Four-mile Town and the coastal resorts.

Val drove and I woke at services somewhere. The toddler was sleeping in a nest of rugs and cushions near me in the back of the van. A copper rapped with his leather knuckle against the driver's window and when I'd climbed up and wound it down he was already reading the licence number into the radio on the back of his bike.

'It's not my car, officer,' I told him.

'Would you mind telling me whose it is, sir?'

They have different ways of saying sir. I gave him Vic's name and the address of the yard.

He looked past me into the back. 'Is the child yours?'

'His folks are inside.'

'People place a lot of trust in you, don't they?'

The check took about five minutes. He was careful not to look at me until the answer came.

'Well, it seems the owner is happy for you to drive his vehicle . . . The reason I woke you up is that I spotted a bit of damage on the front wing. Were you responsible for that?'

'I don't think so. There's damage all over this thing, anyway.'

'He might not be happy to hear you say that, sir . . .'

Ray drove for a couple of hours and I took the next leg between fields which had a bluish shine when the light caught them. Then a long grade with the land dropping away on either side so that the road tracked across blue-brown moor.

'Look out!' Valerie called.

I barely felt the bump through the spongy suspension. I looked in the mirror but I could see nothing on the road. 'What was that?'

'You got a fox,' Val said. 'Do you reckon that's good luck or bad?'

'We'll find out, I suppose.' I caught her eyes in the mirror. They were level for a second and then she lowered them. 'You should sleep as well.'

'Someone has to tell you where you're going!'

'I know this part of the country anyway. A funny thing is, I used to live around here.'

She yawned, looking about, not much interested. The road lowered us into a shallow valley. The sun went in and the bluish tint of the fields deepened. Dead things were spread on the tarmac – little scraps of rabbits and birds. A low, grey house was set close to the steep verge, washing flapping on a slack line at the side. A collie dog stood with splayed white front legs and watched us. A saloon car with a new, mismatched wing was parked behind the gate.

Rhona sat up and blinked. The little boy was droning a song. We passed another group of houses – raw-looking brickwork behind low walls of neatish stone. The windows of one still had tapes across the new glass.

Ray reached from the back to tap my shoulder and point.

A drive was set at a narrow angle to the road – soon lost behind trees so that I might have missed it. I had to back up a little before I could turn and then I was soon involved in black mud with an oily shine in its hollows. There was a bend where I had to squeeze past a red van and then a house came into view – peaked roofs behind trees then walls of narrow, dark brick with windows set in stone embrasures.

'Is this where she lives now?'

'It doesn't look so good when you reach it,' Ray said. 'There's a lot needs doing to the place. Helluva lot.'

'I was starting to worry – I thought she might be lady of the manor nowadays.'

'Oh, that's her friend,' Valerie said.

I saw how a lean-to had been added to one side of the house with fresh timber stacked below the shelter. A cement-mixer stood in a tread of sand and mud. A woman of about fifty in a dark coat waited beside it – square on to us, her arms folded.

20

You fell asleep, John. You said you heard a snatch of song. You couldn't fight the voice that sang you into sleep.

'He told us he was sleeping when she must have wandered off,' David Ordish said. 'But why when it was the middle of the day?'

'Oh, he couldn't explain it to himself. He never could. Maybe it had to do with the medication he was on – the painkillers or the antibiotics. Remember he wasn't allowed to drive . . .'

'And you'd left her with him?'

I glanced at his face to see if it was accusing but there was no particular expression as he watched the road. He's good at that, John – leaving his face in neutral.

'He told us there were signs of a struggle.'

'He didn't say that! He said he found her shoe.'

You were gripping it so hard that the buckle drew blood from your palm. You could feel the pain but it didn't matter. The pain was sweeter than your thoughts.

'And he had a dental card for her in his coat pocket. An appointment for a check-up. We asked the postman and he said he would have delivered it that morning . . .'

Pearl Lilian Drean. Please give at least a week's notice if you cannot keep this appointment. *You slipped it into your pocket on the way out – like you'd do with bills or junk mail. You'd turn them out weeks later, creased and grubby with the dirt from your work.*

'And it was a couple of hours before he contacted the police, anyway. Why didn't he go back to the house and do that as soon as he knew she was missing?'

But you couldn't credit the silence, John. Every-thing that had been alive and moving was still. Everywhere you looked the angles would change, the trees would be different. You thought you would find her kneeling somewhere quietly, absorbed in a mush-room or a flower. She would look up at you, surprised and becoming afraid. The fear would show on your own face and she might mistake it for anger.

Why are you angry, Daddy?

You went down to the wooden bridge over the nameless little beck. You knew she was attracted by the water. It seemed deep now, powerful, rattling its yellow stones.

'Then when he did walk to a phone he called you and not us. That lost us more time.'

The box on the edge of the wood. Only for emergency. You had to go through the forestry switchboard in Berwick and ask for an outside line. I was talking to Mr Natta – a problem with the wages, they were complaining that their overtime was short. The phone went on my desk, a partition away. 'That will be your young man,' Mr Natta said kindly. Psychic, you see.

I walked towards the house, so as to give them time to talk. The line of the roof was jutting and I noticed broken windows in the upper storeys, as if whatever work they'd done hadn't extended that far. The roof of the deep porch carried what looked like a child's rocking-horse – splashed with white emulsion but still airborne and miraculous-looking. A youngish man watched me from the doorway, then reached unconcerned for a pair of boots. Ray and the tall woman were still talking and then she turned to me and managed to smile – like a cheque she might cancel.

Ray wandered up to me, dragging his feet in the sludge and builder's sand, smiling. 'Claire owns this place, you see. She said it's okay if you stay for a night.'

'A night would be fine,' I said.

The man in boots laughed and slapped his hands. He was smooth-cheeked with a wispy goatee growing down from his lower lip. The woman was talking to Val now and she laughed – a loud bark that I wouldn't have expected. Then she walked back towards the house, the smile clearing from her face.

'You're a friend of Enid's?' she asked and I wondered what Ray had told her.

'That's right. Is she here now?'

She shook her head. 'She's found a job for herself. She'll be back in a couple of hours if you want to wait.' She looked like she didn't care and then smiled at me, as if she'd decided to make the effort.

'What does she do?' I asked.

'Oh, it's a hotel job – reception and waiting sometimes. It depends. I do some things there as well – just to make a few pounds.'

The man laughed again and I stared at him, irritated now. There was a child standing under the porch in a suit of blue, pilled wool. His feet were bare and the white electric cable of the mixer ran between them. Val saw him at the same time and ran with a cry to pick him up. He seemed to float in her arms, weightless and surprised. She squeezed him to her chest while he looked open-mouthed over her shoulder at the mud-splashed van and Rhona getting down from the cab, holding his near-brother.

I sat in their hall which had plastic sheets at the windows. Wood panels were missing from the walls, showing the brick with its soft mortar. Grey blankets hung at the open doors to check the draughts. There was the sense of a great weight above, its fall arrested by the internal walls. It was built around the time of Whiteheads, I thought – some wool merchant's mock-baronial pile.

Claire lit a candle and shared out the last of a bottle of red. There was a creeping summer darkness but Rhona and the two boys were still outside, playing in an area to the side of the house that had plastic cars and a slide, a sand-pit between walls of railway sleepers. I was listening to their shouts and chatter and Claire must have noticed the concentrated look on my face.

'Are you worried this place'll fall on our heads, John?'

I took another look at the ceiling. 'Oh, I reckon it'll be a while yet – another few years, say.'

She sat on the rug with one hand on the ankle of the other man, stroking his skin with the tips of her fingers. He lolled back against the side of the fireplace, looking half-asleep in the heat from a log. Warren, she called him, whether it was his first name or surname wasn't clear. 'Warren and me lived in a caravan at the back through the winter,' she said. 'At least I could heat the thing and I had somewhere to wash my face.'

'This is a great place!' Ray told her, sitting with his back to the table. 'There's nothing here that couldn't be fixed, given time . . .'

I saw Val roll her eyes. Claire laughed and nosed into her glass again. 'That's right – Warren will see to that. Warren and a bit of cash . . .'

Warren sighed and she smiled at him, then at me. 'You could move here as well, John. This place has a dozen bedrooms, so you could make your choice.'

'If you don't mind the damp,' Warren said, 'and the falling plaster.'

'I invite people and he warns them off,' Claire said. 'That's how we work together.'

'I've a house of my own, anyway.'

'Oh? And a family?'

222

'A father and a sister.'

'Ah, you should avoid families,' Claire said. 'You should give yourself plenty of distance there . . .'

'Why?'

'Well, I hated my father because my mother was a martyr to him. Then later I worked out it was a game they had between them and after that I hated them both.'

Warren stood up, as if he were tired of listening to her. He stretched himself and back-heeled a log further into the fire. Sparks streamed up the chimney and I heard the children yell as a car came into the yard. A loose two-stroke – 2CV or similar. I could see its yellow headlights through the patched window and then it stopped close to the wall and the engine died with a shudder.

'I'll go and say hello,' Val said.

She went outside and I could hear their low talk. I thought she might be warning her about me. Enid said something back and then laughed and it sounded low and clear. Then she was under the porch and Rhona came into the room before her, carrying something which she put to her eye.

'A small present for a big girl,' Enid announced. 'A kaleidoscope from the gift-shop.'

I thought that her hair was different – longer and a different shape. She stood a cardboard box on the end of the table and a bottle clinked against another. She wore khaki-coloured jeans and a top of pale blue wool buttoned to her throat. I wondered if they were the clothes she wore at work or if she'd changed into them before the drive home. She looked too neat for the house, anyway. It would be an effort to keep herself clean inside its flaking walls.

Val followed her into the room with one child in her arms and the other trailing behind. For a second I couldn't distinguish and then I saw she was holding the younger child, Enid's little boy. Ray held up his hand and Enid took it and kissed him on the lips. Val smiled down at them then glanced at me and set the child on the floor. He went to Claire with a staggering, sliding walk and she caught him up.

'You can see he's exhausted!' she said. She kissed him on the cheek. 'All the excitement today, isn't it, Solly?'

Enid was still looking about the room, smiling but as if her mind was half elsewhere. I wasn't sure then if she hadn't seen me or if she had deliberately passsed me by. I stood up, so that she wouldn't have an excuse.

'Hello, Enid.'

She took my hand – frowning, drawing me towards her. Ray reached into the box and pulled out a bottle.

Then she was smiling at me, grinning.

We had a few glasses of wine with the meal, together with a damaged cake she'd brought from the kitchens. Enid sat cross-legged near the fire with the child in her lap wrapped in a woollen blanket except for one bare foot. She was talking to Val mostly – question and answer. Val had drawn her chair close and their hands were clasped. I could tell when the conversation changed from words to looks.

Claire was weaving Rhona's hair into thin little spikes of plaits. 'I'll be glad when it's longer – you look too much like a boy.'

'Don't tell her that!' Ray said. 'That's her aim in life.'

Claire kissed her on the nape of the neck and pushed her gently away. 'Look, forget about your work tonight, Enid sweet – I'll go in and take your shift.'

Enid looked up. 'Why should you?'

'No reason – only that I'm kind.'

'I could give you a lift there,' I said. I was thinking about how much she'd had to drink. I'd been keeping my head clear, I didn't know for what.

'Thanks but no thanks,' Claire said.

'I'll step out with you anyway.'

'Why?'

'Just for the air.'

The car was a slope-nosed Citroën. Claire turned it

slowly in the mud and found the entrance to the drive. Firelight from the window was pulsing on the tops of the trees. When she'd gone I turned around and saw Enid standing under the flying horse.

'Do you think I'm following you about?' she asked.

'I'm not complaining.'

'Ray said you might be going back in the morning.'

'If there's nothing to keep me.'

She looked away, as if what I'd said was too stupid for comment. 'Will you help me put the boy to bed, John?'

I carried him while she led the way upstairs, reaching to boards of clustered brass switches to turn on bare lights hanging from black, braided cords. On the landings you could see the lattice of timbers behind broken plaster.

'Is he heavy?' Enid asked, teasing a bit.

'No, he weighs nothing at all.'

'You thought he was lost, didn't you? You thought he might have gone up with the rest of it,' she said as if she were asking something light.

'No . . . I knew I'd find him.'

'Do you know his name?'

'Rhona told me. Sol. Is that short for Solomon?'

'Because of the sun – because he was born on a Monday . . .' She smiled over her shoulder. 'You don't like it, do you?'

'It's unusual.'

'And you don't like unusual things?'

'Oh, I can get used to it.'

She laughed, stepping exactly on the creaking treads. The children's room was on the second floor and she reached in to turn on the light. The square room seemed taller than it was broad. It had a single window and a low-hanging lamp with a blue, conical shade. There was a divan bed and then a smaller, narrower bunk against the other wall.

'The two boys can go in together,' Enid said. 'He'll like that when he wakes up.'

225

She turned back the bedding and I lowered the child. He rolled on to his belly, groaning and drawing up his legs. Enid bent to kiss the side of his face. I felt empty-handed without him.

'I sleep in the next room myself,' Enid said.

'Can I see?'

I didn't know what she was thinking. Her neat self with the new hairstyle. We kissed just outside, lightly and gently. She had kept the door open an inch, letting out the light breath of the little boy.

'Does his father live here?' I asked.

She shook her head. 'He used to. But he brought the police to the place and Claire asked him to leave . . . He was frightened of her, I suppose.'

'She has that effect on me. So what did he do?'

'He stole from a couple of places. The locals don't like that kind of thing . . .'

'Where is he now?'

'I'm not sure . . . I don't specially care. Does that surprise you?'

'It's no business of mine.'

Smiling at me. 'So, I'll show you my little home.'

Drapes of gold-brocade curtain made the room look small as a nest. Enid moved about quietly, turning her back to me, arranging little objects and ornaments. There was a thump on the other side of the wall – the little boy's elbow or knee – and she glanced towards it with such a concerned look that I kissed her again, just at the angle of her jaw. When I put up my hand I touched the soft pad under her hair.

'Sorry.'

'I was turned that way when the heater blew up. Luckily I was already stepping out the door.'

'And you started it yourself?' I asked. It didn't seem so difficult with the wine and her being so close. These things that I had to ask her.

She nodded. 'My own work, that's right . . .'

226

'Weren't you scared of being hurt?'

'Oh, I was the one I was after – that's what the last fire taught me. When I finally caught up with myself . . .'

'Where was the boy?'

'I'd already passed him on to Ray and Val, you see. I could feel the thing coming on, like you can a cold . . . They'd bring him back to see me, on nights when he couldn't settle. That's when you saw us together – as I was walking him to sleep.'

'And you thought you'd burn me first?'

'I didn't think. Not until afterwards.'

She was still busy with her hands and I took hold of her arm to stop her. I could feel how nervous she was.

'So why then?'

She shrugged, not facing me. 'Because I wanted to share it with you . . . I wanted you to know that feeling.'

'Pain, you mean? Did you think I didn't know that already?'

She turned around and took hold of my hand, teasing apart the fingers that were still stiff sometimes. 'I'd seen this, you see. That's what made me think you'd understand . . . It's a different language, isn't it – fire?'

'So you set light to your caravan?'

'I waited for you a couple of days. I thought you might come to see me. I'm not sure if I'd have stopped then or asked you to help me . . . But then all you need is a light.'

'And it was my lighter you used.'

She took my hands again, rubbing the fingers between hers, as if she were trying to soothe the damaged skin. 'Did you really do this putting a fire out?' she asked.

'I burnt a house down once – not far from here. I didn't want to see it any longer and that was the easiest way.'

She smiled as if she were pleased. 'It *is* easy, isn't it? An easy way of changing the world . . . Once you realise that you become very dangerous – you start to follow the train of thought that ends in that . . .' She nodded, recalling, still holding my hands. 'I started with a box of matches I'd found and hidden. I think they must have been my dad's because they were the sort he used – smoker's matches. I was about six then. It took me a while but I managed to strike one and then I knew I could do everything. That single little thing made me so strong . . .'

'But you had to use it, try it out?'

'I started with an edge of the curtain and watched this line of fire creep up the material – very fine so that you could hardly see it at all, only this bright line before the material turned to smoke . . .'

'There were other things you could have done, though.'

'Cooked my own dinner? Invented the steam engine? No, I knew this was the best thing. Nothing else was so easy and clean . . .'

'Did you tell all this to the people at the hospital?'

'As far as the hospital were concerned I was some stupid cow who nodded off with a cigarette in her hand.'

There was another noise in the next room and then a child's cry.

Enid sighed and smiled. 'I'd better see to him.'

I waited. I lifted a part of the heavy curtain and looked out of the window. I could see nothing at first but then I made out a light. It looked far away – on the slope of the next hill, say – but bright and clear because of the country darkness. It made me think of a lamp burning in a narrow window – someone working late, reading say, studying. A lamp over a desk surrounded by the quiet, country night.

Enid came back after five minutes. She stopped to listen, leaning close to the wall, smiling, nodding to herself when it was silent. Then she smiled at me and pointed to the alarm-clock beside the bed. The thick hands showed a couple of minutes to midnight. The light went out suddenly and after a second of pitch black I could make out the faint shine from the window. The tick of the clock was very loud.

'Warren turns off the generator at midnight,' she said.

'That's good of him.'

'He worries about the house, you see. He thinks Claire has no head for money.'

'If she's sunk it in this place, I'm not surprised.'

'We'll survive. I think we will . . .'

'You could come home with me. You and the boy . . . It isn't as big as this place but we'd find room for you.'

'I want to stay here.'

'Why?'

'I don't want to always be moving, even with you. You could keep me company, anyway.'

'Dad's ill. I have to go back.'

She was looking for something now, distracted. 'I don't suppose you've a cigarette, John?'

'I left them downstairs. I need one myself.'

I started to walk to the door but she stopped me, holding on to my arm – the urgent grip between fingers and thumb that's better than a caress. Keeping me there. 'It's okay. I can do without.'

21

Sleeping – the woodsman and his love. The clock with its heavy tick, the vertical night behind the window. Their room is high among the trees, her body in the curl of his own.

He feels the heat on his back, the hairs along his spine lifting. And he turns – drowsy, blinking. The hands of the clock lurch to midnight.

A house on fire! He runs through the rooms. Flames grow from his finger-tips and he knows that he's the source of the blaze. Whatever he touches – door-jamb, stair-rail, wall – curls and buckles with flame. His bare feet wade through sheets of it. His toes are individual tongues. He shouts and it bursts from his throat.

The house is burning behind him, sending flares into the hillsides, floating out sparks like burning hair. The flames stream up through all its openings, then unite above the roof in a top-knot of fire. The walls are liquid sheets of it, sealing the doors, windows. Fragments of slate fly from the roof like crippled bats.

He raises his hands. His palms are flames. The skin is blistering, lifting away. He can see the blue pulse of veins.

Father, she says.

He turns in the small garden – to the gate and the road leading to the woods. The hills are quiet with their reflections, folding. Sweet. Sweetness comes from her. She stands with her back to the woods and sings.

The woodsman drops to his knees in the damp grass. The hollow crack of the fire like snapping bones is behind him. She sings and with careful hands unfastens the little brass hook at her chest. The doors of her ribs swing open of their own weight, swivelling on the long hinges along her spine, showing a rosy, hollow space lit by soft light.

Pearl?

A flame. A perfect, single flame. The song fluttered it, like it was a reed and itself the breath. He had hold of her hand and he could feel it slipping away. A touch against his palm, his wrist. A whisper. The last warmth he felt leaving. Atoms of warmth passing like coins between them.

She smiled at him and the song stopped. The song stopped. The garden was empty, quiet. The sweetish smell of soot was in the air and he felt it falling as the blaze subsided – big flakes settling on to the grass – thicker and thicker, softly.

I thought we hit something as we were leaving – just as we were coming out of a bend. What happened was that David Ordish looked over at me – his short lashes make his eyes seem naked, the mildest blue possible – and blinked as the car passed over something. I had that strong feeling, though there was no noise and barely an impact: I knew we'd killed something and left it behind.

I asked where we were going, because I knew it wasn't home.

He let go of the gear-lever for a second and tapped on my thigh with his finger-tips. 'Trust me, Anna – I shan't take much more of your time!'

I was soon lost on the minor roads. A few miles and then a few more. An hour maybe, less. No sense in talking to him with him in this mood. I'd see things which seemed familiar – a tree at a crossroads, some

232

broken farm machinery in long grass. Then nothing did and I wondered what it was we'd run over – that smooth impact like a knot of air. More than once I'd run over a fox myself – the low rush like rusty mercury and the barely felt death. You stop and get out of the car but you can never find them. Even dead they keep running.

David stopped in a lane, drawing the car on to the narrow verge. I could see the ridge of a felt roof through the spikes of trees.

'There's nowhere to park in the grounds,' he said. 'And everyone who comes here has to travel by car. You can picture what it's like when we have a full congregation . . .'

I couldn't though, even seeing the dried wheel-ruts along the verges. It might have been the way the sky had turned white and glassy but it was hard to picture this place as being anything other than empty. David put on the brown sports jacket he keeps folded on the back of the seat and used the bleeper thing to lock the car. He crooked an arm for me.

The chapel was built of unpainted boards stained dark with age and preservative. It had the look of a scout hut except for the little carved crosses on each end of the roof-ridge. It was the sort of place you might be given precise directions for and still not find. The land around had little folds and dips, stands of trees which hide things.

David took out a bunch of brass and silver keys, just as a tall silver-rinsed woman of about sixty opened the door under a porch at the side.

'Sorry to trouble you again so soon, Mrs Woodhouse!' he said, smiling.

She shook her head. 'No trouble at all, David! And I'm glad you've brought a friend with you.'

He introduced us and Margaret Woodhouse glanced openly at my belly. But then I knew that she'd noticed my little bump so that to ignore it would have been pointed also. She smiled and led the way inside.

A door with a panel of wired glass opened out into the main hall, where the walls were painted a thick white. A dark wooden cross on a stepped base stood in the centre of a long table draped with a shiny blue cloth. Shallow brass bowls were set on either side heaped with dried flowers. Despite these the strongest smell was of mansion-polish. We walked down an aisle between rows of metal stacking chairs. Daylight came through narrow windows set with grilles.

'Anna is interested in my work, Margaret,' David said.

'Oh yes?' She picked up a yellow waxy cloth from the seat of a chair. 'Then I'm sure there's plenty you'd like to show her.'

David stopped and pointed to a panel of brushed silvery metal set at chest-height in the far wall. Thin neutral-grey cables led from its side to every part of the hall, stapled neatly into the angle between wall and ceiling. 'As you can see, I've had to use my skills to protect this place. Unfortunately we had a burglary a while ago . . .'

'About a year ago now,' Mrs Woodhouse said.

He nodded, taking the correction. 'As long as that? Although we had nothing to steal they managed to leave their mark on the place.'

Mrs Woodhouse turned to me. 'What sort of mark I wouldn't like to tell you. The police were convinced it was local people – those in the area who might hold a grudge against our faith.'

'To be fair that was only speculation,' David put in. 'What they said was that they wouldn't rule out the possibility – which they'll never be able to until the culprits are found.'

'If and when,' Mrs W. said. 'I have my suspicions,

as you know . . .' She gave a heavy-chested sigh. 'Well, if you'll excuse me.'

David nodded. 'I'll show Anna around and then we have some work to do.'

But she seemed not to hear, turning her back as if we were already forgotten. David took my elbow and guided me to an archway behind the long table leading to a windowless room studded with rows of metal coat hooks. An earthenware handbasin with a narrow mirror fixed above occupied one corner. One tap made a busy hiss and David stepped over to turn it off. Panelled doors were marked GENTLEMEN and LADIES in worn greenish gilt paint and a new door with an unpainted plywood face had been let into the wall opposite. I could see where the frame had been cut into the old woodwork. David cleared his throat and got busy with his keys again.

We entered a small room with a tiny, square window guarded by bars, a pair of shrivelled pot plants decorating the sill. The daylight didn't reach the dark corners and so he snapped a switch and a fluorescent tube sparked the width of the ceiling. Its brightness made my eyes start to water.

'This is where I spend more or less every spare minute, Anna. Sometimes it's barely more than that. Other times I'm more fortunate . . .'

The walls were of cinder block, painted a light blue-grey that was restful at first and then oppressive. Air came through a plastic vent let into one pane of the window. I could smell dregs of coffee, stale food. A plate balanced with the crusts of a meal stood on the top of a desk not much bigger than a schoolboy's. A hotplate stood on a table in one corner and something had boiled over and burned black against the enamel. A bigger desk set against the wall carried a pair of monitor screens.

'You should let your friend in for the afternoon,' I told him.

'Mrs Woodhouse?' He leaned over the larger desk. 'Oh, I'm aware of the squalor of my life, Anna. That's when I need to remind myself of the importance of what I'm doing. Margaret is a valuable ally but she finds it difficult to accept that there are things she doesn't need to know. Even someone as well meaning as her might destroy years of work.'

'How many years?'

He didn't answer but touched a keyboard. One of the screens filled with smooth light. Because of the sealed window I could hear nothing from the outside – no birds, not the wind. Just the rattle of the ventilator as it spun. David slipped in a disc and columns unreeled. I watched his bent back in the brown jacket.

'You should find yourself a wife, you know, David.'

'Thanks, Anna . . . Thanks for that thought. But I couldn't expect a woman to share my particular interests.'

He beckoned me to a swivel-chair. A mug on the edge of the desk showed an inside furry with mould. He sent a cursor down long columns. Names.

'Like a war memorial,' I said.

He prodded the keyboard. A change on the screen. Pearl Lilian Drean. He leaned by my elbow. 'I hope you don't mind, Anna.'

'Why should I?'

'Some people would think of it as a kind of theft, you see. Our information is all we really own. Our particulars.'

Pearl Lilian Drean. b. 18/1/85.

'A lovely name,' he said.

'Thanks. Pearl was my choice. John had his way

236

with the other one. Lilian was his mother's name, you see.'

He reached past, his arms on either side of me. Height and weight. Colour of eyes. Birth marks if any. Allergies.

'You were very thorough, David.'

'Oh, I still am. I'm still thorough.'

'Did John tell you all this?'

'You as well, Anna. The rest we took from her medical history, dental records. John was very helpful at first. Up to a point . . .'

'He had to ask you if he was a suspect.'

'But we had to cover that – that's sometimes the easiest solution.'

'How is it easy?'

'I mean as far as we were concerned it would have been. Keeping it in the family, you see – father, mother, sibling. Affectionate uncle. Doting grandparent. A little circle. After that we consider, say, a friend of the family, a neighbour, a child-minder. We move out in circles. We trace the path of the victim and try to have no opinions, only method. A shopkeeper, a plumber, delivery-man, scoutmaster. It's not very often that we reach the outer circle of the complete stranger . . .'

'But you did with Pearl. You had to.'

'That's right.' He shook his head, as if he admired that. 'Sometimes people can escape entirely.'

Height in centimetres. Body type. 'What do you mean escape?'

'They go out into the world in a path we can't follow. They become permanently lost. We have to assume they're out there but we can't say where or how.'

He reached past me again. A sound of electrical churning – the screen turning itself inside out.

'This is based on a photograph that you gave us. To

help with the search. I made a copy and then I was able to enhance the original image, key in photographs of you and her father to see how she might have changed . . . Of course you have to know when to stop.'

Pearl looked at me with so much expectancy and David's hand hovered, chose another combination. The little snigger of the machine. She was turning, shining.

'The original programme was developed by the Danish police. For some reason the Danes have the initiative in this kind of work . . .'

She offered her half-profile, the child's face sharpening with age. When she looked back her eyes were mournful, the mouth starting to be deceitful.

Was it my mouth?

'You've only to say if this is distressing,' David Ordish said.

The baby moved in me then, did one of its free-fall turnings, dragging the hard little point of a heel across my belly. Little informer – it could feel my fear. David touched the screen with his thumb and the tips of his fingers, made a snooker-player's bridge there. I could see the brightness of the image in the shade of his hand. If I leaned closer I would be able to make out its tiny, individual pulses.

'What else have you got?' I asked.

'Let's see . . .' Working with his ringless fingers, calling up directories and sub-directories. Moving the blunt little arrow of the cursor. He smiled. The screen had a flicker at one side that I found distracting.

'So, have you found any of them, David – any of your . . . children?'

He waved his hand as if it didn't matter, waiting while the machine organised itself. 'No, not yet . . . no actually. A few have been found by other people, of course. By accident.'

238

'How do you mean found?'

'Oh, traces. Physical remains. Some of the cases go back thirty years, you see . . .'

The screen steadied but I didn't want to look for a second. I could see the light on his face as he watched over my shoulder. 'How old are you, David?'

He looked surprised. 'Thirty-eight next birthday.'

Like a child would answer and I laughed. 'Oh, David!'

He looked mystified for a second and then he must have thought I was making fun of him because his eyes went back to the monitor. Names and times. Routes. What looked like map coordinates. Do you remember how you taught me to read a map, John? Use a compass and make the adjustment for true north?

'What's this, David?'

'Oh, I set myself the task of reconstructing that day through individual witnesses.'

'But no one saw her . . .'

'Well, that's a piece of information in itself.'

'Like the dog that didn't bark, you mean?'

'What?'

'Nothing – just a story I read.'

He gave me a look of patience. 'This is what I began in the police investigation but it's now in much greater detail. It's what's called low-level information – details of what went on in the area on that day which probably mean nothing in themselves but might become significant when taken together. I've written to local firms, haulage contractors, cab firms, walkers' organisations, cycling clubs – tried to find everyone who might have been in the area or passing through at that time . . .'

'And you're still doing this?'

He lowered his head. 'It becomes more difficult as I carry on, but I think it becomes more valuable. I wait

239

and sometimes there's a phone call. A letter drops through my door . . . There might be a memory, a detail – a car parked by the road, something half-seen through the trees, a woman buying milk at a garage – which will act like a seed crystal in a solution. Everything will form around it, clarify.'

I turned the squeaking chair. 'You mean you'll find her then? You'll know what happened?'

'The picture will be more complete, yes.'

I was angry with him now, getting that way. 'What use is that, though?'

'What I mean is we'll never know everything, Anna. We shouldn't expect that.'

I could see he was pleased with himself – with his own humility. He stepped back a yard to let me watch the screen – the routes and times, grids of the maps. A place from where she had gone outwards, along the trunk roads, towards the cities. Or another way she had escaped and my fingers searched for that, keyboard-knowing: the buried lands that we had found on our walks – farms that had been covered by the new plantations, lanes and fields under a mulch of pine-needles, rocks marking submerged heights.

One map replacing another, drawing itself in light. A scale and date of survey. A change of view. Then the beck that freed itself from the darkness under the rows of conifers, followed its own path brown and shining in the shadows, gliding over boulders speckled with grey crystals.

He came forward again, as if it were time to intervene. 'There,' he put his finger to it.

The dotted plan of the house that would have had its own road and pasture, a stone outcrop where the children played games and skinned their knees. Where you slept, John, and she was lost but then only to us. Because whatever happened was something different and she exists to this day but behind or beside us, somewhere else . . .

A respectful but sharp rap at the door startled us. 'Excuse me a second, Anna!'

He opened it a foot and spoke in a whisper, made arrangements about times, keys. He laughed at something she said, then came back, his face in its serious lines again.

'Mrs Woodhouse wondered how long we might be staying. We don't like to leave the place unattended for too long, you see.'

'In case the burglars come back?'

'You shouldn't laugh at her, Anna. This place is nearly her whole life.'

Which made me wonder about the rest of it, and his. 'D'you often bring people back here, David? Relatives?'

He shook his head. 'You're the first, Anna. Probably the last, I might say.'

I wondered if I should be flattered. He leaned over me again, caught by something on the screen, and I took his hand, the cold fingers.

'Don't you ever heat this place?'

He laughed awkwardly. Maybe he was worried about Mrs Woodhouse. 'There's an electric fire somewhere. Shall I find it for you?'

'Don't bother . . .' I rubbed the white ends of his fingers, trying to bring the blood back to them. 'Are your hands always this cold?'

'Not always.'

I leaned towards him and the chair swivelled under my weight. He stepped back as I stood up, freeing himself, glancing towards the door. So nervous that I almost laughed.

'Wasn't that what you wanted, David?'

'This isn't the place, Anna.'

'Where then? Your room? The back of your car?

241

Don't you want us both now – a mad woman and a dead child.'

He was thinking about that now, considering. His mouth must have been close because I kissed him. Because I wanted to draw the chill from him, the doom. I wanted to suck her cold little ghost from his marrow.

22

Light at the curtains. I saw the boy beside the bed. When I sat up he stepped back shyly and looked beyond me for his mother. She propped herself on her elbow, stretched an arm past me.

'What is it, Sol?'

'Maa . . . ma.' More a cry than the word – a sad bird cry. He leaned at the edge of the bed and struggled towards her. I took the little twisting body and lifted him over me. He was scared for a second, of the stranger. He let out a wail and then Enid had him in her arms. She held him to her and I could hear the working of his greedy little mouth.

'He still likes to feed sometimes,' she told me, 'if he's had a dream or something. I've no milk left but he just likes the comfort. I like it too . . .' She sighed and yawned. 'What's the time?'

The clock's thick, painted hands were ticking towards five.

'You should go back to sleep, John . . . I'll put him back in his bed soon, because I might already be gone when he wakes up.'

'Why?'

'I'm taking Claire's shift at the hotel today – that's the price I pay for a night off, you see.'

I listened to the hungry sound the child was making, the ticking of a valve in his throat. 'I'll give him his breakfast then.'

She shook her head. 'Claire'll see to that . . . You don't have to act as father, you know.'

243

'I'm not trying to. I just thought I'd lend a hand.'

She turned away with him, snuggled her back against me. 'You're warm as toast,' she said.

'Good – I'll keep that up, shall I?'

It was nearly ten o'clock when I woke again. I hadn't meant to sleep so long. I drowsed for another few minutes and then went downstairs. The fire was out and the leftovers of breakfast were still on the table. I could hear Rhona shouting from somewhere at the back of the house and when I stepped outside I saw how the tyres of Vic's van were sinking into the mud, so that I thought it might be difficult to move. One of the back doors was open and I looked through. The back was empty except for a roll of striped mattress they must have decided they didn't need. The litter of the journey was still on the floor – food cartons, cups.

I went back into the house and walked through into the kitchen at the back. The window had been repaired by tape that the breeze sucked at. I filled a kettle and put it on the stove. Bacon fat was congealing in a pan, scraps of white gristle embedded. I found a box of kitchen matches and lit the gas. The flame was yellow and noisy. While I waited for the water to boil I walked along the hall. Letters were pinned to a board – water and gas bills, edged with red. I wondered about the state of the plumbing.

A little room like an office and a radio playing. The window was open at the top and I heard a noise from outside, a squeak like greased machinery. The radio stood on a narrow mantelpiece with a flex trailing to a brown socket in the skirting-board. Turned low, it was lisping music and local traffic. A desk was spread with documents – invoices, solicitor's letters – a striped mugful of pencils and ball-point pens. There was a calendar on the wall with dates circled and a view of Ribblesdale viaduct. I spotted a red compact phone and picked up the receiver to see if it was live: a cool buzz from the rest of the world.

I dialled the number of Whiteheads.

'Hello?'

'Is that you, Rosemary?'

'Where are you, John?'

I sat at the corner of the desk, picked up a quote for damp-coursing. I heard the kettle start to whistle but decided to ignore it. 'Oh, somewhere . . . It doesn't matter.'

'Marion was worried sick about you. She reckoned you might have gone off with some rubbish from the caravan site. She said a bunch of them did a flit the other night and left three months' rent owing.'

'Well, I'll stay clear of that bunch, Rosemary. Is Marion there?'

'She's taking a trip with her friend.'

'Tony?'

'Mr Gosse to me.'

'How long for?'

'Not long, she reckoned.'

'She should stay away. They both should. What's the point of them coming back?'

'I thought you'd never liked him,' Rosemary said.

'She'll only damage herself if she stays.'

'I think she's worried about your father,' Rosemary said gently.

'I can look after Dad. Between the two of us we could.'

'Thanks for including me in that.'

'Is Dad there?' I asked. He would have finished breakfast and now he would be taking his walk in the garden. He went as far as the fence, then stared moodily at the overgrown land at the back of the caravan site.

'He's upstairs dressing. I'm taking him into town in a while to see his friend Teddy.'

'Ah . . . That's good news, Rosemary.'

She was quiet for a second. I could still hear the peep of the kettle. I wondered how long it might take to boil dry. 'Did you know that he'd had a stroke, John?'

'Teddy? No, I didn't . . .'

'Alice phoned last night. He was taken into hospital early yesterday morning. She asked where you were and I had to tell her I didn't know.'

'Did Dad speak to her?'

'They were talking for about half an hour. I don't know what about.'

'Is it a serious stroke?' It sounded ridiculous as I said it. You'd brush someone with a feather and they'd fall down dead.

'I think it's bad enough, John.'

I saw a face at the window then. Warren smiling through at me and holding a wood-plane in his hand. I nodded at him. 'I'll be home tonight, Rosemary. Tell that to Alice if she asks. Tell it to Dad as well . . .'

She was anxious now, I could hear it in her breath. 'I don't know what seeing Teddy like that might do to him, John. He thinks he'll live forever, you see – that's what keeps him going.'

'I think he'll survive, Rosemary. I really think he will.'

I put the phone down and went back to the kitchen. The kettle was light when I picked it up, just a swill of hissing water at the bottom. I stood it among the dishes in the sink and steam lifted up. A door with coloured panels of rosettes and stars was open to the back and I stepped out on to a terrace overlooking what must have been the ruin of a garden. Warren was working at a bench with his back to me, planing one side of a window-sash held in the vice. The new frame was leaned up against the end and the unprimed timber was fresh and white, smelling of resin. He threw his weight behind the plane and a tongue of shaving curled away. He turned to me, grinning – a big, jowly face in the daylight, red stubble spreading up his cheeks.

'Did you get a good connection?' he asked.

'Clear as a bell . . . D'you have trouble sometimes?'

'It's just that we haven't had a proper line installed yet.

246

The cables are all left over from the last owner and he's been dead for twenty-odd years. They just never got around to cutting it off . . .'

He laid the plane on its side on the bench. I could hear the children somewhere in the tangle of the garden now – Rhona's call, then the breathless laugh of one of the boys. 'Kids are having a good time . . . Where's the rest of them this morning?'

'Claire wanted to pick up a few things and Val and Ray went along for the ride. I think Enid had told them to let you lie.'

I looked up at the back of the house. Scaffolding had been erected to the second floor and ladders sloped from one level to the other, tied into the framework. Clouds were disappearing behind the eaves and the back wall had a look of constantly falling fowards. Tall weeds waved from the troughs of the lead guttering. 'How did Claire come into this place?'

'Her dad died and left her something. Claire's family have always been big in vending machines.'

'Is there that much money in it?'

'I think they sold this house to the first fool that came along. There's about enough left over to get the place weatherproof.' He clicked his tongue. 'This is going to be her little therapeutic kingdom, you see. She'll fill it with every lost soul that manages to walk through the door . . .' He smiled again. 'Sorry, am I offending you?'

'Not exactly.'

He laughed and looked down at the work on his bench. The breeze was carrying curls of wood-shavings along the terrace. 'I keep trying to introduce a bit of reality but I'm not hopeful. Trouble is, the only way with a place like this is to go in over your head.'

'And that's what you've done?'

'That's what I've done all right.'

'Because of Claire?'

He stared at me, as if he felt he didn't need to answer.

'This house would bury her otherwise – she knows that . . . You might get involved if you aren't careful.'

'And I've stopped being careful,' I said.

He shrugged, then peered over the tangle of the garden, listening. 'I don't trust them when they're quiet. They'll be difficult to find, you see – there's a maze at the back . . .'

'A real one?'

'Oh yeah . . . It's overgrown now – a kid might squeeze through it but you couldn't. Whoever built this pile went for the full country-house bit. There's a fishpond in the middle with nothing but fifty years of dead leaves in it . . .'

I walked to the edge of the terrace and looked out. The coping was cracked and fat stems of weeds were pushing through. Shallow steps of grey stone led down between leaning stone urns. There was a row of beeches at the bottom and the white shell of an elm. I could hear a lorry changing gear in the valley. 'I'd like to see them before I go.'

He looked up. 'When are you going?'

'Soon as I can . . . Will you tell her that? Enid?'

He nodded, picking up his plane as if he'd spent enough time with me. 'If you want to find them then try the scaffolding.'

I looked up at it. I could see where a ladder was missing a rung. A board didn't span, left one end in mid-air. 'Is it safe?'

'It's all right. Ray and me put it up last summer.'

My foot slipped on a damp board and I hung on to one of the poles. The iron was chilly and rough with scale. The empty space of a window opened into a disused room – rags of sheets across a bed, a wardrobe with a grey upright of mirror. That smell of dust and pigeon shit. I climbed to the next walkway – near the roof now and the waving stems of weeds in the trough of the old lead guttering. Pigeons flew off in a staggered group, catapulting themselves like thrown hymn-books. Grey torpedo-shapes of sash weights stood in a tin pail below one of the sills. I pulled one out to test its weight, swinging it at arm's-length.

Fifty feet below Warren bent over his bench in the way my father would lean studiously over the snooker-table. The terrace jutted like a stone raft into an acre of thistle and flat crowns of nettle that must once have been the lawn. Then the maze – like the whorls of a green thumbprint scarred by ruts of water, tyre tracks crossing in an arc where a lorry had backed. Behind that the ground seemed to fall away on three sides as if the house and garden were built on a headland. Where the land started to rise on the other side of the dale I could see a house in a clearing through trees. Not really a house but a dark, low building with a steep, slate roof and the little shapes of crosses at the ends of the ridge. I thought it might have been where I'd seen the light the previous night – the student's lamp shining through the night. A car was parked in the road outside and the ground to one side was a smooth green around outcrops of grey rock. A sheep or a goat was grazing placidly nearby.

There was a shout from below, sharp and single. I saw how Warren glanced up from his work and then clubbed the chisel with the side of his hammer. A lighter blow and then a stronger, spitting off white wedges of wood.

Tap-TAP.

Rhona was guiding the younger children between the rows of overgrown bushes, hands on their shoulders, steering them away from the patches of dark mud and water. One of them broke away from her and she reached down and caught his arm. He struggled and I could see his pale scalp through his thin hair. Finally she picked him up and carried him while the other followed behind. Warren had put his hammer down and was watching them now. He called out and Rhona smiled. The child she was carrying was the youngest – Enid's child. I swung the weight in an arc at shoulder-level and struck one of the upright poles. It shivered and I could feel the force of the blow in the bones of my wrist and then along my arm. There was the slither of loose rust and then a note burst out of the pole as if it had been trapped inside and I'd sprung it – a loud tone like a cracked bell. Rhona looked up at the scaffolding, surprised, not seeing me at first but then spotting me as I brought back my arm. I struck again and a second later the echo of the first blow came back to me from across the dale. The child was struggling in her arms now, wanting to be put down. The second echo came back and I swung again, weaker this time because my wrist was aching and my arm was getting tired. But the note broke crisply and he stared up at me, his little mouth open.

23

A bell chiming. Was it a bell? I could hear it even through the breeze-block and the tight little window.

'What was that, David?'

He pushed back his head to listen. 'I'm not sure – some work they're doing across the way, maybe.'

He laughed, drawing himself in, making himself awkward . . . The noise came again, longer this time – a shivering stream of air passing over the roof. Then, because my ears were strained, a fainter sound that was like a child crying.

I didn't ask. I could see that he was starting to worry about the time and Mrs Woodhouse who was busy in the cloakroom behind the door. So I reached up and smoothed back his hair.

'You want to go, don't you, David?'

He nodded, not looking at me. 'It's best if we do, Anna.'

'That's right – it's best.' *I pulled back my sleeve to glance at the little watch that Gerald had given me two Christmases ago. Even then I hadn't liked it – that look of dull gold and the face trapped behind its glass.* 'We'll need to start for home now, anyway. Well, thanks very much for bringing me here, David . . .'

Sometimes the worst word is thanks.

He gave me a kiss with dry lips, then nodded towards the screen with its threads of light. 'Would you like to take that with you?'

'Her file?' It seemed so ridiculous that I had to laugh. 'What use is it to me, David?'

He looked awkward again, shrugging. 'I'd like you to take it anyway.'

'Take her off your hands, you mean? Okay . . . Is that why you brought me here? Or did you hope I'd tell you something?'

He looked towards the door again. I could see how this was difficult for him, that his hands liked to be busy. Pearl Lilian Drean. Lit by a luminous bar. 'There's always more to tell.'

'But there isn't, David. I think you have it all now – more than you'll ever need. John fell asleep and she was lost, but even that's saying too much . . . All we can do is put one thing next to the other, David. One thing and the other but there's no connection – however hard you tried you wouldn't find one.'

'God connects things, Anna. He fills the spaces.'

'He shouldn't then. The spaces are where we breathe.'

He made his reasonable noise again – biding his time until he thought I'd calm down. But I felt quite calm and indifferent. Indifferent to him and to you, John. To Pearl. Even to the child in my belly. It might not last but a second would break the chain.

I held out my hand. 'You can give me it if you like.'

He swivelled the chair and sat down. The back of his head was always so neat, with clear furrows from the comb. Even as I'd kissed him I'd been reluctant to put my hand there. He responded to the prompts and messages: No (Yes), leaning forward so that I felt a sympathetic ache in the small of my back.

A map reference. An arm and a leg. A womb. A face: EXIT. The columns on the screen turned to a grid of lines which folded like the legs of a tripod. The machine cleared its throat and David sprung the disk.

He looked about the desk, among papers, apple-cores. 'I'll find a case for you . . .'

'Don't bother – I'll take it like it is.'

It had hardly any weight. I don't know what I'd expected – the density of lead? David went to the door and whispered something to Mrs Woodhouse, who had approached us silently. She whispered back.

'Margaret will be leaving soon,' David said. 'She has just a couple of things to take care of.'

We went into the cloakroom and he leaned back to check the room, then turned off the light. Mrs Woodhouse had hung her dust-grey smock on one of the pegs and a door I hadn't noticed before was open to the outside. Sunlight crossed it, then darkened. I heard the cry again – like a baby's but thinner and with less hope.

'Would you like to meet our goat?' David asked. 'We used to keep her for her milk but now she's more of a pet, really.'

We stepped outside. I was ready for graves or monuments but instead I saw a sloping field and a few grey rocks darkly flecked. When my eyes started to water in the bright light I was worried that David might think I was weeping.

He pointed. 'That's Charles – a strange name for a goat, especially a nanny.'

She came towards us, as if she knew her name. The other end of her rope was tied around a stone which was ridiculously small to tether her to, so that she dragged it behind her across the turf which she'd left as short as the pile of a rug.

'Margaret called her that,' David said. 'After her late husband.'

'That was very nice of her.'

I looked back towards the chapel. I could see Mrs Woodhouse cleaning the bottom corner of one of the windows, pretending not to look towards us. Her cloth squeaked against the glass. Then the nanny nuzzled at my thigh and when I petted her silky little head her eyes brimmed with grateful light.

'She needs company, I think,' David said. 'We've thought of finding her a companion.'

I still had the disk in my hand and I held it towards her but she turned away her face with a delicate, disdainful look which made me smile. 'Maybe she's better as she is, David . . .'

He laughed and I could see he was uneasy again. The sun came out and flamed the rocks and grass, the animal's queer squarish pupils. I started to examine the casing and found the seam with my thumbnail.

'What are you doing?' David asked.

'You said it was mine, didn't you?'

I tugged at the two halves until there was a gap wide enough to push in the tip of my finger, then levered them apart. There was the disk on its bed of felty paper – the etched grey of lines too fine to see. Light and dark – information. I must have looked strange for a second because the nanny skittered back on her precise hoofs.

'I've another copy,' David said.

'I knew you would have.'

I let it fall, knowing he would carefully dispose of it the second my back was turned. Over his shoulder I could see roofs on the opposite side of the valley – about half a mile away, behind trees. Tall chimneys with a twist to them like old-fashioned table-legs. I started to walk towards the car and David followed. The nanny watched us from her mound and I saw how her stone anchor had scraped a little path in the turf. Mrs Woodhouse squeaked her cloth again, polishing a last inch of glass.

24

Dad tapped me gently on the forehead. I looked up from the chair to see him with his hand still out, the first two fingers extended with a tremor in their ends.

'You could have let him sleep!' Eric told him. 'It's a slow time of day and I wouldn't have minded.'

Dad sniffed. 'He'd spend his life asleep if I let him! He has some tart tucked away and she draws the life out of him.'

'She isn't a tart,' I said.

Dad nodded, willing to be corrected. 'Then I'm sorry that I spoke. If that's what she isn't.'

I rubbed my forehead. I could still feel the light touch of his fingers. He was pacing the worn lino behind the chairs now, a rolled magazine in one hand. *Practical Photography*.

He smiled towards Eric who was shaking out a towel. 'His mother used to wake him like that. Every bloody morning – even when he was a teenager.'

I stretched out my arms from the sheet, turning my wrists. My head felt small and damp, cold at the nape and temples. 'I don't remember that.'

'Of course you don't – you remember nothing!' He pointed with the end of the magazine. 'She was the finest woman alive, Eric – and it was wasted on this one!'

'I'd agree with you there,' Eric said. 'With the first part anyway.'

He smiled at me and retrieved the sheet, letting fall hanks of my hair. 'Will you be there yourself, Eric?' I asked.

He handed me a towel so that I could wipe my neck. 'At Teddy's send-off? No . . . But I've cut a lot of the heads, so I'll be present in that way.'

'Your shortcomings will all be visible,' Dad said.

Eric shook his head. 'If that's how you see it, George!'

Dad tested the hair at his nape with the edge of his thumb. 'Well, if I'm going soft in the head then I've the haircut to match, don't you think?'

'I wish him rest anyway,' Eric said. 'Teddy, I mean.'

We waited for Rosemary in the car outside. Twelve o'clock and I listened for the voice of the talking clock and then remembered.

'Don't you miss it, Dad?' I asked. 'Hearing your friend John Gosse?'

'I never missed him while he was alive,' Dad said. 'Why should I start now?'

'They're installing a set of chimes for next season.'

He nodded. 'That's what they should have done in the first place! That thing was only fit for frightening the pigeons . . .' He sighed. His head looked damp and narrow. I could still see the tiny scar at the tip of his ear where the scissors had caught him. 'You keep looking at me,' Dad said. 'Is my hair sticking up?'

I wet my thumb and slicked down a strand at the back. He pulled a face and then submitted to it.

'I might go away for a couple of weeks,' I told him, 'take advantage of this fine weather.'

'With your fancy piece?'

'Her and the boy, yeah . . . If she wants to come along.'

'First Marion and then you! I'll be alone in that big bloody place!'

'Just you and Rosemary . . .'

He pointed a finger. 'Now, don't you start that!' He frowned through the windscreen. 'How much longer will she be?'

'She said she'd aim for twelve. She has to find an outfit for the funeral, and one to meet her son in.'

He started to grumble, tugging at his jacket pockets. 'Wouldn't the same do for both? He's only a bloody comedian, isn't he? You'd think there were enough of them in this town already . . .'

'One less since Marion went.'

'Does that mean we need a replacement?' He looked mournfully over at the front of the hairdresser's shop. I could see the white reflections in the mirrors on the far wall and Eric still cleaning the glass shelves.

'So did you see her today?' I asked. 'Did you see Pearl?'

Dad's ears stood out like a sign of his suffering. 'I could have. I could have easily . . . You can't prove that I didn't.'

'Why did you tell me that?'

'I didn't tell you – I told your sister.' He flapped his hand. 'Oh, you know what she's like! She *presses* you! She won't take no for an answer . . .'

'So you came up with that?'

'I had to say something, didn't I? I suppose I might have been thinking about her at the time – about little Pearl. I don't remember . . . I was sitting in the chair one second and the next there was nothing. Nothing!' He looked across the car at me, pleading. 'You have to explain away nothing, don't you, John? Because nature abhors a vacuum.'

I laughed and at the same second saw Rosemary turn the corner. 'You're a bloody liar, Dad!'

He shook his head, standing his ground now. 'Now, you can't say that about me, son! Not really.'

I opened the back of the car for Mrs Shand and she put her shopping on the seat, then sat down. A parcel and a couple of paper carriers. She'd told me it was ten years since she'd bought a hat.

'Well, I *think* that was a success . . . You're both looking very smart, I must say.'

I turned on the engine and put the car into gear. The

clutch was new and savage. 'Dad reckons you're wasting your money, Rosemary.'

He cleared his throat and she stared at the back of his head. 'Well, it's mine to waste, isn't it, George?'

'I daresay it is,' Dad said. 'It just seems a shame to be buying dark stuff in the middle of summer.'

She laughed. 'You were saying it wasn't like summer only this morning.'

'Oh yeah . . .' He smiled. He was indulgent now – with that softness he had in reserve. 'That summer we were all out of the army – me, Teddy, and Johnny Gosse. They'd done something to the air, I think! You'd only to take a breath and you thought you were bloody immortal!'

'Well, you remember that, George!' she told him, settling back in her seat.

He nodded, convinced by himself. 'Oh, I will – no fear of forgetting!'

Also available in Vintage

Stephen Blanchard

GAGARIN AND I

'An extraordinary piece of writing. Beautifully observed
and lovingly constructed'
Sunday Times

*Winner of the Yorkshire Post
Best First Book Award
Shortlisted for the Whitbread
First Novel Prize and the
Dillons First Fiction Award*

'Through the eyes and overkeen ears of 14-year-old
Leonard, we absorb the early Sixties, a time harking back
more to the War and the Fifties than the carnival to come.
The space race is young. Leonard observes the night sky
with devoted fascination, knows every crater and ocean on
the moon. His hero is the cosmonaut Yuri Gagarin, whose
picture is pasted on his wall...A clever and evocative book,
with its combination of delicacy and density that reverber-
ates after the last page'
Independent

'Very funny, very artful, very accomplished'
Daily Mail

VINTAGE

Stephen Blanchard

WILSON'S ISLAND

'Brilliantly crafted, perfectly observed...compulsive'
Literary Review

'Blanchard follows his excellent first novel, *Gagarin and I*, with this equally good, dry study of grubby provincial life. Ralph, a darts virtuoso and lowlife drifter, returns after four years to his family – his grandmother, living in a miasma of cat food over an amusement arcade, and his dodgy father Cliff...A startling, claustrophobic novel; [Blanchard's] dog-eared, side-of-the-mouth quality is already memorable and will soon be unmistakable'
Mail on Sunday

'As superb as its classy precursor...*Wilson's Island* purrs with menace and decay, spitting its sparks of comic brilliance, like barbs of light, against the dank setting of grubby streets...Blanchard's exactness of description...is beautifully judged...The writing sings'
Scotland on Sunday

'His apprehensive powers are of the highest order...The concentration and imagination, the wit and the propensity for things melancholy and strange raise expectations. Could Blanchard be the new, desperately wanted, Mervyn Peake?'
Times Literary Supplement

VINTAGE

A SELECTED LIST OF CONTEMPORARY FICTION
AVAILABLE IN VINTAGE

☐ GAGARIN & I	Stephen Blanchard	£5.99
☐ WILSON'S ISLAND	Stephen Blanchard	£6.99
☐ THE MERCY BOYS	John Burnside	£6.99
☐ DISGRACE	J M Coetzee	£6.99
☐ A HARLOT'S PROGRESS	David Dabydeen	£6.99
☐ EVERYTHING YOU NEED	A L Kennedy	£6.99
☐ THE ROSE GROWER	Michelle de Kretser	£6.99
☐ ENDURING LOVE	Ian McEwan	£6.99
☐ PARADISE	Toni Morrison	£6.99
☐ MASON & DIXON	Thomas Pynchon	£7.99
☐ AMERICAN PASTORAL	Philip Roth	£6.99
☐ THE WAY I FOUND HER	Rose Tremain	£6.99
☐ TIMEQUAKE	Kurt Vonnegut	£6.99

- All Vintage books are available through mail order or from your local bookshop.

- Please send cheque/eurocheque/postal order (sterling only), Access, Visa or Mastercard:

☐☐☐☐☐☐☐☐☐☐☐☐☐☐☐☐

Expiry Date:_____Signature:_____

Please allow 75 pence per book for post and packing U.K.
Overseas customers please allow £1.00 per copy for post and packing.

ALL ORDERS TO:

Vintage Books, Books by Post, TBS Limited, The Book Service,
Colchester Road, Frating Green, Colchester, Essex CO7 7DW

NAME:_____

ADDRESS:_____

_____

_____

Please allow 28 days for delivery. Please tick box if you do not
wish to receive any additional information   ☐

Prices and availability subject to change without notice.